Wandsworth Common

ROBERT NUTTALL

authorHOUSE

AuthorHouse™ UK
1663 Liberty Drive
Bloomington, IN 47403 USA
www.authorhouse.co.uk
Phone: UK TFN: 0800 0148641 (Toll Free inside the UK)
UK Local: 02036 956322 (+44 20 3695 6322 from outside the UK)

© 2020 Robert Nuttall. All rights reserved.

No part of this book may be reproduced, stored in a retrieval system, or transmitted by any means without the written permission of the author.

Published by AuthorHouse 12/01/2020

ISBN: 978-1-6655-8302-2 (sc)
ISBN: 978-1-6655-8301-5 (e)

Print information available on the last page.

Any people depicted in stock imagery provided by Getty Images are models, and such images are being used for illustrative purposes only. Certain stock imagery © Getty Images.

This book is printed on acid-free paper.

Because of the dynamic nature of the Internet, any web addresses or links contained in this book may have changed since publication and may no longer be valid. The views expressed in this work are solely those of the author and do not necessarily reflect the views of the publisher, and the publisher hereby disclaims any responsibility for them.

Dedicated to Dorothy Booth (Grandy) RIP.

To my Family, wife Kim, Children Guy & Lucy Myles, and dogs Billy & Pablo.

Contents

Prologue xi

Chapter 1	The Early Days	1
Chapter 2	Meeting the Love of His Life	6
Chapter 3	Climbing the Ladder	10
Chapter 4	Good News	17
Chapter 5	The Homecoming	23
Chapter 6	The Life Changer	26
Chapter 7	New Home, New Life	35
Chapter 8	London Life	39
Chapter 9	The Present Day	48
Chapter 10	The World Changes Forever	52
Chapter 11	Coming Home	65
Chapter 12	The Funeral	77
Chapter 13	Life Goes On!	87
Chapter 14	The mystery text messages	96
Chapter 15	The Debt	110
Chapter 16	Mattie Patterson	113
Chapter 17	Meeting Sammy Bloom	122
Chapter 18	Business as Usual	139
Chapter 19	The Campbells	141
Chapter 20	Who Is He?	146

Chapter 21	The Realisation about Gill	149
Chapter 22	Sunday Lunch	161
Chapter 23	A Trip to Clapham	166
Chapter 24	A Serious Warning	168
Chapter 25	Face-to-Face Confrontation	179
Chapter 26	Revenge	200
Chapter 27	The Camden Meeting	211
Chapter 28	A Job for the Campbells	219
Chapter 29	A Relaxing Weekend	223
Chapter 30	The Recon	226
Chapter 31	Hello, Mrs Harrison	229
Chapter 32	The Day of Reckoning	237
Chapter 33	A Problem Solved	239
Chapter 34	Wimbledon Parkside	246
Chapter 35	The Aftermath	250
Chapter 36	Convalescing	257

Prologue

He lay on the grass with the warm sun bathing his face. Looking up at the cloudless blue sky, he thought what a beautiful day it was—one of those perfect, balmy South West London summer days that made people feel glad to be alive and want to be outside enjoying the warmth. Grunting a short laugh, he thought, *How ironic!* The pain was unbearable, and he could feel the blood running down his side, soaking his shirt and running onto the grass beneath. The sickly smell made him retch, and retching made the pain more intense. He closed his eyes, trying to replay what had just happened, trying to make sense of it all. After the events of the past few weeks, what he had thought was his perfect "normal" life had ceased to exist. How could he have been so blind? How could he not have seen what was happening? Had he been so wrapped up in his work or himself that he had not seen any signs? Did that make him a bad person or just a damn fool?

He looked around, but any movement just brought more pain. From what he could see, there wasn't anybody close. No one would hear him if he called to for help. How bloody ridiculous—normally there were people all over the common at all times of the day and night. His mind began to wander. He had passed this spot so many times—walking with Gill, playing with the children, at weekends exercising Max, the family wheaten terrier—and it was always busy. Closing his eyes, he lay back and tried not to concentrate on the pain as he decided what to do. More to the point, just what could he do? He couldn't stand or even crawl, and calling for help would be challenging. His mouth had started to go dry, and he let out a sigh. He looked back up at the sky, thinking, *Little did I know this would be the spot where my life would come to an end.*

He had always said he wouldn't want to know the future, when the subject came up with friends over drunken dinner parties, when the boozy conversation turned to life, the future, fate. Some friends wished they could see into the future while others told of their "amazing experiences" visiting their psychics and what they had been told about their future lives. Utter bullshit! All bullshit. Also, he would argue, why would you want to know the future? What had just happened proved his point. He wouldn't have wanted to know this was where he would eventually die. Who in their right mind would want to see the future, especially to know when and even where they were going to die? If he had known, he wouldn't have come within a thousand miles of Wandsworth Common! Would that have changed his life and ultimate death?

He felt the pain washing over his sweaty, bloodied body. He tried to be calm. He had worked hard throughout his life, trying to provide the best life he could for his family. And now he was left bleeding to death within view of the family home, the source of so many happy memories. He hadn't been in control of anything that had happened, even though he thought he had. His close friends had told him to let it go, but he wouldn't. Had he caused all this because of his stubbornness or because of his love for his family? He wouldn't just let it go … he couldn't … let it go … If only he had taken their advice, it would have all been so different.

Chapter 1

THE EARLY DAYS

Little Frank Junior, the second son of Frank and Anne Quinn, was born and raised in a modest end terraced house in the Elland area of Leeds. Frank Senior was a stocky six-footer with dark hair, hazel eyes, and an olive complexion, as they said in those days. A fine figure of a man. He was built like the proverbial brick shithouse, as his old pals described him. At the age of fifteen, straight from school, he had started work at a local steel foundry. By the time he was twenty-five, he had worked his way up to foreman—the youngest foreman ever, he would proudly tell people. He was a hard worker and always willing to put in overtime to provide for the family, even more so now he had an additional mouth to feed. He was a Yorkshire man through to the bone, and proud of it! Straight-talking, hardworking, honest as the day was long, he had never got a lucky break in all his life and never expected one. His dad had always told him, and he would tell his own children, "It's not where you start off in life, but where you end up." Frank Junior; his sister, Lucy; and the elder brother, Joe, had it drummed into them that, with hard work, you could achieve anything. "Remember that, and it will stand you in good stead in your adult life," Frank Senior would say.

Little Frank's mum was Anne, a loving wife and a good mother who devoted herself to her family. She prided herself on turning the children out clean, tidy, and most importantly, with impeccable manners. Her favourite saying was "Good manners cost nothing." A good-looking woman, she and husband Frank made an attractive couple. In her younger days, Anne had been a real head-turner: five six; a good figure; long, shapely legs; small waist; and thick, wavy blonde hair. She could have been a fashion model, if only those opportunities had been easier to come by in her time. She was still a very attractive woman for her age, though a little bigger now, as was to be expected after three children. She had looked after herself over the years and was quietly pleased with her looks and figure, which could still turn heads.

Frank and Anne were both born in St James's Hospital and raised in Leeds. Frank grew up in Holbeck, and Anne on the other side of the city in Harehills. She met and started dating Frank Senior when she was nineteen, marrying him three years later when she was three months pregnant. The pregnancy caused a big falling out between her family and husband-to-be, and it never healed. Her father never forgave Frank for getting his only daughter pregnant or for all the shame it brought upon the family, and they never spoke to each other again.

But Frank Senior was a good man and a devoted husband. He looked after her well, worked hard to provide for the family, and never complained about whatever life threw at him. In the early years of their marriage, he didn't have much to give her except love, kindness, and a humble home, and that was enough for her—she was happy with what they had. Things naturally improved over the years; they had a reasonable working-class lifestyle and were able to tuck away a bit of savings for a rainy day. The three children were well brought up, and the family were well respected and liked in the neighbourhood. The children were taught right from wrong, to be polite and caring, and to be respectful to grownups. They enjoyed holidays each summer at Butlins holiday camp in Skegness. That was the highlight of the year for the children; many of their school friends never had a family holiday.

Frank Junior did well at school and was a bright, popular boy, willing to learn and always asking questions, so much so that his classmates called him "Frank Why." In his final year at school, he captained the football team and was also head prefect, which made his mum and dad very proud.

At night in bed, his parents would chat about the family business and the children. It was the only time really that were alone together and out of earshot of the children. Frank's dad would always say, "I've got a feeling young Frank will make something of himself in life. Anne, he's got a good head on his shoulders."

Anne would smile in the darkness of the bedroom and reply, "So long as he's happy however his life turns out. That's all I want for him and his brother and sister."

When Frank Junior was young, an elderly Jewish man named Nat Margolis would call at the house every other week to collect life insurance money for a policy his mother had taken out with his company. It was common in her day to pay weekly, as the shame of "something" happening and the family not being able to afford a decent funeral was unthinkable. The insurance company Nat worked for was The Victoria, one of the biggest in the country. He had worked for them since what was left of his family fled Germany during the war to settle in England. He was a kind, friendly man, but Frank's mum said he had great sorrow in his eyes. He always wore a long, dark-grey woollen overcoat, even in summer. Frank's mum told him Nat had lost a lot of his family in the war in Germany, and she always made Nat welcome and fussed over him when he called. Frank always looked forward to Nat's weekly visit, as he made the children and their mum laugh.

Nat would relax over a cup of tea with Frank's mum, and they would discuss all the local gossip. Before he left, "Uncle" Nat would do a magic trick for the children and tell them a silly joke.

Frank always remembered something Nat once said to him in one of his rare serious moments. They were walking down the street together, and he said, "When you grow up and leave school, young Frank, get a job in a business that people will always need. People will always need insurance. If you're lucky enough get a job with a good insurance company, you'll have a job for life."

It was the first and only time that Uncle Nat ever talked seriously with him, and Frank would remember and heed his words. When he left school, he got a job with the Leeds branch of a multinational insurance company just as Uncle Nat had advised him to. He enjoyed working and especially earning a real wage. Work life was so different to the restraints of school life. He'd had two part-time jobs when he was at school, so he was used to earning money and having savings, but he loved the freedom of being a "grown up" in a full-time job. His curiosity about how things worked and why they were done a certain way and his curiosity to learn about processes helped him to quickly pick up the role he was given. He was also interested in what other people did in the company and was always asking questions. Despite what a teacher had once told him— "Your curiosity will get you into trouble one day"— the trait helped him learn about different aspects of the company and also the insurance business. His work and enthusiasm to learn were noted by his immediate superiors, and he stood apart from the other young employees who were happy just to do the job in hand and take the money at the end of the week. Frank's thirst for knowledge and his natural curiosity paid off; he was promoted six months after joining the firm.

Chapter 2

MEETING THE LOVE OF HIS LIFE

Frank was in his early twenties when he met Gill, a real blonde beauty—five foot eight, fabulous figure, pale blue eyes, and full lips. When he first saw her, her stunning looks put him off even thinking of making a move on her. She was two years younger than he and lived in Manchester with her mother. She was in Leeds on a night out with friends from the Yorkshire office of the travel company she worked for. An only child, her father had died when she was four and her mother, Betty, had done a very good job of raising her on her own. They dated despite the Pennine Hills separating them. Nothing serious in the early days; they got on very well and enjoyed each other's company.

Gill would travel over to Leeds one weekend, and he would drive over to Manchester the following weekend. During the week, they would talk on the phone about how work had gone for each of them and what they were going to do at weekend. As time went by, they went away on holidays together and spent Christmas and New Year's Eve together. Frank realised he could see himself spending the rest of his life with her. She was kind, funny, and a lovely-looking young woman. She was popular with most people she met and came to know. She reminded him a lot of his mother—her kindness, her attitude, and her outlook on life.

Gill was prepared to work hard for the things she wanted in life, but most importantly she had the same feelings for Frank. After they got engaged, Frank's friends would tease him saying he was punching above his weight with Gill. He didn't mind them ribbing him because he was a reasonably good-looking lad. He had enjoyed a fair bit of success with the girls before Gill came on the scene. Standing five feet ten, he had thick black hair, hazel eyes, and a decent build with wide shoulders. He was happy with his lot. However, secretly, he did feel lucky and so glad that he had gone over to speak to Gill in the nightclub. When he first saw her that night, after he caught her eye, she had smiled back at him. He'd been as nervous as hell, but he knew if he didn't go over to her quickly, somebody else would swoop in, and his chance would be gone. *Fate lent a hand*; he would always say to himself. And he'd smile when he thought back on how they'd first met.

They got engaged two years after meeting, and they married the following year in August. They bought a little terrace in Roundhay; the mortgage seemed enormous at the time.

They had saved up for a deposit, with additional money coming from the sale of his beloved car. He loved his car, an MBG Roadster, and had saved up hard to buy it. It had been his dream since he was sixteen, but it had to go despite his love for it. He loved Gill more. The house in Roundhay wasn't anything fancy—a terraced house with two bedrooms, a bathroom, a small back garden—but it was home, and most importantly, it was theirs. Roundhay was a good area to live as it was dominated by the big park where festivals and the odd summer pop concert were regularly held.

They moved into their home with a new bed—a wedding present from his mum and dad—two borrowed armchairs, and a TV—a present from Gill's mum, Betty. That was it! They had nothing else except each other, but they didn't care. They were happy starting their new life together, and most of their newly married friends were in the same position.

The carpets being fitted and the three-piece suite arriving just before Christmas gave both of them the best feeling ever and turned their little terrace home into a palace, certainly as far as they were concerned.

They had a wide circle of friends. Some were recently married like themselves, and their outlooks were all similar to Gill and Frank's. They were enjoying married life and building a home and careers for better things in the future; they were sensible young people.

Neither Gill nor Frank had gone to university. In their family backgrounds, universities were for posh people, not the working classes like them. When children left school, they got a job straight away to help out with the family bills, giving most of their money to their mums. It was the "done thing" in those days. Frank worked as a loss assessor for PSB, one of the biggest international insurance companies in the UK. They had six offices in the main cities, and the northern regional office was situated in Leeds.

When they married, Gill got a transfer from her travel company's Manchester office over to their Leeds branch. She didn't want to a career change; she was happy working in the travel business and for her present company. She enjoyed her job and especially the good staff discounts they got on holidays.

Frank and Gill were both dedicated to the companies they worked for and were both good at their jobs. They worked hard and progressed in their respective roles. Eventually their salaries and savings enabled them to move up the housing ladder.

In 1987, they bought a semi-detached house in the posher part of Roundhay, not that far from their first home but closer to the park. It was in need of some modernisation. The elderly lady who had lived there had gone into a care home, and her family had decided to sell. A reasonably sized family house, it had a good-sized kitchen, a lounge, a dining room, three good-sized bedrooms, and fairly large gardens front and back.

Their savings paid for the modernisation, and Gill turned it into a lovely home. She had a good eye for interior design. Frank often said she should take it up professionally. She was a natural and a very good homemaker just like his mum. Frank enjoyed tending the gardens and built a patio area where they could have friends around for barbeques. Sitting in the garden on balmy evenings eating and drinking with friends or family members was the highlight of their weekends in the summer months.

Chapter 3

CLIMBING THE LADDER

With Frank's latest promotion, he was visiting their head office in London on a regular basis and sometimes staying overnight in the capital. He loved the buzz of the head office, and he started to get noticed by the head office management. Once they got to know him, they liked what they saw. It wasn't just because of his work and the innovative ideas; it was also for his Yorkshire straight talking. He didn't kiss arse or creep like most of the other guys his age looking to climb the corporate ladder. If he thought something could be improved or he saw a problem, he would speak out, always respectfully as he had been brought up to be. His boss, Simon Taylor, always encouraged him to speak up, and when he took Frank's ideas to his bosses, he always made sure to give the credit to Frank.

Apart from the buzz of working in the head office and being involved in middle management meetings, Frank really enjoyed London life. He felt like a real grown-up standing there with his briefcase and overnight bag on the platform at Leeds Station waiting for the early-morning

London train. He felt so excited arriving at Kings Cross Station and walking out into the throng of commuters making their way to work. He would be the one smiling face in a sea of people who were busily going about their commute with no smiles and no eye contact. It would amuse him why people walked around looking so miserable when they lived and worked in one of the greatest cities in the world.

The capital was such an exciting city. He remembered watching films when he was young that had been shot in London. Here he was walking past famous landmarks and even getting quite good at finding his way around the city … well, to a certain degree. He even enjoyed walking back to the hotel after work instead of taking a taxi or the tube. He would wash, change his clothes, and head straight out again. He would walk around soaking up the atmosphere—theatre land, Covent Garden, the Thames Embankment, and Chinatown. He would often eat dinner in one of the many restaurants, and on his way back to the hotel, he would stop off and have a drink in an old pub. He loved the really old ones that looked as if they hadn't changed in a hundred years.

Over time, because of the nature of his role, he would go out for business dinners with his boss, Simon Taylor, entertaining clients after business meetings.

He loved this part of the job. Apart from gaining additional insight into the business, Frank got to eat in top restaurants that were far and away above his salary and where he could only dream about dining on his own.

His favourites were Quaglino's and Scott's of Mayfair. The food was superb, and there was always a celebrity or two eating there, which added to the excitement of the visit. When he got back to Leeds, he would tell Gill all about it—what he'd had to eat, who had been dining there. Sometimes Gill would take a few days' holiday and travel down on the train with Frank. She would fill her day shopping and sightseeing while Frank worked. In the evenings, they would go out to dinner, and when they could afford it, take in the occasional show. If finances allowed, Frank would take Gill to one of the smart restaurants where he and his boss had entertained clients. They were always cautious what they ordered, making sure the bill wasn't too expensive. He was becoming a bit of a foodie and liked impressing Gill. She loved the shopping and their evenings out; it was evident she enjoyed visiting London as much as he did.

On the train going home, Frank would daydream of living in the city enjoying the good life. He had discussed his dreams with Gill, and the thought of living there appealed to her too. Frank's love affair with London continued and indeed grew deeper, despite the fact that he was mugged one night on the way back to his hotel. He was walking up Bloomsbury Street past the British Museum having said goodbye to his boss and clients after dinner. He had just turned left onto Bedford Avenue, pleased with the way the dinner meeting had gone, when he was suddenly aware of how quiet and empty the street was—apart from the two young guys laughing and joking as they walked towards him on the same side of the street.

The two young men seemed to pay no attention to him at all until they drew level, and then it was all over in a matter of seconds. The smaller guy asked Frank for the time, and as he lifted his arm to look at his watch, the bigger of the two punched Frank on the side of his face. His legs buckled, and he dropped to his knees. The young men were shouting and swearing at him as they aimed sharp, quick kicks into his ribs that took the breath out of his lungs. Gasping for air, he could feel the big thug's hands frantically tearing at his pockets, screaming at him, "Where's your fucking money, you bastard? We'll fucking kill you! Do you hear?"

It was all over so quickly. They had found his wallet and his phone and appeared satisfied. They gave him one last kick for good luck and ran off down the road. Frank rolled over onto his back sore and probably bruised, feeling sick, although he was relieved to see the muggers running away.

The road was quiet again, the silence deafening. The thugs had stopped running; they were now strolling along as if nothing had happened. *Bastards!* thought Frank. But he didn't shout the word out after them in case it prompted them to come back and give him another good kicking. He lay there breathing heavily and trying to focus on the streetlight above him. It was shining down on him like a spotlight on a stage. He waited for the black spots darting in front of his eyes to disappear. He mentally assessed his body for any damage, and then he slowly got up. His ribs hurt like hell, and his left cheek was throbbing. He didn't feel seriously damaged. His hand hurt; it was grazed and bleeding from where he had fallen to the pavement. He felt lightheaded and thought he was going to be sick. He carried on walking up Bedford Avenue. At the junction with Great Russell Street, he managed to hail a taxi. He asked the cabbie how the much it would cost to take him to his hotel. Checking he could cover the fare with the change he had in his pocket, he climbed in, he didn't fancy walking anymore.

When he got back to his room, he painfully took off his suit jacket, checking to see if it was ripped anywhere after its encounter with the pavement. His ribs hurt where they had kicked him. He looked at himself in the wardrobe mirror. He was still very pale. He had a red mark on his face where he had been punched; it had started to swell a little bit and would probably turn into a bruise. But at least he had stopped shaking.

Frank hated violence. He must have looked rough. On the drive back to the hotel the taxi driver kept looking at him in his rear-view mirror and nervously asked him twice if he was okay. He was obviously more worried that Frank might be sick in the back of his cab than he was about his passenger's well-being.

Frank sat on the edge of the bed for a minute running his fingers across his forehead, looking down at the carpet as he recalled the mugging. Then he quickly jumped up and ran to the bathroom. He threw up twice into the toilet. As he wiped his mouth on the hand towel, he thought, *What a waste!* He had really enjoyed the food at dinner.

He assured himself his upset stomach was probably caused by shock from the mugging. He washed his face and sat on the cold bathroom floor with his back against the bath. *It could have been much worse*, he thought. *If they had been carrying a knife, I could be dead now, and for what? A few quid and a mobile phone? What a stupid way for someone to die!*

When he finally felt a little better and was sure he wasn't

going to be sick again, he phoned Gill just as he always did before he turned in for the night. He told her of the drama but played it down. He didn't mention throwing up because he didn't want her to worry. And, more importantly, he didn't want her to be put off about moving to London in the future. He said, "Gill, anyone could be mugged in Leeds or anywhere these days. I'm fine—really." She asked him a few more times if he was okay, wanting to convince herself there was nothing to worry about. He told her he was and would just end up with a bruise on his face. Trying to sound blasé about the whole incident, he asked her how her day had gone and what she had done. He told her about the evening and the meal, who the clients were. When he was satisfied that she had calmed down about the mugging, he told her he loved her and to have a good night's sleep. Blowing a kiss down the phone, he hung up.

In the office the next morning he told his tale without trying to big himself up. He wasn't a fighter—never had been! His boss, Simon, scolded him for not reporting the attack the night before. Then he sent Frank to see the company nurse. After checking him out, she told him he had a few bruised ribs, but he would live. He set off to the nearest police station to report the mugging.

The desk sergeant, sitting at a desk away from the glass window where Frank was standing, kept him waiting for a few minutes. When he finally looked up, he looked annoyed that Frank was still there. He took a loud slurp of his coffee, set the cup down, and finally walked over to the window. He looked Frank up and down whilst wiping his mouth on the back of his hand.

He listened—or appeared to be listening—to Frank's

account of the mugging. At one point, he walked back to his desk to get his cup of coffee. He recorded the details—the address, the approximate time, a vague description of the muggers. He seemed totally uninterested. He was obviously annoyed that Frank had interrupted his attempt to get up to date with his paperwork. The last thing the sergeant wanted was to add to that stack of papers, and he wanted to get back to his half-eaten tuna-mayo sandwich that was waiting for him in his top drawer.

When Frank was telling him of the previous night's drama, the sergeant, whom Frank by now had mentally nicknamed Fat-Arse, glanced at Frank's bruised cheek. Frank thought he detected a bit of a smirk. Fat-Arse was totally bored now and brought the report to an end. Taking another loud slurp of his coffee, he wiped his mouth again on the back of his hand and then wiped his hand on his trousers. He was definitely smirking as he took a final glance at Frank's cheek. Putting the pen behind his ear he said dismissively, "Any news we have regarding the attack, we'll be in touch, son."

Frank thought, *why didn't you just add "northern bastard" on the end of your sentence instead of "son"?* That's what the sergeant's smirking face was saying. Frank gave him half a smile and curtly replied, "Thank you. I'll wait to hear from you." He turned and left, thinking what a bloody waste of time that was. And he would tell his boss that when he got back to the office—a morning totally wasted.

Chapter 4

GOOD NEWS

Gill collected Frank from the station at the usual time after one of his trips to London. On the way home, she was her usual chirpy self. He was quite weary from work and the train journey. It had been a busy couple of days in the office. Reluctantly he talked about what he had done in the office. She always took an interest in his work and colleagues and where he had eaten, but he was tired and just wanted to have a shower and crash in front of the TV. She was always bubbly and excited when she picked him up after his London trips. He felt guilty, so he asked what she had been up to whilst he was away. At least all he would have to do would be listen and not make conversation.

She pulled up at a red traffic lights not being able to contain herself any longer. She looked at him and blurted out, "You're going to be a dad! I'm pregnant!"

Frank just stared at her trying to take in what she had just said. Suddenly, he wasn't tired anymore. His jaw had dropped open. After what seemed like an eternity of looking at her in disbelief, he finally laughed and said, "Are you sure?"

They had been sort of trying but not seriously; Gill had just stopped taking the pill a month or so earlier. They had friends who had been trying for quite a while but without any success, so this news came as a bit of a shock.

She nodded, giggling fit to burst with excitement, and said, "Yes. I'm well and truly pregnant. I've done two tests."

They hugged each other, both talking at the same time. The sharp toot from the annoyed driver in the car behind brought them both back down to earth. Gill looked up at the green traffic light. She laughed and quickly put the car into gear. But when she stepped onto the accelerator to drive off, she stalled the car. Restarting the engine while listening to another longer angry toot from behind, she finally pulled away. They looked at each other and burst out laughing again.

When they arrived home, Frank followed her into the kitchen and made them some coffee. She excitedly told him all about doing the test and realising that she was pregnant.

Then she'd gone out and bought another kit and did a second test just to make sure. The second test confirmed the first. She was having a little Baby Quinn. They both laughed and hugged each other. Frank put his hand on her tummy and kissed Gill tenderly. It was the start of a new chapter in their lives. They were going to be a family; they were growing up and couldn't wait for Baby Quinn to come along.

Gill begged Frank, "Please don't say anything to our friends or at the office until it's confirmed. Things can and sometimes do go wrong early in a pregnancy. I don't want to tempt fate."

Frank hugged her and reluctantly agreed. He wanted to tell everyone and anyone. He did tell his boss, Simon, in the London office and a few close friends in the Leeds office, swearing them to secrecy, especially if they spoke to Gill should she call the office. He couldn't help himself; he was so happy and really proud that he had done the deed and that he was going to be a dad!

When they did announce the pregnancy, their family members and friends were delighted for them; they were congratulated by all. Two couples in their circle of friends had already beaten them to it and had young children. They told Frank and Gill that having a child was the greatest experience, and their lives would change forever. It would be a lot of hard work, but definitely a change for the better.

Thomas Benjamin Quinn introduced himself to world on 19 November 1992 at 7.10 pm. With ten fingers and ten toes, he weighed in at nine pounds, seven ounces. He certainly was a bouncing baby. They had both liked the name Thomas. They had chosen Eli as a girl's name. So, baby Thomas had two good strong names. His parents had chosen his middle name, Benjamin, after Gill's late father. It was a nice touch that wasn't lost on Gill's mum.

Gill and baby Tom were both doing well. Once they were settled on the ward, Frank left them and headed to his mum and dad's house having already phoned around with the news from the hospital.

Frank's dad answered the door. He shook Frank's hand and hugged him. Tom wasn't his first grandchild, but Frank Senior was proud that another little Quinn had come into the world to carry on the family name. Beckoning Frank into the house, he asked "Are they both okay?" He had a big beaming smile on his face.

"Perfect. Just perfect," replied Frank Junior.

Frank's mum, Anne, let out a squeal when he walked into the lounge. She jumped up out of her favourite chair and rushed over to him, hugging and kissing him. "A birth in the family always makes for a very special day," she said, sitting back down wiping away a tear in her eye.

Frank talked them through all the details over a coffee and sandwiches—the waiting, then the birth, and how good Gill had been, so strong and calm throughout it all, which was so unlike him as he had panicked at anything and everything, driving the midwife crazy. At the end of it all though, he and Gill finally saw their son and got to cuddle him at long last. His parents smiled as Frank described who the baby looked like—his dad's nose, his mum's eyes. But basically, just a beautiful new grandchild—just a perfect baby.

After all the excitement of describing the birth and answering all his parents' questions, Frank started to fade. He was tired after all that had gone on in the hospital after all the waiting around. It was a fantastic experience and one he would never forget. Strangely, he had felt a little redundant and on the edge of it all during the final half hour of the birth.

He kissed his mum and hugged his dad at the front door, saying his goodbyes. As he headed off home, he was conscious that he had to talk Gill's mum, Betty, and go through it all again. She was over from Manchester and had been staying with them for the past few weeks, helping Gill in her final stages of pregnancy before the birth. Despite all the stereotypical mother-in-law jokes, Frank really liked her. He got on really well with her, and she had done a great job of raising Gill single handed. He appreciated her helping to look after Gill towards the end of the pregnancy as he was still spending a couple of days a week down in London.

A short bundle of energy standing at five two, Betty never stopped. She was always rushing around doing this and that, and she was always helping people. She was also a great cook. Frank really looked forward to her dinners when he got home from work in the evenings. Gill's cooking was good, but her mum's dinners had the edge. Not that he would ever tell Gill that. She opened the front door before he could put his key in the lock. She hugged him and asked, "Hello! How does it feel being a dad?" Beaming a big smile, Betty hugged him and helped him off with his jacket. "Would you like a coffee and something to eat?" she asked.

"No thanks, my love. I've just had something to eat at Mum and Dad's." Frank smiled and plonked himself down in the armchair.

Betty settled down on the sofa opposite Frank and listened intensely as he went over the birth again, more or less word for word exactly as he had told his parents half an hour earlier. He reassured her that Gill was fine and had been very calm throughout it all, after Betty had asked him a few times if Gill was okay. When he described his new son, Betty's eyes filled with tears and she had a little cry. She assured Frank they were happy tears. She was a lovely mum-in-law and a lovely lady.

"My mum and dad are coming to the hospital with us tomorrow to visit Gill and baby Tom," said Frank, kicking his shoes off and putting his feet up on the stool.

"I can't wait to see them both," replied Betty, picking up Frank's shoes and placing them near the door. "I bet you Mum and Dad can't either. They must be so proud."

The nursery was the first thing Gill's girlfriends had asked to see when they came to visit her after she had finished work and started maternity leave. *Obviously a girly thing*, Frank thought to himself when he heard the squeals of delight and the oohhs and the arghs. It made him laugh that a room could reduce women to tears when a some of them cried and said how the beautiful nursery was. It just amazed Frank when he thought about all the equipment they needed. He couldn't believe how much stuff one small baby required: cot, crib, changing mat, buggy, car seat. Then there were all the clothes. The list was endless, and all for one tiny little person. Incredible!

CHAPTER 5

THE HOMECOMING

Gill and baby Tom came home four days after the birth. Everything had been ready for his arrival weeks before. There was a steady stream of girlfriends, again bearing baby gifts of all shapes and sizes. Clearing away the presents after they had left, Frank was worried at one stage that they would need a bigger house. A week after Gill and baby Tom came home, things started to calm down as fewer visitors arrived. Gill, being Gill, got into a routine very quickly. She had always been very well organised at everything she did. Frank was back to work on the Monday after a week off. He had taken Betty back home to Manchester on Sunday afternoon. Gill and baby Tom had stayed at home in Leeds as the weather wasn't too good and Gill was feeling a bit washed out.

Gill loved her mum very much but had confessed to Frank when they were in bed that, as much as Betty had been a great help, she was getting in the way a bit now. Gill wanted her own space with some Mum-and-baby time without Betty. Frank said he understood, but secretly he was disappointed that he wouldn't be savouring Betty's dinners anymore!

Gill was enjoying her maternity leave and loved being a mum. She confided to Frank that she wasn't sure she wanted to leave baby Tom with someone when the time came to go back to work. After listening to Gill's concerns about going back to work again, Frank assured her it wasn't a problem as far as he was concerned. He told Gill it was completely her decision; at the present time, they were okay moneywise. If she didn't want to leave Tom, that was fine. She could be a stay-at-home mum. After all, she could decide nearer to the time. She might feel differently then.

Christmas soon came, and it was a magical time with little Tom. They both said it was the best Christmas ever. They felt like a real family now they were three, even if Tom was too young to really know what was going on. Gill's mum, Betty, came to stay for the Christmas holidays. They didn't want her to spend Christmas alone in Manchester. She gladly babysat on New Year's Eve so Frank and Gill could go to a dinner dance with all their friends. It was really their first night out together since the birth. They had a great night but laughed at breakfast the next morning when they both admitted to Betty that they couldn't wait to get home to baby

Tom. On the way back from Manchester, after driving Betty home, they talked about how life was good and they were so happy and lucky to be having such a wonderful time. Gill said, "I hope this never ends. I'm so happy and content. I just love being a mum and wife!"

Pulling up at traffic lights, Frank leaned over and

kissed Gill tenderly on the lips telling her, "I promise you, darling, I will make sure our life will always be this good, if not better. I will do everything in my power to see that it is. Trust me."

Chapter 6

THE LIFE CHANGER

Late one Friday afternoon in January, Frank was working in London. It was his second visit in three weeks. He still enjoyed his time in the head office, but he really hated being away now even though it was only for a few nights every week. He felt he was missing out on baby Tom and family time. Gill would put the phone next to baby Tom when Frank phoned to say goodnight each night he was away. He could hear Tom breathing or gurgling if he was still awake, which just made him miss his son all the more.

Frank was busy wrapping up for the weekend and looking forward to catching the train back to the North when his boss, Simon Taylor, called him into his office. Sitting back down behind his big dark walnut desk, Simon adopted his usual pose, leaning back in his chair with his hands behind his head. He looked at Frank silently for a while and with a big grin finally said, "Sit yourself down, young Frank. You know you are well thought of in the company and considered by some people to be a good asset

Wandsworth Common

for the future. Well, good news! I would like to offer you a new job role within the company."

Shocked at the news, Frank asked, "Is it promotion?"

Simon laughed. He loved dropping bombshells and catching people off guard. He replied, "Oh, it's promotion all right. Oh, yes! It's definitely promotion. It's here in head office, and it's been approved upstairs. We just need you to say yes, if you want it."

He had caught Frank off guard. Frank just stared at Simon for what seemed an eternity. Finally closing his mouth he replied, "Wow! Really, I don't know what to say. What's the role?" He was still trying to take in what he had just been told.

The job was in a different division. Frank had been in life, accident, and health. This was an underwriter's position in the speciality lines division—the big league of the company, the biggest trading team at PSB based on gross written premiums. Overall, this would be a bloody great step up in the company.

Frank sat looking at the carpet, deep in thought, letting it all sink in. Rubbing his fingers across his forehead, he looked up at Simon, who had quietly sat there enjoying every minute of shocking his young protégé. Frank finally said, "When do need an answer? Err, I would like to discuss it with Gill over the weekend if that's okay with you? Will Monday be all right to get back to you?"

Simon smiled stood up and replied, "Of course. That's fine. I wouldn't have expected anything less. But tell Gill to seriously consider this offer. It's a great opportunity for both of you, Frank, but, hey, no pressure. If the answer is yes, I'll be sorry to lose you from my team. I was hoping that, eventually one day, you would take over from me, but you have been spotted and observed by the king makers on the ninth floor. It would be a great career move for you. You really don't want to turn it down, Frank. I know you both love London, and you'll love the life down here. Well, this is your chance to finally come down here, and with the family. The promotion will change your life and for the better in more ways than one. You'll see."

Simon stood six two. At thirty-eight years old, he had a good head of dark brown hair, with surprisingly a few grey flecks running through the sides now, which he thought made him look quite distinguished. He didn't carry any excess weight; he was in good shape and was considered quite dishy. He always got admiring glances from the ladies in and outside of the company. He was polite and always charming with the ladies, so most of them considered him quite a catch. He was also someone the men described as "a real bloke's bloke", which made him very popular with both sexes. Very good at his job, he was well respected and liked by the people who worked with him and for him.

Simon lived in a smart two-bedroom apartment in Canary Wharf, overlooking the river, which he had bought in the early days before the prices went crazy. He also had a beautiful, three-bedroom apartment in Bournemouth with stunning sea views that his mother had left him when she died. After a few years of spending weekends down there, he decided to rent it out. When he was younger, he would take his girlfriend's down to the apartment in Bournemouth for the weekend. It was a beautiful part of the world—a beautiful sea with the long sandy beaches, the New Forest a few miles inland, Sandbanks and Poole

Harbour just up the coast. It was an ideal relaxing retreat. Spending the weekend down there was always a welcome change of scenery after the hustle bustle of working in London all week. Despite his many girlfriends over the years, he had never married. When the subject came up, he would always say he had never dated a woman with whom he wanted to spend the rest of his life. So, with no wife or family to rush home to in the evening, he was a company man through and through.

In fact, the company was his life. He had a big love for sea fishing, which he always described as his "only vice", though even his fishing trips took a back seat if and when work called.

Simon had grown to like Frank a lot over the few years he had known him, and he was quite protective towards the young Yorkshire man. Simon knew Frank always did his best for the company and was ready to go the extra yard for his protégé if need be. The feeling was mutual. Once when Gill had spent a few days in London with Frank, Simon had taken them out for dinner. They'd had a good night out, and Simon had charmed Gill just as he charmed most women he met, but in a nice way, not flirty. They got on well, and she really liked him. Frank and Gill asked Simon to be godfather to little Tom. He said it would be an honour and gladly accepted. He assured Frank it wasn't a problem travelling up to Leeds for the baptism, and he stayed at Frank and Gill's home for the occasion.

Despite the close bond with his boss, Frank was never too familiar with Simon, always remembering that he was his boss. This wasn't lost on Simon; it just made him like Frank all the more. He knew Frank had a great future with the company, and he took him under his wing more than he did with any of the other young employees who worked for him.

Simon had come to think of Frank more as the younger brother he never had. He liked the way Frank conducted himself. In spite of his young age, Frank was very focused. He took his career seriously, and indeed took his life seriously as well.

Because of this attitude, Simon knew Frank was a good asset to the company and had a good future ahead of him. The glowing terms in which Simon spoke about Frank to the directors when he nominated Frank for the job confirmed he was worthy of the role. Some of the directors had met Frank previously from presentations Simon had asked him to carry out and also from a few high-level meetings that Frank had been involved in. They were impressed with how he handled himself, especially for a young man. They knew a good prospect when they saw one and told Simon to go ahead and offer Frank the role despite his tender years.

Simon walked around from behind his desk and shook Frank's extended hand. Smiling, he said, "Go home and speak with Gill. Sleep on it over the weekend. If the answer is yes, we can get things rolling early next week when you're back down here. We'll get Hillary in HR to go through the personal details with you. Also, there's a very good relocation package. Now go on. Sod off home before you miss your train!" Jokingly, he pushed Frank out of his office.

Gill was parked at the station in her usual spot in the line of pick-up cars as she waited for Frank. It was a miserable night. After checking on Tom in the back seat, she started up the engine when she saw the London train pulling into the station. The weary commuters came rushing out of the entrance braving the pouring rain. Once out of the entrance, they split into two groups, one heading for the taxi rank, the other group looking down the line of cars trying to spot their pick-ups. Frank waved at Gill and dashed over to where she was parked. He jumped into the passenger seat, rain dripping down his face. Leaning over, he kissed her on the cheek. She laughed and pulled away from his wet face and coat. He looked around at Tom, who was fast asleep in his car seat. As they pulled out of the station, he fastened his seatbelt and pushed his wet overnight bag down in between his legs into the footwell. Letting out a huge sigh, he proclaimed, "It's always good to get home. What have we got planned for the weekend? Nothing, I hope."

Gill smiled and replied, "It's funny you should say that. We are completely free. We can do whatever we like!"

A big smile appeared on his face as he looked around at Tom again. The baby always looked so comfy when he was sleeping. Frank turned around and said to Gill, "Have you both been okay while I've been down in London?"

Gill shot him a smile and replied, "Yes, we've been fine. Good to have you home though!" On the way home, they talked about how Tom had been and what he and Gill and he had done whilst Frank was away in London. Frank had decided on the train journey home that he would wait until they got home before telling Gill his news about the job offer. He desperately wanted the job and thought it was the right move for them as a family. However, he wasn't sure how keen she would be moving down to London now Tom had come along. Everything at home in Leeds was perfect. They were close to their family members and friends who also had children, and they were both really enjoying family life.

Gill gave him a sideways glance. He had gone unusually quiet and was looking out of the passenger window into the dark wet night. She broke his thoughts saying, "You're quiet. Is everything okay at work? You're looking a little pensive."

Turning to look at Gill, he forced a smile and thought, *Well, here goes nothing.* Taking a deep breath, he replied, "Simon called me into his office and offered me a promotion. It's a great role and a brilliant opportunity. We would obviously have to move down to live in London, though. What do you think?"

He didn't have to worry. His fears had been unfounded. She loved the idea. "That's brilliant! I'm so proud of you, darling. Well done, you! To be honest, I've been expecting it from what you've said recently." Gill beamed.

Frank was so relieved that she was open to the idea of moving south. He asked, "Yes, but only if you are you okay with it. Do you still like the idea of living in London?"

Pulling up on the drive, she turned and kissed him passionately. Ruffling his hair she replied, "Of course! I love London as much as you do. I always have done. Also, it's the perfect time to move down there now before Tom starts his school days. What's more, it will be a better future for him in the city when he grows up. Also, the added bonus is you'll be home every evening when we are living down there."

"True," he replied. "Although, with the new position, I would probably have to go to the States on business from time to time just as I have been going down to London over the past years."

Smiling she teased him replying, "Ooh, listen to the jet setter here! Anyway, I enjoy a break from you now and again. I might be out in London with my newfound friends every night you're away!" They both laughed.

Gill settled Tom down in his cot for the night while Frank opened the bottle of champagne he had bought at Kings Cross Station to celebrate his promotion, hoping that she would say yes. They chatted excitedly into the night about where they wanted to live and what type of house they would be able to afford with Frank's salary increase. They had a pretty good idea of the house prices in London and roughly where they would like to live if they could afford to.

"These are such exciting times," Gill said.

"Another milestone in our lives. Tom coming along and now promotion with a move south to London," Frank replied.

Lying on the sofa with her head on Frank's knee, Gill thought, *It doesn't get much better than this*. She smiled to herself and asked Frank for a top-up of champagne, asking, "Do you think we'll still see all our old friends when we move down to London? Do you think they'll come and visit us?"

Frank laughed, "Knowing that lot and how they like to party, they'll be down every weekend. I'm sure we'll never get rid of them!"

Gill laughed and said "Also, we'll make new friends down there, from Tom's nursery and your office!"

They went to bed and made love before falling asleep content and happy in each other's arms.

CHAPTER 7

NEW HOME, NEW LIFE

After three months of exhaustive house hunting, which they grew to hate, they had looked everywhere—Inner London, Outer London, Essex, Kent, Hertfordshire, Surrey. It was hard work and soul destroying. They just wanted to put down roots in a house that they could call home instead of viewing other people's homes and seeing how settled they were. At the worse times, they questioned if they had made the right decision agreeing to the move to London. All the upheaval was draining.

After four months, they finally found a house that they really liked in an area in which they could see themselves living. It was also a good commute for Frank. They decided on a smart, modernised, white-painted Victorian terraced house in Wandsworth, South London, on Belle Vue Road. It was on a main road, but that wasn't a problem. It was not a quiet road that they originally wanted, but the big plus point for them was that it had great views out across Wandsworth Common—seventy-one acres of trees and grasslands right on their doorstep—who could ask for more? Wandsworth was becoming very popular with young professionals. Its close proximity to central London made it ideal for commuting. Named after the river Wandle, the borough stretched from Battersea Park to Wimbledon Common on the south side of the River Thames.

It was fast becoming the latest fashionable place to live, with wine bars, high-end restaurants, and boutiques opening up all the over the area. It was becoming as popular and trendy as neighbouring Clapham. Frank and Gill were getting on the London property ladder in the right area at the right time, just as Wandsworth prices were on the rise.

Their real estate find was all thanks to David Williams, a pal and work colleague of Frank's in the head office. David lived in Wandsworth with his wife, Susan. She had spotted the house in the window of the local estate agents, and knowing Frank and Gill were house hunting, she told David about it. They lived close by in a similar terraced house around the corner from the common on Wexford Road. The fact that they would be close neighbours was a real bonus. Frank got on really well with David and had also met his wife, Sue, at several company dinners. Sue was good fun. He liked the couple, and he could see Sue and Gill becoming good friends. He thought it would help Gill settle in quicker and not be so lonely having a "readymade" friend living close by.

Gill came down on the train on Friday evening with young Tom and checked into Frank's hotel. Frank finished work for the weekend and went to the hotel to meet Gill and Tom. After a dinner at a restaurant close to the hotel, they turned in for the night ready for the viewings the next day.

They'd had two viewings in Balham. The houses were okay, but Frank and Gill weren't very keen on the area. Then they had the viewing at the house opposite Wandsworth Common. The area was very nice, and the house ticked all the boxes. Afterwards they were invited to David and Sue's for dinner. They had a few drinks and sat down to a lovely meal that Sue had prepared. Apart from being a looker, she was also a great cook.

The evening went well. During the meal, David caught Frank's eye. He smiled and winked at David as the two girls ignored them and chatted away like old friends reunited. They appeared to have a lot in common. Frank had been right; they got on famously, and Sue couldn't leave young Tom alone, hugging him and kissing him, making a huge fuss of him. Gill told Frank in the taxi on the way back to the hotel that she really liked Sue and David and could see them becoming firm friends.

Frank and Gill both loved the house. It was in a good area for shops, restaurants, and potential schools, and it was a fairly short tube journey into the city. With David and Sue just around the corner, their minds were pretty much made up. Frank's salary increase and his bonus were very good. He had also received a generous removal package. It included all legal fees, all removal costs, and a £2,000 soft furnishing payment. The company also bought their house in Leeds at the current market value. Frank and Gill made quite a reasonable profit over what they had paid for it.

With the move and Frank's new London pay grade, their finances were looking healthy, so much so that Frank reminded Gill that she could be a stay-at-home mum if she wanted to, even with the move. It was completely her choice. She quite liked the idea, having already discussed it with Sue on the phone one night over a few glasses of wine. Sue convinced her they could buddy up and go shopping and lunching together. Gill could join Sue's gym and sports club, and Sue would introduce her to all her friends. She made it sound so good Gill couldn't wait and definitely didn't want to go back to working in an office, leaving someone else to look after baby Tom.

After all the legal work done and contracts were signed and exchanged, they finally moved south and into their "new" home over the August bank holiday weekend.

Frank had taken his two-week summer holiday from work so they could get things sorted out in the house. They hoped they would settle in quickly before he had to go back to work. The weather was good, and they were fine in the house. Gill quickly had it feeling like home. That done, they decided to have a few days' rest and take young Tom down to the seaside—Brighton one day and then West Wittering and Bournemouth. Frank thought this would probably be the only holidays they would have until the following year. Everything and everywhere was new, and they spent happy, fun family days. It seemed so natural coming "home" at the end of the day to Wandsworth Common.

Chapter 8

LONDON LIFE

They settled into life in London with great ease. Frank threw himself head long into his new job. He had started travelling to the States on business three or four days at a time usually every three or four weeks. He enjoyed visiting the US offices and got on well with his American counterparts. However, the best part of the trips was coming home. He missed Tom and Gill. He always brought them each a little present from his business trips—nothing extravagant. He might choose a toy or kiddies' book for Tom and perfume or something for the house for Gill. The gifts just added to the excitement of his homecoming.

Frank loved being a dad and coming home from the office in the evening. If he wasn't too late, Gill would keep Tom up so Frank could bathe him and put him to bed. He especially enjoyed the weekends, spending family time together, going for walks on the Common, nights out in town, dinners and suppers with their friends, David and Sue. It was just how he had imagined life would be living and working in London. Gill had settled in really well. She was enjoying a good social life, making friends at Tom's nursery, coffee mornings, lunches, and shopping with Sue.

They joined David and Sue's club, working out in the gym, playing tennis and squash together. Frank would get the tube in to the office with David each morning, and they'd travel home again together in the evening if they finished at the same time. They became good friends. Their offices were across from Liverpool Street Station, a modern glass building, nothing too grand but certainly befitting a successful insurance company.

The visits from Frank and Gill's friends from Leeds tailed off after about six months. When the couple had first moved down, friends had come to stay nearly every other weekend. However, as time progressed, there were fewer visits. It was to be expected, really. People get wrapped up in their own lives. It was sad, really, but understandable. It meant they had more time for their newfound friends in South London. Gill's Mum would visit once a year for a week in summer. Gill loved taking her into London shops and having lunch in nice restaurants. Frank's mum and dad weren't big lovers of London; they weren't big lovers of anywhere outside Leeds. And they didn't really like leaving Yorkshire. So, the "southern" Quinn family would journey north to Leeds a couple of weekends a year to visit Frank's family, calling in on Gill's mum in Manchester on the way back to London.

Most of their social life included Sue and David Williams, including a close circle of friends from the gym and sports club where all four of them were members. They enjoyed each other's company despite the menfolk coming from different professions and walks of life. The "gang" became closer and started enjoying family holidays abroad together. One of the couples owned a fabulous villa in Barbados where they would all take off to for their summer holidays. The husband was a successful medical consultant, and his wife was a stay-at-home mum like all the other mums.

Sometimes, for a change, they would hire a villa in Europe that was big enough for ten or twelve adults plus children. They preferred the villa lifestyle as opposed to hotels; it was more suitable with all the children. After a day on beach, the mums would prepare food for the men to barbeque, or sometimes they'd get a local chef to come in and cook for them. Dinner would always be followed by long, boozy evenings on the terrace whilst the children played in the swimming pool, the men put the world to rights, and the women caught up on all the latest gossip. These were happy, happy, relaxing days.

Sue was a "local" girl from Wimbledon, a year older than Gill. She was the same height as Gill but had dark, long hair. Basically, her figure and looks would stop a riot in a prison! A real stunner. She had a bubbly personality, but with a bit of an edge; she could be quite feisty when something upset her. If she didn't like someone, that person would certainly know about it very quickly. An only child, she had been raised in Wimbledon Village close to the Common. Her family home was an older type large detached house that had once been owned by a famous old music hall entertainer. The star's identity would change depending on how much wine Sue had consumed when she told the story. However, the truth was that it was a fine old pile on Somerset Road on a third of an acre with outdoor swimming pool and tennis court. The house had been expensively modernised by her mother, Brenda.

Her daddy, Henry, was managing director of some big family financial house in the city. The family were described as "old money" and well known in the high society circles of London life. Sue had been spoilt from birth. She was an accomplished horsewoman and had been given her first pony when she was seven years old. Later she had graduated to a beautiful chestnut horse called Ralph. She would ride him on Wimbledon Common like most of her rich girlfriends in the village.

Sue's school days were very colourful; she had boarded at the prestigious girls' school Roedean on the outskirts of Brighton on the South Coast. She'd narrowly avoided being expelled on two separate occasions thanks to the intervention of her father and his generous donations to the school. She'd gone to Bristol University, the only reason being that her two best friends were going there, and the three girls were inseparable—the three female musketeers.

David was born and raised in Guildford, Surrey, also an only child born into a middle-class family. His father, Ben, was a bank manager, and his mother, Marie, a nursery school teacher.

He went to Charterhouse Public School following in his father's footsteps where he excelled academically and also in sports, much to the delight of his parents. His education continued at Bristol University where he studied economics, and that was where he first met Sue. They started dating in year one and remained a couple throughout their three years studying there.

They say opposites attract, and it was definitely the

case with David and Sue. He was the exact opposite to Sue, academically and personality wise. David was a likeable young man, very placid. He never had a bad word to say about anybody, which made him very popular. Also being a six-foot-four second-row rugby player usually made up people's mind on liking him too. Sue, on the other hand, didn't take her studies very seriously at all. She was too busy partying with her close circle of friends. The other students just thought of them as spoilt little rich girls. They believed the girls were just at uni to enjoy themselves and have fun, which was about right really.

David would often speak to Sue about her attitude to university life and try to get her to take her studies seriously, but she would just laugh and say to him, "You're only here once. Don't be so stuffy!"

Despite their different personalities and outlooks on life, they did love each other very much; it was evident to all who knew them. After graduating, they continued to see each other; six months later, they decided to get engaged. They lived together and were blissfully happy; a grand marriage followed two years later. Sue's parents liked David; he was a polite, serious young man, and they thought he was a good, calming influence on their daughter. They were disappointed at first thinking she was marrying beneath herself, but their opinion changed when they got to know him. Equally, David's parents weren't sure about Sue. She was a typical little rich girl who didn't take life or anything else seriously. However, after a few meetings, they fell in love with her too. She was good fun, kind, very bubbly, and very affectionate. She soon became the daughter they never had but had always longed for.

The newlyweds set up home in Wandsworth, buying their house outright. They put down the deposit, paid the stamp duty, and the remainder of the money was a wedding gift from Sue's parents.

After the honeymoon, Sue worked for a law firm in the city as a personal assistant. David was employed by PSB straight from university. He was working his way up the management ladder just like Frank. After two years, they started trying for a family. Sue gave up work to concentrate on getting pregnant—or so she told everyone. It was partly the truth, but the whole truth was that she didn't like working—not one iota. Unfortunately, she couldn't conceive. There didn't appear to be a medical issue with either of them according to what their consultant told them.

Sue was heartbroken. She had her heart set on being a mum and desperately wanted to give David a child. They had in vitro fertilisation treatment at Listers Fertility Clinic, one of the best clinics in London. Their lack of success started to affect her health; she began drinking heavily. This put tremendous pressure on their marriage. They loved each other but were quarrelling a hell of a lot. Sue's drinking caused even more arguments and trouble. They finally decided to get help and see a marriage guidance councillor in an attempt to save their relationship. It helped. They realised that the root of their problems was their inability to start a family, so they resigned themselves to being childless. They decided not to try to adopt but just to get on with enjoying the good life they had made for themselves, and if a baby came along, well great!

Frank and Gill's arrival with Tom made so much

difference to Sue and gave their marriage a big boost. They doted on Tom, taking him on days out, and they loved having him for a sleepover when Frank and Gill were on a night out in town. David always felt bad when Tom went home; he couldn't bear the sadness on Sue's face after the Quinns had left.

For a long time, Sue had not been negative to David about not being able to conceive, but he knew she would have been a great mum. She loved playing mum with Tom when they had him. She was a natural, and they both enjoyed him running around the house. They both loved the noise and the laughter. It was just like a family home should sound, but then the quietness was deafening after Tom had gone home with Frank and Gill!

Deep down, David blamed himself for not being able to give his wife a baby. She had long stopped talking about it with him. She loved having Tom for sleepovers, but she hated giving him back afterwards.

Frank and Gill had often spoken about Sue and the sad look she tried so hard to hide when they were ready to leave and little Tom kissed and hugged his "Aunt Sue", thanking her for his sleepover. They always felt so sorry for her; it was heartbreaking to see her. They would purposely leave him at the Williams' home a little longer sometimes before going to collect him.

Gill had spoken to Sue about it in depth when they had a coffee after one of their classes at their gym. The pressure on her and David had been very difficult for them both in the early days—more so on Sue. She even told Gill about the problem nearly ruining their marriage; she had never told anyone about that before. Her smile couldn't hide her sad face. She said, "But like the saying goes, time heals all wounds, doesn't it? Well almost!"

Gill tried to lighten the mood. She leaned across the table, held Sue's hand and replied, "You and David can borrow Tom whenever you want to. I promise!"

When Gill fell pregnant again, David and Sue were the obvious choice for godparents. They were totally thrilled with the idea when Frank and Gill told them over dinner one Saturday night. Sue became very emotional, bursting into tears and hugging everyone.

The pregnancy went well without any problems. Sometimes Gill would catch Sue looking enviously at her. She was obviously wishing she was the one with a baby bump. Sue was a great help, doing everything she could to help Gill as the birth got closer. She was practically living at Gill and Frank's house and loving every minute of it.

Little Eli was born on 7 November, two weeks late. At six pounds and four ounces, she was a delicate, beautiful little baby girl with a shock of black hair, which was a big surprise to the parents! Tom had been born with very fine white hair and had practically been bald until he was two years old.

Sue was a great help after the birth, taking Tom to school in the mornings and collecting him when school was over. She would bathe little Eli, feed her, and take her for walks on the Common in her buggy so Gill could rest. She was in her element playing mum, and she was loving every minute of it.

She would excitedly tell David what she had been doing during the day with Tom and Eli. David was delighted to see how happy she was.

Wandsworth Common

Gill would tell Frank what Sue had done when he got home from the office and about how happy she had looked being a mummy. Gill was so pleased and commented on how lovely it was to see Sue so happy. It was such a shame she couldn't have children of her own.

Frank smiled and replied, "We wouldn't have a worry about who would look after the children if anything happened to us, would we?"

Gill looked shocked and replied, "What a morbid thing to say!" She laughed and said, "I'm only joking. You're right. They would both make lovely parents."

Chapter 9

THE PRESENT DAY

"Well that went well," Frank said in a low voice has he and David walked briskly out of the boardroom with the rest of the board directors after presentations on the departmental financial plans for the coming year.

"Like a charm," replied David, winking at Frank. "What time's your flight?"

"Two thirty," replied Frank, adding, "But back in time for our game of tennis and dinner afterwards on Saturday evening."

"Have a safe trip! See you on Saturday," shouted David over his shoulder, but Frank had already disappeared into his office.

Time had been good to them. They were both eager, fresh-faced young men, starting out on their careers with PSB. They had worked hard for the company and had risen through the ranks to become directors. Being paid and bonused handsomely along the way, they enjoyed the lifestyle that big-money salaries and bonuses could provide. Frank used to tease David saying how well he had done for a working-class boy from Yorkshire, and he was always quick to add that he hadn't been to university himself, unlike David, who had been to uni and whose wife came from a wealthy family and whose in-laws had paid the largest chunk of the cost of their home in Wandsworth when they got married. David always took it in good spirits, telling Frank he had to prove to them he could keep their "little girl" in the manner she was accustomed to!

They were both still living in their fashionable Victorian terraced homes in very fashionable Wandsworth. They'd never had the urge to move out of London to the home counties; they were all true Londoners now. Their homes were large enough for their needs, and besides they had always enjoyed living where they were and having some of the best amenities and restaurants in the world on their doorsteps in London. Both couples were totally settled in Wandsworth opposite the Common. All their friends lived locally, which made the place perfect for their socialising, which centred around town.

David and Sue had no need to look for anything grander or larger, not having any children, and it was handy for Sue to visit her parents in Wimbledon, which she did religiously two or three times a week. The family visits gave her a perfect excuse to shop at all the expensive clothes shops in the village.

Tom was living in a flat in Clapham not too far away from the family home but just far enough. His career was going well; he had a good job in banking in Canary Wharf and was well thought of within the company. Eli was in her second year at Nottingham University studying to be an interior designer. She was very close to her mum; when she was away at uni, Gill missed her tremendously. Gill would often travel up to Nottingham to see Eli when Frank was away in America on business. Gill was happy with the way their life had turned out and especially, as any parent would, that her children were doing well in their lives. But deep down, she missed the years when her children were little innocent things and totally depended on her.

Gill often thought it a shame that children had to grow up and leave the nest. She had adored being a mother; she had been born for the job. Her life seemed to lose some purpose when they stopped depending on her as much. She would never say it, but she felt lonely at times without the children, and it didn't help that Frank was away so much in America. She would think back to the family holidays—not the "big gang" ones in the later years, but the earlier holidays when there were just the four of them. The children would love to play on the beach and swim all day. They all enjoyed the dinners in the evenings—the fun, the laughter. She really missed those days. Sometimes memories just weren't enough, and it made her sad that part of her life had gone forever. She missed being really needed; the family unit had been so special back then.

Gill had a good social life with a wide circle of friends. She got on so well with Sue even though they were different characters. Gill was the serious one, very pedantic. Everything had to be just so! Sue, on the other hand, didn't have a care in the world. Everything in life was good even though she was heartbroken at not being able to have children. Even so, her attitude was "Oh, well. Let's get on with life and enjoy ourselves." It was amazing that the two got on so well. Gill did see Sue's mask slip on occasion and saw her Sue upset about the baby thing. Especially being drunk caused her to be melancholy. However, Sue was a very good friend and absolutely doted on Tom and Eli. Sue and Gill had become like sisters over the years. They enjoyed lunching together and with friends, shopping in London, and keeping trim with their classes at the gym and playing tennis.

CHAPTER 10

THE WORLD CHANGES FOREVER

All Saints Church in Wandsworth is a beautiful listed place of worship. It shares its parish with the nearby church of Holy Trinity. There has been a church on the site since at least 1234, when John de Panormo was granted dispensation "to hold the Church of Wandsworth." The present church originates from 1630; however, only the tower actually dates back to this period. The north aisle was built in 1716, with most of the remainder of the church dating from the rebuild of 1780. The interior has Robert Adams–like marble columns, with a frieze and enriched cornice. Some monuments from the original church still survive in the present building. These include a brass soldier of King Henry V and monuments of Susannah Powell, the daughter of Thomas Haywood, a yeoman of the guard to King Henry VIII. All that said, it's a truly beautiful church.

The vicar, the Reverend Edward Pickford, had presided over All Saints for only nine months. He was very proud to hold the office in such a prestigious and historical church. Reverend Pickford stood only five foot four and, at thirty-five years old, had, surprisingly, lost most of his hair. He was quite overweight and, given his height, he looked very much like a Weeble. However, his strong, deep voice boomed out from the pulpit every Sunday. His voice was amazing considering the size of the man, and it always brought smiles, grins, and even stifled laughs amongst his regular congregation.

Today, though, was not a day for his usual popular booming fire and brimstone voice, but for a quiet, sincere, caring voice. He looked around at the faces before him. It was not a huge congregation for the service, but still a good turnout, he thought to himself, and a very well-heeled one. He had visited the family to discuss the arrangements and the service. They appeared to be really nice people. Truly tragic circumstances had hit the family, he'd thought when he said goodbye and left their home.

Loudly clearing his voice, he drew the attention of the congregation. He gave his best sympathetic smile as he looked around at the faces that looked back at him. His eyes focused on the front pew as he made eye contact with the family members, the two children first and then the husband. He nodded very gently to the husband, the prearranged sign that the vicar was about to begin.

Reverend Edward Pickford announced in a not too overly loud voice but perfectly clear one, "Good afternoon. We are gathered here today to celebrate the life of Gillian Quinn. Gillian recently passed away leaving behind her beloved family, husband Frank, and children, Thomas and Eli."

Frank had returned the discreet nod from the vicar, but as the vicar started the service, Frank quickly drifted away, lost in his thoughts. He sat in the pew bent slightly forward and towards the right, running his fingers across his forehead as he always did when deep in thought or especially when something was troubling him. It had all been so sudden. He and Gill had never discussed one of them dying. Why would they? They had both always enjoyed good health, and they were quite young still. Was he doing the right thing having Gill cremated? He didn't even know if she wanted that, or if she would have wanted to be buried.

They were too busy living to discuss what to do if one of them died! He started replaying the events over in his head again, just as he had done so many times over the past weeks.

They had just returned from their annual ten-day fun break in Palma with David and Sue. They had been going there ever since the children had grown up and started holidaying separately with their own friends. Gill had mentioned to Frank a few times before the holiday about feeling unwell and being exhausted. Frank had asked her several times if she wanted to cancel the holiday. He couldn't remember the last time she had been ill; she was always fit and well and in the rudest of health. She always exercised, looked after herself, ate all the right foods, and maintained the perfect weight. Apart from the occasional cold, she was never ever ill.

She didn't want to make a fuss, and each time he had asked, she said wanted to keep their plans. She said the holiday would probably snap her out of it. And she didn't want to spoil it for everyone. They always had such a good time together. Frank remembered she had perked up at the beginning of the week but then had felt ill again part way through. Gill had told Frank she had been feeling like that on and off for some time now. They always had a great time with David and Sue. After just a few hours of flying time, they were there. No eight-hour long-haul flight that they had been used to in the past. Palma was perfect for a short break before summer really started back home. They all liked Mallorca and enjoyed fine dining, drinking a bit too much, and letting their hair down in the high-end bars and night clubs.

Frank sat in the pew deep in in thought. He unknowingly shook his head. *It's crazy*, he thought. Here he was now a short time afterwards at her funeral. It just didn't seem real!

None of it made any sense to Frank, least of all the speed in which it had all happened. She had made an appointment with Mark Postlethwaite, their consultant. Mark was an old friend from the sports club they all belonged to. It was Mark's family villa they all used to go to in Barbados for the gang's summer holidays when the children were young.

Frank hadn't gone with her to see Mark; Gill had told him there was no point. She told him not to fuss; he should go to the office as usual. Gill had driven herself the short distance to the Bupa Hospital where Mark had his consultancy. After a brief chat about how she and Frank were and what the children were doing, Mark told her she looked very healthy with her fabulous Mallorca tan, but then he asked her what the problem was. He listened intently as Gill explained what had been going on and what the symptoms were. Mark asked a few questions and then examined her. He told Gill they should carry out some blood tests that could help establish the problem. His secretary booked a return appointment the following week when they could discuss the results of the tests. After the blood was drawn, she thanked Mark for his time. He walked her back to the reception, kissed her on the cheek, and they said their goodbyes. On the drive back to Wandsworth, she replayed the appointment over again in her mind. It hadn't gone unnoticed by Gill that Mark hadn't once said to her "I'm sure it's nothing to worry about" to try to reassure her!

When Frank got home from the office that evening, they discussed the appointment with Mark Postlethwaite over dinner. Frank asked looking a bit concerned, "Did Mark give you any indications what he thought it might be?"

Gill smiled, took a drink from her glass of red wine, and replied, "No, he didn't say, and really I didn't think he would. He's not going to speculate in case he's wrong. That's why they're testing some blood samples."

"Okay, but did he say it's nothing to worry about or anything like that?" asked Frank, rubbing his forehead.

Gill shot Frank an annoyed look. He stopped rubbing his forehead immediately and took a drink of his wine. She replied, "No, he didn't, but I'm not worried, and I don't want you to be either.

Everything will be fine. I know you don't like doctors' surgeries and hospitals. You're very lucky you've never really been ill apart from your man-flu. But I'll be fine—really. So don't start worrying yourself now. The last thing I want is you getting all agitated and worrying needlessly."

Frank got up to clear the dinner plates from the table.

Kissing the top of Gill's head he whispered, "Never been ill, hey? Really? Man-flu can be very serious I'll have you know."

Gill laughed and jumped up, following him into the kitchen to the sink where she playfully hit him with the tea towel.

A few days later, Mark Postlethwaite's secretary had called Gill to say they had got the blood results back and could she call in to see Mark the following day. When Frank got home in the evening and heard about the appointment, he told Gill he would go with her even though she insisted again that it wasn't necessary. He said he felt it was his duty, and after all he would want her to go with him if the tables were turned and it was he who was ill. She laughed, shaking her head in disbelief. Walking past him, she stopped and kissed him and called him a big baby.

Mark greeted them, walking around from behind his desk to kiss Gill on the cheek and shake Frank's hand. After seating them, he sat back down at his desk. His smile faded as he looked at Frank, who was watching him intensely, and then at Gill. He spoke in his deep, authoritative voice. His words were like a bomb going off in Frank's head: "I'm sorry, Gill. It's not the good news you wanted. I'm afraid it's cancer." He paused to let what he had just said sink in as he always did in these circumstances.

Frank's jaw dropped, and the colour drained from his face. He looked at Gill in horror. She just smiled at him and reached for his hand, squeezing it gently. Breaking the silence after a few moments, Mark asked, "Would either of you like a coffee or a glass water?"

It was Gill who answered, letting out a heavy sign has

she spoke, "No, we're fine thanks, Mark. So what happens now treatment wise?"

He began explaining to them both that the cancer was an aggressive form that had already started to spread, and they really should make arrangements for the treatment. He said he would arrange for an appointment with Kate Newman, the top consultant at The Royal Marsden Hospital in Chelsea.

She would then arrange treatment to start as she saw fit, which in Mark's mind would probably be straight away. Frank missed most of what Mark had just said. The word *cancer* just kept bouncing around in his head.

Once he had refocused on what was being said in the room, Frank was amazed at Gill's' calm attitude as she discussed the pros and cons of the treatment with Mark. She was unbelievable. Frank had always tried to be the eternal optimist, but he accepted that Gill was in for a rough ride over the coming months. Looking back now, Frank realised he had been shell-shocked and hadn't taken in the severity of Mark's prognosis. But Gill had. She had known it was bad news but was being so brave—probably for him.

Acute Myeloid Leukaemia is an aggressive form of that starts in white blood cells called granulocytes or monocytes in the bone marrow. AML progresses rapidly, and depending on the growth, is fatal within weeks or months if left untreated. If caught early enough, it is treatable with chemotherapy, although the five-year survival rate of AML isn't good at only slightly higher than 26 per cent! It is caused by damage to the DNA of developing cells in the bone marrow. When this happens, the blood cell production goes wrong and the bone marrow produces immature cells that develop into leukemic white blood cells.

Mark and his wife, Jennifer, had been part of the Quinns' close circle of friends for many years. Mark played tennis with David and Frank and the rest of the gang at the club. He was six foot two, and his premature grey—almost white—hair was in contrast to his fitness and strength for a man of fifty-four years. Mark was the one to beat on the tennis court, but none of the gang ever did; he was a fantastic player. Everybody liked Jennifer. She was a short lady, a little on the tubby side, dark haired, and quite scatty. But her heart was in the right place. She was a fabulous hostess at dinner parties at home and at their family villa in Barbados when the gang had gone there with all the children when they young.

The meeting with Kate Newman at the Royal Marsden in Chelsea went more or less as Mark had explained it would be. Kate recommended that the treatment should start straight away after explaining the procedures in depth to Gill with Frank listening on intently. Gill had taken a liking to Kate and connected with her immediately. She was very professional but also pleasant and genuine. Gill was quite surprised Kate was in charge at the Marsden; she looked far too young, Gill guessed she was only in her mid-thirties, but she looked much younger.

Kate was an attractive woman with shoulder-length mousy hair; a neat, trim figure a little on the boyish side; and a lovely face. When she smiled, her face lit up the room. Gill noticed that Kate wasn't wearing an engagement or wedding ring, so she was still single probably, married to her job—consulting, lecturing on the dreaded disease, busy saving people's lives, Gill thought, which she found very reassuring.

Mark was at the Marsden hospital in Chelsea to greet Frank and Gill when they arrived for her first treatment. He wanted to be involved and felt it would be good for them both to see a familiar face. Gill appeared radiant as ever, Mark noticed, but Frank wasn't bearing up that well at all by the look of him. Frank was fidgety and nervous. Wearing a smart business suit, shirt, and tie, he kept fingering his collar as if it was too tight for his neck. Gill looked at Frank and tutted. She shook her head and then turned to Mark. She smiled and said, "He really doesn't like hospitals, Mark. You'll have to forgive him. You wouldn't think he was here to support me, would you?"

They both looked at Frank again and laughed. Frank laughed too, finally, although it was a completely false laugh. He was so nervous he hadn't slept at all, and he kept feeling quite sick and a little dizzy at times. All in all, he was an absolute wreck. To the best of Frank's knowledge, he had never suffered a panic attack, but he wondered if that was what he was experiencing now! To make matters worse, he wasn't very good at waiting or "hanging around" as Gill always reminded him of when he got too impatient. Today was no exception. He finally settled down and started to read the newspaper he had brought with him. After about an hour, and trying his best to do the crossword, he heard footsteps and talking outside the room. Frank looked up from his paper as the door opened. He saw Mark Postlethwaite's troubled face as the man came striding into the room. Quickly rising to his feet, Frank could tell something was wrong.

"I'm so sorry, Frank. There were complications."

"Were …? Why are you speaking in the past tense? What are you saying to me, Mark?" he heard himself say. The words seemed to echo around his head. He realised he was shouting. He felt dizzy again, lightheaded, and thought he was going to throw up. He tried to unscramble his brain. He realised Mark was speaking to him. Trying hard to refocus on what was being said, he stood up and murmured. "I'm sorry, Mark. What? What did you just say?"

Mark took the newspaper from Frank's hand. Placing his hands on both shoulders, he sat Frank back down in the chair. "Frank, I'm so sorry. There were complications. We've lost Gillian."

Frank rubbed his forehead and looked up, confused, at Mark, who stood closely over him in an effort to stop Frank standing up again. "Complications? Lost her? What do you mean you've lost her, Mark! I … I don't understand!" Frank was getting agitated; his head was spinning.

Mark was worried about how he had broken the news of Gill's death to Frank. Instead of being his cool, calm self, as he had been trained to be in these situations, he was coming over as quite agitated. This wasn't normal patient bad news, though. He and his family members considered Frank and Gill good friends, and had done for many years. Mark didn't feel calm, detached, and sympathetic as he always was with patients' relatives. Gill's death had affected him emotionally, and he had to try to hold it together and be calm and professional for Frank. "Are you okay, Frank? Do you understand what I'm saying to you? Do you understand what I have just told you?" whispered Mark, fighting to control his own breathing and placing his hand on Frank's shoulder.

Mark took a seat next to Frank and explained slowly and calmly that Gill had developed bleeding complications and had died during the induction therapy—chemotherapy. They had tried to save her with blood transfusions, but it was too late. Standing up, Mark apologised again. "I'm so sorry, Frank." It seemed so futile just repeating those words. Mark turned and quickly wiped away tears that were gathering in his eyes, hoping Frank wouldn't see that he was upset also. *Not very professional*, Mark thought to himself.

Frank felt as if he had been hit with a sledgehammer. A nurse appeared as if by magic from behind Mark. Frank hadn't noticed her before. She handed him a glass of water. He tried to sip it, but his hands were shaking so much all he managed to do was to spill it on to his trousers and the floor. He felt as if he wasn't in the room or even the hospital, but in a drifting world of his own, not hearing what was being said because it was all just faint background noise. He heard Mark telling him to take long, deep breaths. Finally, his mind returned once more to the room. The nurse had taken the glass from him and was wiping his hand and then the wet floor in front of Frank's feet.

She died all alone, was all that kept going through Frank's' mind. He felt so guilty that he had failed her by not being by her side when she needed him most.

He shook his head and said, "I was sat here waiting for her to come back from having her treatment. I should have been with her." He thought, *Tom's at the office. Eli's in*

Nottingham in her studies. Oh my God! How I am going to tell them their mother has died? Gill had spoken with both of them when she was diagnosed explaining the details of the cancer very calmly. She had played down the seriousness of the situation, but apart from that fact, she had been very honest with them. After all, they weren't little children anymore. She had told Tom and Eli not to worry, insisting she would be okay. She'd told them to come home at the weekend after she had her first course of treatment. Her plan was that they could all discuss her illness and the treatment fully and have a wonderful family weekend together. Now she was dead, and Frank had to tell them when, at the present moment, all he wanted to do was to die to and be with Gill!

They never got to see her one last time or to say goodbye—none of them did. She had died alone. The last words she'd said to Frank as she walked off for her treatment as he fussed about trying to fold his newspaper to do the crossword was, "Don't worry. I'll be fine. We'll get through this." She'd kissed him on the cheek and left the room.

How he wished he could change places with her. If he had been the one to die first, she would have known what to do and would have coped so much better with it than he could ever do. He would be lost without her. He started to quietly cry. Mark placed a sympathetic hand on his shoulder and asked Frank if there was anybody he wanted him to call to be with him—Tom or David?

Frank shook his head and wiped his mouth on the back of his hand. He felt foolish for not paying attention and said, "No. I will be fine thanks, Mark. I'm just ... When can I see Gill?"

"I'll go and check for you. I'm sure you'll be able to see her soon," Mark replied. As he turned to leave the room, he whispered something to the nurse who looked sympathetically over at Frank. Then she sat down on one of the chairs on the other side of the room.

Chapter 11

COMING HOME

Frank walked into the hall and closed the door behind him with a bang by leaning back onto it. Max, the wheaten terrier, came bounding down the hall wagging his tail wildly to greet him. Frank was absolutely exhausted. The drive back from the Royal Marsden in Chelsea had been torturous. How he hadn't had an accident was anybody's guess. So many thoughts were going through his mind as he tried to make sense at what had happened. He certainly hadn't been concentrating on his driving; he should have let Mark drive him home when he offered.

After tossing the car keys on the lounge coffee table, he watched them skid across the glass and fall on to the carpet. He stood there confused for a moment looking at them before deciding to leave them where they had landed on the floor. He turned and walked over to the drink's cabinet. Opening the doors, he took out a glass and poured himself a large malt whisky. He took a big gulp. It burned the back of his throat. It hurt like hell and made him cough. He wiped his mouth on the back of his trembling hand

and sank into the chair. Max had been patiently waiting, watching Frank closely. He trotted over to Frank. Wagging his tail, he placed his head on his master's knee. Frank patted Max on the head and looked down into his dogs' big dark brown eyes. He let out a big sigh and asked his trusty friend, "What the fuck are we going to do, Max?" Letting out another deep sigh, he looked at his trembling hand and held it up in front of his face.

Hearing his name, Max wagged his tail and leaned into Frank's legs. Frank smiled at his dog and ran his trembling fingers across his forehead. He said to himself, *Come on, you need to concentrate. What do I do now? Phone Tom first I suppose, then Eli. And then let David and Sue and the office know. That sounds about right, I suppose.*

After going over the plan again in his head, he dragged his top teeth across his lower lip. He decided he would get David to tell Sue and to let the company's directors know about Gill. The ringing of his mobile made him jump up with a start. Cursing, he picked up the whisky glass from the floor. Looking at his phone, he saw it was Tom's number, and his heart sank.

He'd been building himself up to break the news to the children. He needed a few more drinks first. He wasn't ready yet. He was tempted to let the call ring out, but he felt embarrassed even thinking that. He had to man up and tell his children their mother was dead. Frank answered the phone. "Hello, Tom."

"Hi, Dad. How you doing? How did Mum's treatment go? Is she there?" Tom enquired. Tom went on to explain he thought he would ring as he had just come out of a meeting and was heading straight off to another one.

"Son, I need you to sit down and listen to me."

Picking up on the tone of his dads' voice, Tom said, "Dad, what's wrong? You're worrying me. What's happened? You never call me son unless you're cross or something's wrong. And why do I have to sit down, Dad—"

Frank cut Tom short. "Tom, just listen to me. I've only just got home. Son, I'm afraid your mum died this afternoon at the hospital while she was having her treatment. I'm so sorry, son."

Frank sat back down in his chair, giving Tom some time to take in what he had just been told. Frank went on to explain to Tom that there had been complications during the treatment. It was something that could happen in these situations. His mum had developed bleeding problems, and despite blood transfusions, the medical team hadn't been able to save her. He actually felt better in a weird way for sharing the news. It was as if a weight had been lifted off his shoulders. Frank took a deep breath and waited for Tom to speak, but it was completely silent on the end of the line. "Tom, are you there? Are you okay, son?"

Tom's emotional and shaky voice came over the phone. "Yes, Dad. I'm here. Sorry. I'm just trying to take it all in. I can't believe it. I'm just shell-shocked. Mum told us both to come home this weekend so we could have some family time together. Oh, my God. Have you told Eli yet?"

"No. I was building up the courage to ring you first, when you called me. I'll phone her next when we've finished talking." Frank sighed.

Tom, holding back tears, said, "I'll leave the office and come home straight away. Are you all right, Dad?"

Frank reassured Tom he was holding up and said, like him, he just couldn't believe it.

Phoning Eli to break the news to her was the hardest thing Frank had ever had to do in his whole life. His heart was beating so fast he thought he would have a heart attack. He knew Tom was strong and would hold it together and would do his crying in private. Eli was completely different; she responded in floods of tears and just kept screaming "No! it's not true!" to everything Frank told her. It broke his heart listening to her.

After half an hour, he finally calmed her down at least so they could talk rationally. She refused Frank's offer to drive up to Nottingham to bring her back home. She had calmed down and reassured Frank that she would be fine getting the train home. It would give her time to try to come to terms with everything. Although Frank wasn't happy about it, he was too drained mentally and physically to try to argue the case with her. Reluctantly he agreed, saying he would meet her at the tube station as usual.

Frank called David at the office and caught him just as he had got back from a meeting. This was his third call now, and it seemed easier speaking to David about it than it had been with Tom and Eli for obvious reasons. He had unknowingly developed a pattern of what words he started with and how he reacted to the shock and sadness and the condolences. David's first words were to ask after Gill. Frank told him the bad news and waited for the words to sink in. "What? Bloody hell, Frank! What? I didn't realise it was that serious from what you and Sue told me. Shit! We were all in Palma having a ball only a short while ago! I just can't believe it."

Frank went through everything from going for the first appointment to Mark Postlethwaite rushing in, ashen faced, to seeing Gill's body. She'd been as beautiful as ever and just looked as if she was sleeping.

Letting out a huge sigh of disbelief, David said "Oh, my God, Frank. I'm so sorry. Is there anything you want me to do?"

"Thanks, David. Actually, there is. Would you tell the MD and the other directors and everybody in the office and whoever else you think should know what's happened? And tell them I'll send along the details of the funeral when I get it all sorted out."

"No problem. Consider it done. I'll deal with everything, and I'll also tell Sue. God! She will be devastated. Do the children know?

As Frank rubbed his fingers across his forehead, his mind drifted. He looked out of the lounge window over to the Common at two young children playing happily with their dog. People sat on the grass and in deckchairs sunbathing. Then he realised he'd been asked a question. He refocused. "Sorry, David. Yes. So bloody hard telling them. It was the worst thing I've ever had to do—especially Eli, as you would expect. She wouldn't believe me. She just kept 'No! It's not true!' They are both on their way home. God, the next few weeks are going to be so bloody awful. What will we do without her, David?"

Standing up from his desk and looking down at the traffic on the road below, David replied, "We'll all rally round to help as much as we can, Frank. Whatever you want us to do for you, consider it done. That's what friends are for at times like this. I'll do my utmost to keep Sue from calling around for a few days so the three of you can grieve as a family, but if Eli does need Sue, Frank, please just tell her to ring, and she'll be straight round to yours."

"Thanks. I'll let Eli know. It might help. I'll ring you tomorrow and have a chat with you if that's okay." With that, they said their goodbyes and hung up. Frank thought that he actually felt a little better after his conversation with David. He was a good friend. He half smiled to himself—the first real smile since they got Gill's prognosis.

Max's barking brought him back into the real world. Frank had been staring at the framed family photo on the coffee table—all of them on holiday in Florida. It was one of Gill's favourites. The children were so young then. Putting his whisky glass on the table, he looked at the clock on the fireplace and realised he had been lost in his thoughts for almost thirty minutes. *Happier times*, thought Frank as he walked into hall following the excited Max.

Max had heard Tom's key in the lock and was now dancing around at the bottom of the long hall excited to greet him. The front door opened, and Tom walked in, pulling his key out of the lock and putting it in his pocket. Putting his briefcase down, he looked up and saw Frank standing at the top of the hall looking at him. Tom smiled and said, "Hi, Dad. How are you?" Closing the door behind him, he ruffled Max's ears. The dog was making a nuisance of himself around Tom's feet, leaping up to greet him.

"I've been better, son! Thanks for coming straight home. Are you all right?" replied Frank. He walked up the hall to greet his son, who towered over him and had done since he was about fifteen. They hugged affectionately as they always did, only this time the hug was a little longer than usual. Tom took off his coat and shoes. He left them with his briefcase at the bottom of the stairs as he always did when he came home. It annoyed his mum every time, and she would tut-tut and take them up to Tom's room.

Loosening his tie and undoing the top button of his shirt, he joined his dad in the lounge at the front of the house. Frank poured two more drinks. He turned and handed Tom a glass of whisky. Tom was looking out across the Common. Sitting back down in his chair, Frank asked Tom if his superiors at the office were okay about him leaving early. He asked what Tom had told them.

Tom smiled, walked over to the sofa, and plonked down. He replied, "Don't worry. They were fine, Dad. Believe me, I told them the bad news. They were very sympathetic and quite understood me leaving for home." Tom took a sip of his drink and added in an emotional voice, "It's such a shock, Dad. I don't think I've fully taken it in yet, to be honest. I expected to see her come walking out of the kitchen or standing with you when I walked in. Mum seemed so upbeat when I spoke with her after she was diagnosed."

Leaning back in his chair with his drink, Frank looked up at the ceiling and gave a wry smile at Tom's words. He explained wistfully, "That was your mum all over, son. She didn't want to tell you and Eli her cancer was a bad one. She didn't want you both worrying, especially Eli. And she was always so positive. She was certain she was going to beat it. She had felt tired and not herself for a while, which we didn't realise at the time were the early signs, but why would we suspect it could be cancer? I just wish she had told me earlier. We could have checked it out earlier. But she kept it to herself and just got in with things. Typical of your mum. Although the consultant at the Marsden told us it's known as the hidden cancer because of the lack of early symptoms."

Tom sighed heavily and had a gulp of whisky. He looked across to his dad and said, "I just wish we could have had more time together as a family before she … You know—before it happened. It's just so sudden and so bloody final." His voice tailed off. He thought he should try to change the subject because he felt he might start to cry again. "What time is Eli back?"

"She'll be another hour or so I suspect. She said she would text when she was close. I'll take Max down to meet her at the tube station as usual," Frank replied, taking another sip of his malt.

Max, hearing his name, jumped up and padded over to where Frank sat enjoying the warmth of his drink, which was going down rather a little too well. He was glad Tom was home. Gill wouldn't have approved, Tom thought to himself—drinking whisky so early in the evening. Tut, tut!

"How will you cope without her, Dad? You and mum were so close and always did everything together when you were home."

Frank looked down at the carpet and rubbed his forehead. Then he stopped and put his hand on his knee. He had remembered Gill always told him off for rubbing his forehead. She would say, "It's your one and only annoying habit!" Frank looked up at Tom and answered, "I'll have to, Tom. I need to be strong and be here for you and your sister, especially for Eli. She will miss your mum so much. When she was home, they were always out shopping with

Wandsworth Common

Sue, lunching, and doing all those girly things together. I used to call them the three musketeers!"

"Bloody hell—Sue! Does she know, Dad? She and Mum were like sisters!"

"Yes, she will know by now. I spoke with David. He said he would tell her. I didn't want to; it was hard enough telling you and Eli. She'll be heartbroken. She really will," replied Frank.

They sat there in silence for quite a while enjoying the warming taste of the whisky, lost in their own thoughts and memories. The silence was broken when Frank's mobile went off. It was Eli to say she was getting on the tube and was about twenty minutes away.

Frank finished his drink and put the glass down on the coffee table. After ten minutes or so, he went to get his coat. He was ready to walk down to the tube station to meet Eli. It was their little ritual; he and Max would always wait outside the tube station to greet her when she came home from uni.

"Do you want me to come with you?" Tom shouted to his dad, who was in the hall. Tom sneakily got up and poured himself another whisky, fully taking advantage of his dad being out of the room. He sure felt that he needed it.

"No. It's okay. You sort your things out and take all your stuff up to your room please, so the hall's clear when we get back." Frank worked at putting the lead on Max, who was making it so difficult by jumping around excitedly at the thought of going out after seeing Frank put on his coat and hearing Eli's name mentioned.

Eli came out of the station entrance, her face as lovely as ever. She obviously tried to manage a little smile when she spotted Max and her dad standing there in their usual place, but when she took off her sunglasses, her red eyes gave her away. She must have been crying all the way home. She would always make a big fuss of Max first. Frank was used to Max getting all the attention while he stood there smiling, holding the lead, and waiting for his turn for a hug and kiss. This time, however, Eli fell straight into her dad's arms in a flood of tears. He just hugged her tightly, quietly saying in her ear, "All right. It's okay. Let it all out, darling."

After a few minutes, conscious of the looks they were getting from some of the commuters coming out of the station, Frank finally said as he gently rubbed her back, "Come on. Let's get you home. Tom's there waiting for us." Taking Eli's backpack and holdall, he handed her Max's lead. He could never get over how alike Gill and Eli were in both looks and personality. Even wearing a simple pair of faded jeans and a cable jumper, her brown hair pulled back in a simple ponytail, Eli looked beautiful. She always did, just like Gill. Sue always said Eli would still look fabulous if she was dressed in a bin liner.

On the way back, they walked slowly, long silences interrupted with some small talk. He asked about student life in Nottingham, the latest news on the boyfriend front, how her studies were going—anything to stop her asking about the details of what had happened, afraid it would upset her and start her off crying again.

Eli looked at her dad and said, "I can't believe it, Daddy. She was so young!"

"I know, darling. Let's wait until we get home, and the three of us can talk about everything," replied Frank, getting hold of her hand and giving it a gentle squeeze. He wanted to go through everything that had happened just one time with Tom and Eli when they were all together in the privacy of their own home. At this moment, it was too painful, and to see Eli so upset would start him off crying as well.

"We're home!" shouted Frank. As he opened the front door and dumped Eli's backpack in the hall, he heard Tom shouting at someone in the front room. He walked down the hall and looked into the lounge just as Tom ended a call on his mobile. "What was that all about?" Frank noticed that Tom was red in the face and quite flustered.

"Nothing. Just work," replied Tom.

"It didn't sound like work," said Frank, studying Tom's face. From the time when Tom was a little boy Frank always knew when Tom was lying to him.

Ignoring his dad's comment, Tom walked over to Eli. As he pulled her towards him, gently kissed her on her forehead, and hugged her, she buried her sobbing face into his chest.

Frank looked at the two of them there in the middle of the lounge hugging each other while Max sat there looking up at them both. He swallowed hard. It broke his heart to see them like this. His eyes filled with tears. He said to himself, *God, help us get through the next couple of weeks please!* Clearing his throat and discreetly wiping his eyes with his handkerchief, he said quietly, "I'll take your bags up to your room, Eli darling."

In the hall he took a deep breath, picked up Eli's backpack and handbag, and walked up the stairs with a heavy heart. He thought, *What would Gill do to get the family through this? Probably just be her normal, cool, calm self—the way she always was in a crisis.* He thought to himself, *That's what I've got to do—keep cool, rational, and calm. Easier said than done at the moment!* He placed Eli's bags on her bed.

Frank crossed the landing and walked into *their* bedroom—the room he had always shared with Gill. Some of her creams and makeup were on the bedside cabinet where she had left them before they'd left for the hospital. He sat down on her side of the bed and gently stroked her pillow. *We were lying here talking only a few hours ago*, he thought. *And now we'll never talk again. What the hell am I going to do when Tom goes back to his flat and Eli returns to uni?* He sighed heavily. *The house is going to be so empty without her. She won't be here to greet me when I get home from the office. It'll just be Max—that's all. God! What will I do with Max when I go back to the office? I need someone to look after him. I'll sort that out before I go back to work*, he reassured himself. Standing up, he hung his jacket up in the wardrobe, checked in the mirror to make sure his hair was tidy, and went downstairs to re-join Tom and Eli, who were both sitting together on the sofa talking.

Chapter 12

THE FUNERAL

Eli shouted down the stairs from her room. She was getting dressed to walk Max. "There's no point me going back to uni in Nottingham after the funeral. Uni finishes in a few weeks, and I can do what studying I have to do here at home, Dad. Honestly."

"Well, if you're certain that's the case. You know your studies are very important to your mum and me." Realising what he had said, Frank winced and waited to see if there would be any reaction from Eli. The words had just come out! He had tried to be so careful not to mention Gill's name or say "your mum" recently for fear of upsetting Eli. He hoped it wouldn't start her crying again. She had been surprisingly upbeat today. It was just something he would have said when Gill was … well … still here.

"Besides, I can look after you, Dad. You need someone to take care of you now," she shouted back.

Frank was so relieved he hadn't upset Eli, he shouted back up to her, "Well, if you're sure your studies won't suffer. And for the record, young lady, you're the one who needs looking after, not me, you cheeky little bugger!" After jokingly scolding her, he turned away from the bottom of the stairs and headed into the kitchen, a little smile across his face.

It was the day before the funeral. Everything was arranged. It had been a long hard slog to deal with the grieving and especially the inquest. A lot of tears had been shed and a lot of anguish suffered, but it looked as if they had made it and come out the other side intact. Frank was sure that, if Gill was looking down on them, she would be proud with the way he had coped and managed everything, especially looking after Tom and Eli.

He was normally always at the office or in America, and it would fall to Gill to sort out family "problems." Frank usually heard about them after they had been successfully dealt with and put to bed, after he had returned home.

Tom had gone back to his flat, it was quicker for him to get to his office, and there wasn't really any need for him to stay off work too long.

Frank had told him to go back to work, saying it would be good way to take his mind off his grief. He had a feeling that Tom had really wanted to get back to work but didn't like to suggest it in case he offended him or Eli.

They'd had a good family chat about grief and that people handled it in many different ways, and however they wanted to grieve and deal with their mum's death individually was fine. There was no right or wrong way. It had been a good conversation, and it had brought their individual feelings out into the open. Frank had got the idea after speaking to David who asked how the children were coping having never lost anyone close to them before. They had lost their grandparents, but they hadn't been really that close to them. They had spoken on the phone occasionally, usually to thank them for birthday and Christmas money. Frank and Gill rarely went north to visit their parents; they were always too busy with school events and sports at the weekends. Frank realised that it was a good point, so he had raised the subject of grieving with Tom and Eli, and it appeared to have helped, not just the children, but also him.

Tom appeared to be coping reasonably and seemed relieved to get back into a normal routine before the funeral. Frank was convinced something was troubling him, though, and it wasn't just his mum's death. There was definitely something else going on in his life. Tom seemed worried and tense about something, but he was keeping it to himself, just as he always had done since he was a little boy.

Frank had heard a few more angry phone conversations—once when he was passing Tom's bedroom and another time when he was in the kitchen and Tom was in the garden. When he asked Tom if there was a problem regarding the heated phone calls, he just said it was to do with work and then quickly changed the subject.

One thing Frank did know was how his children reacted when either of them had a problem, especially Tom. It wasn't like Tom to become annoyed. If Eli had a problem, she would share it with her mum and dad, but Tom was a closed book.

For Eli, her mum's death was obviously still very raw. She could be fine, and then something would remind her of her mum, and it would start her off in floods of tears again. Hearing her cry like that would break Frank's heart. He was devastated that he couldn't fix it for her. He had always been able to "fix" problems for his little girl, and it had become a joke between them.

Eli had been out with Sue for lunch several times and also shopping to buy an outfit for the funeral. The lunches had appeared to help Eli. She would talk with Sue about her mum. David had told Frank the reminiscing about good times appeared to be helping both of them, Sue just as much as Eli.

Frank and Eli had walked Max on the Common each morning and again early in the evenings. They had lots of long conversations about past family holidays and happy days they had all spent together. Eli had developed a thirst for all the family details—when Frank and Gill first meet, when they decided to get married, how Frank proposed to her mum. They laughed together and cried together, but it all helped the healing process and the aching pain that they both felt about losing Gill so suddenly and unexpectedly. Frank hadn't realised just how much Eli had grown up these last few years whilst she had been away at university. She had blossomed into a lovely, caring, intelligent, and strong-willed young lady. Frank thought that, when she was eventually ready to settle down, she would make some lucky man an excellent wife and also a great mother to their children.

"Now, I would like to call on Gill's husband, Frank, to come up and say a few words." The vicar's mention of Frank's name quickly brought him back into the present. Eli squeezed her dad's arm as he straightened his tie and stood up to walk to front of the chapel. It was a hot summer day outside, and the long rays of bright sunshine poured in through the stained-glass windows behind the alter. The sunrays gave the effect of spotlights bathing the pulpit in a warm glow.

Frank took out his notes looked at them. Pausing and looking up, he scanned all the friendly sympathetic faces looking back at him—friends from the sports club that they both belonged to, close friends they had made in their years down south, several old friends from the north who had made the long journey to pay their respects, parents of Tom and Eli's school friends with whom they had kept in touch after the schooldays were gone, and also quite a few of Frank's colleagues from his office. Some people there had never met Gill but were obviously in attendance to show their support and respect to Frank. Simon Taylor's face smiled back at Frank from the third row. Frank gave him a little smile back and gently nodded his appreciation. He cleared his throat ready to start his eulogy. "I would like to thank you all for your support today at what has been a very difficult time for Eli, Tom, and myself. Those of you who knew Gill will know the big void she has left in our family. We will miss her terribly."

He looked at Eli, who was sitting next to Sue dabbing her eyes with a handkerchief. Tom was looking down at his feet. *Probably trying to concentrate on the poem he was going to get up and read next*, thought Frank.

Taking a deep breath, he continued: "Even though Gill was taken from us so quickly and, without a doubt, far too soon, I have a lot to be thankful for—the wonderful years I knew her and got to spend with her, the two beautiful children she gave me, how she brought them up to be good, kind, level-headed young adults, with a little help from me also of course." A small respectful ripple of laughter went around the chapel. "Also, the wonderful times we spent together, just with each other in the early days and then as a family with Tom and Eli—all such beautiful times and memories that we, as a family, and certainly I will remember and cherish.

"Just like most couples, we were expecting to grow old together, see our children grow up and settle down and eventually have children of their own. We were looking forward to being grandparents and having family holidays again and weekends with our grandchildren, watching them grow up—normal family things that all parents look forward to. But, sadly, now that's not going to be the case for Gill.

"However, I'm not bitter. I'm just grateful for all the wonderful times I have had with her. They've been cruelly cut short. However, they were special wonderful years that we shared, and for that I am eternally thankful. I will remember them for the rest of my life."

Thanking everyone again for coming to the funeral and for their support, he smiled, put his notes away, and walked back to his seat. He slowed ever so slightly and looked at Gill's coffin on the right-hand side of the chapel. Eli stood and hugged him so hard as he was about to sit down, it took him by surprise. Tom half smiled at his dad and nodded his approval as he stood up. It was Tom's turn now, and he did a good a job of reading the poem they had picked out. He'd told Eli and Frank that he was worried he would break down in tears; the words were so sad.

Eli had decided she didn't want to speak at the funeral

and asked her dad and Tom several times if that was okay with them. They all talked about it, and both Frank and Tom supported Eli's decision and reassured her, agreeing it would be too upsetting for her and, if she were to break down, she would most likely have had the whole church in floods of tears.

The wake was held in a private room of their favourite local bar and brasserie, Brinkley's, overlooking the Common. It had very pleasant views out over the Common. It was where Frank and Gill had gone for drinks and meals on many occasions over the years, alone, sometimes with the children, and also with friends.

The Long Bar was a bright relaxing room, very popular with the local clientele. In the evenings, people would have a pre-dinner drink up there or just have a relaxing evening drinking with a few tapas that were served only there. The bar, with white leather chrome bar stools, was directly opposite the double entrance doors. On the left-hand side of the room, the wall was virtually one big circular window framed by a taupe-coloured pelmet and matching heavy grey curtains. The view, like the one downstairs, looked out over onto the Common. The huge window made the room very bright and airy. Seating areas consisting of light grey, soft leather two- and three-seater chesterfield sofas together with cream-coloured, glass-topped coffee tables on large square cream-and-black scatter rugs were set around the room, giving it a classy homely lounge effect despite its size.

A long table had been placed on the right-hand side to hold the buffet that Eli had carefully chosen with the owners' wife, Stella. Eli had changed her mind on the menu several times, wanting it to be just perfect for her mum. Frank had arranged a free bar for the guests, not that anybody was really drinking. Most guests just had a single glass of wine or a cold glass of beer whilst chatting. Friends were coming up to the family members and offering their condolences as they recollected stories of Gill, all reinforcing what a lovely person she had been.

Frank, Tom, and Eli smiled, listened, and thanked them for all their kind comments. Frank was hoping it would end soon and that they would all leave so he could go home. He hated every minute of it; he had never been comfortable with wakes. It just didn't seem right to him to have a "party" to celebrate someone's life. It was too much in contrast to their funeral, which had been held just thirty minutes earlier.

After two hours, he'd had enough and just wanted to get some fresh air and go for a walk on the Common. They could all go together—Frank, Tom, Eli, and Max. He wanted to tell his children that he would be there for them as always. He found himself on his own over in the bay window where he had been chatting with one of the directors from the office when Simon Taylor and David appeared at his side.

"Pleased with how the day's gone, Frank?" asked Simon, affectionately rubbing Frank's back. "It was a really good traditional service—just right. Not too sad, but also not one of these modern 'come on be cheerful, everyone, and celebrate!' kind of events that people tend to have now."

"Yes, I suppose it was fine," answered Frank. "I'm not sure if you can be pleased with a funeral, but I know what you mean. It was a very nice service. Thanks for coming,

Simon. How's the retirement going?" enquired Frank, thinking, *Bloody hell, Simon still looks good for his age.* He tried to think how old he would be now.

"Good, thanks, Frank. I still miss the cut and thrust of work, but must admit I do like the leisure time, especially being able to go fishing and do anything else I want to do. I suppose your priorities change when you retire. You begin think more of yourself instead of the company always being at the forefront of your thoughts and your main priority," replied Simon whilst looking around the room and waving to Eli, who had looked over and caught his eye.

"I think Gill would be pleased," said David, changing the subject back to why they were all there. "You have done her proud. You know what a stickler she was for everything being done properly and being just so."

Frank nodded in agreement as he followed Simon's line of sight. He saw Eli sat with Sue chatting away with a couple of friends they knew from the tennis club. His gaze moved on to Tom, who was standing alone at the bar drinking. He looked a little worse for wear, which was unusual for him. He never drank too much at family "gatherings."

"Do me a favour please, David?" asked Frank. "Go over and have a chat with Tom. He looks like he's had more than enough to drink. I really don't want him to have anymore, for obvious reasons."

David replied, "Yes of course I will. He does look like he's had enough." He walked off towards the bar in Tom's direction.

With that said, Frank smiled and excused himself with Simon and walked over to say goodbye to some colleagues from the office who had indicated to him that they were about to leave but politely didn't want to interrupt him.

Joining David and Tom at the bar, Frank patted Tom on the shoulder and said reassuringly, "You did well with your poem, Tom. It's very difficult standing and speaking before people at a funeral. It's so emotional—not like doing a business presentation at the office."

Tom smiled appreciatively and replied, "Thanks, Dad. I can't tell you how worried I was about getting upset while I was reading it. That would have been so embarrassing."

David smiled sympathetically and remarked, "You shouldn't have worried about getting upset, Tom. People would have understood and, as your dad just said, it's a very emotional time for you to stand up and speak in front of people."

Chapter 13

LIFE GOES ON!

"Well, that went as well as could be expected!" said Tom, kicking off his shoes and flopping down on the sofa. He was glad the funeral was over but wouldn't have said it out loud for fear it would be taken the wrong way and upset his dad and Eli.

"Yes, it did," replied Frank, thinking he was glad it was all over and relieved it had all gone off without a hitch. He was not really sure why people said that—what sort of "hitch" could happen at a funeral? He dreaded thinking about it and dismissed it from his mind.

"What do you think, Eli?" Frank asked. "A good choice with the food. It was really nice, darling. Quite a few people commented on it."

Eli was lying on the floor in front of the fireplace stroking and cuddling Max as usual; they were inseparably when she was home. Max would always be by her side and follow her around everywhere like a shadow. He would sleep at the bottom of her bed at night, which Gill had never really approved of, but she had given up complaining about it many years ago.

"Yes, I was pleased with it. I'm sure Mum would have been really proud. It was a touching service, and Brinkley's was a great choice. The room was lovely," she replied wistfully.

"Are you staying here tonight, Tom, or going home?" Frank asked, pouring himself a whisky.

"No, I'll head off back to Clapham later, if we're eating," Tom replied making a mental note that his dad hadn't offered him a whisky, which was always his dad's way of saying, "You've had enough, son."

"What are we going to eat?" asked Eli. "Do you want me to cook something? I really don't mind," she said.

Nobody answered straight away. The room fell silent as they were lost in their own thoughts about the day. After a while, they all decided they weren't really that hungry. Tom said he would head off back to Clapham; he arranged an Uber and then went to his room to pack his stuff. Coming back downstairs with his things, he was ready to leave.

He hugged and kissed Eli, hugged his dad, patted Max, and bid them all goodnight. Then he left for his apartment and Clapham. Eli went upstairs followed closely by Max to change into her jim-jams. The two of them came back downstairs, and Eli made two mugs of hot chocolate for her and her dad. And she offered Max a digestive biscuit. He was allowed only one a day.

They sat quietly together on the sofa, all three of them—Frank, Eli leaning into her dad, and Max leaning into Eli. Hot chocolates finished, they decided to turn in after a long, exhausting, sad day.

The weekend came and went. It seemed strange not having the funeral to discuss and plan. The preparations had taken up quite a lot of their time and effort. It was also just as strange that Gill was never going to walk through the front door or shout "Dinner's ready!" from the kitchen anymore. Eli had tried her best to be upbeat in front of her dad, but he knew she was hurting badly and was really missing her mum. Not that he or Tom had closure with the funeral, but Eli was naturally so close to her mum. These past few years they had been more like sisters really than mother and daughter. When Eli was home from uni, they were always together with Sue. The three of them would go everywhere together—gym, tennis, shopping, lunch. They had so much in common and liked the same things.

David and Sue had invited Frank and Eli over on Saturday night for supper. They had a brief conversation about how nice the funeral was, but after a short time, the conversation revolved around the happy times they had spent together. It was still too soon for Eli. After ten minutes of reliving the happy times and the holiday fun, she broke down in tears and ran to the bathroom. Panic stricken, Sue jumped up to run after her, but Frank stopped her saying, "I'll go, Sue. I've got to get used to dealing with her grief. I think it's going to be like this for quite a while. She's hurting so badly!"

Sue started to cry when Frank left the room. David went over to her and hugged her closely to him. "I'm such a fool!" Sue said between sobs.

"Don't be silly," replied David. "You were only trying to cheer up Eli, and I know you're missing Gill too. You two were like sisters. Come on. Wipe your tears away. They'll be back out soon."

After a short while, Frank and Eli returned from the bathroom. When Sue saw Eli, she started to cry all over again. She hugged Eli and said, "I'm so sorry for upsetting you, darling. I wouldn't do that for the world. In my silly way, I thought being nostalgic and that chatting about your mum and the wonderful times we all had together would help. It was insensitive. Please forgive me."

Eli hugged her back and assured her it wasn't her fault. It wasn't late in the evening, but high emotions had put a bit of a dampener on the night. Shortly afterwards, Frank and Eli said their goodnights, kissed and hugged their hosts, and walked home around the corner in silence. After Eli changed for bed, she came down and made them both their usual hot chocolate drinks. Frank had let Max out into garden for his last pee of the day before bedtime and was standing outside the kitchen door, doggy towel in hand, waiting to wipe Max's paws before he came back into the kitchen.

"Are you okay, darling?" asked Frank. "You look terribly pale and drawn. I'm worried about you."

Eli smiled. Taking a sip of her hot chocolate she replied, "I'll be okay, Daddy. We've all been through a lot these past weeks since we lost Mummy."

"I know we have, darling, but you mustn't make yourself ill. Your mum wouldn't want that," said Frank over his shoulder as he knelt down to wipe and inspect Max's paws.

The three of them sat in the lounge while Frank and Eli enjoying their hot chocolate in silence. Max sprawled out at Eli's feet, more than content to have her back home. After ten minutes or so, Eli got up and went into the kitchen with the cups, followed by Max. Coming back into the lounge, she kissed her dad on the forehead and told him, "I'm going to bed now, Dad. I love you. Goodnight."

"Love you too, my darling—very much," replied Frank, smiling as he watched Max faithfully trot off behind her up the stairs to her bedroom. He sat there still looking at the door into the hall. He could hear Eli and Max making their way upstairs and across the landing. Then he heard Eli's bedroom door closing. He was worried about Eli. The grief was having an effect on her health. She didn't look well; she was very pale and drawn. He wasn't sure what he could do other than keep a close eye on her. He would speak with Sue; she might be able to help and spend some time with Eli to cheer up a little.

Tom checked in with a phone call on Sunday afternoon to see how everyone was. Frank was a little concerned about a really strange question Tom had asked him during the call. Tom had wanted to know if his mum had left him and Eli any money. Frank was shocked and somewhat puzzled by Tom's question. Despite the fact that Gill had died suddenly and prematurely, he explained that she didn't have her own money as such. All that Frank earned was in a joint account at the bank.

They had made wills, but they were just mirror wills leaving everything to each other, as the survivor would look after Tom and Eli. The only stipulation was that, if they died together, everything would be split between the Tom and Eli.

Frank was puzzled by the question, though, and enquired, "Why do you ask? Surely you're not short of money on the salary and bonuses you are on, are you?"

Tom quickly came back with, "No. Not at all. Just wondered, nothing more! Is Eli there? I would like a few words with her."

Frank put Eli on the phone, but the conversation he'd had with his son troubled him. It was completely out of character for Tom to ask about money; he was so independent. Remembering Tom's raised voice during recent phone calls, which Tom had dismissed as "just work", Frank wondered if Tom's problems were money related.

He hadn't mentioned to Tom or Eli that he and Gill had maintained life insurance policies, and that he was expecting a £250,000 settlement. Frank was going to leave it for a month or so before telling them. The funeral had just taken place; there wasn't any rush. Frank had taken out life policies on himself and Gill many years ago, mainly to cover the mortgage if anything happened to either one of them. But the mortgage had been paid off a few years earlier with Frank's bonuses. Now that Gill had died, his immediate intention was to split the money equally between Tom and Eli, hopefully when things settled down and started to get back to normal.

However, after a lot of soul-searching, Frank decided to put that idea on hold until he got to the bottom of the situation Tom had got himself into. Also, there wasn't any rush to load either of them up with money. Tom was earning good money and already had his own flat. His half would help to lower his mortgage. Eli didn't need money yet as she was still at university, so Frank might invest it so it would be ready for when she might look to get a flat in town in the future.

Frank suddenly felt so alone not having Gill to discuss this with. They would always discuss the family's "big things" and come up with the best solutions; smaller problems he usually left to Gill.

Frank would have to find out what was going on in Tom's life all on his own without Gill's input. This was what it was going to be like from now on. The thought of it made Frank go cold with feelings of dread, loneliness, and even hopelessness.

Frank's mind returned to the room has he heard Eli laughing loudly at something Tom must have said to her on the phone. Her laughter streaming in from the hall was so good to hear. It lifted Frank's heart. There hadn't been much of that lately in the house. It felt so good—the way family life used to be when Gill was there and the children were younger. The house had always been busy and full of laughter.

Frank heard Eli saying her goodbyes to Tom. She walked back into the lounge with Max. Smiling, she said, "Tom said bye and he'll ring you during the week." She sat on the sofa with Max. Frank smiled at her. She looked up at Frank smiled back and said, "What?"

Smiling broadly Frank said, "It was so lovely to hear you laughing. What did Tom say to make you laugh so much?"

Eli's face broke into a big grin and she replied, "Oh, nothing really. He was just being daft like he usually is. I think he was just trying to cheer me up, to be honest!"

Frank smiled back at Eli and asked her, "Did Tom recently mention to you about having any problems with money, like owing somebody he's borrowed from or any other problems he might have?"

Eli's looked puzzled as she replied, "No he hasn't recently—or in fact ever. That's a strange thing to say. Why would you ask that?"

Frank played it down and casually explained about the phone calls, not mentioning what Tom had just asked him.

She seemed genuinely puzzled and replied, "I'm sure he can't be short of cash or have money problems on his salary. He's always been very good with money. Even when we were young, he would always have money saved up!"

Frank replied, "Well that's what I thought too, but I heard him have some arguments on the phone recently with someone, and when I asked him about it, he just said it was only work, which I don't believe for a minute."

Eli looked across at her dad. Studying his face, she asked, "What do you think it is, Dad? Do you think he's in trouble with someone who's not very nice and they're chasing him for money?"

Frank smiled, but he could have kicked himself. He felt guilty about making her start to worry about Tom. He tried to reassure her saying, "I'm certain Tom can look after himself, and he wouldn't get himself into trouble with anybody like that. Now don't you start worrying your pretty little head about anything. We'll find out what's going on sooner or later and sort it out, so don't you fret!"

Eli looked at her dad and smiled. "Okay, I'm sure it's nothing really, Dad."

The last thing Frank wanted was for Eli to start worrying about Tom. She'd been through enough heartache recently to last her a lifetime. If Gill had been there, she would have realised this and would have told Frank not to mention Tom's troubles to Eli. *What a dope!* he said to himself. Frank changed the subject by asking Eli, "What do you fancy for dinner, in or out?"

"Let's stay home tonight, shall we? I don't mean to be a misery, but I don't really fancy getting ready and going out. I can cook us something nice."

Frank agreed. "Home it is then. What are you going to rustle up for us?"

Eli jumped and set off for the kitchen shouting back "We've got lots of food in. I'll make us something really nice. I think we deserve it, don't you, Dad?"

"I certainly do, my darling. I'll open a bottle of wine," shouted Frank back to her.

He smiled to himself. He was pleased to see Eli nice and chirpy, especially after his stupidity in asking her about Tom and his problem. It seemed that she had put it out of her mind.

Frank shouted through into the kitchen to Eli, "It's a beautiful evening. We'll take Max for a good walk after dinner." On hearing his name, Max came trotting into the lounge, wagging his tail frantically. "Not yet, Max. After dinner, I promise." Frank smiled, patting Max's back.

Frank had stored his son's "problem" in his mental "pending file" just like he did with troublesome issues at the office. The file label read: "To be reviewed and resolved later."

Chapter 14

The Mystery Text Messages

No man knows when his hour will come.
Good men are trapped by evil times
That fall unexpectedly upon them.
The book of Ecclesiastes 9:12

Frank had intended to book a few weeks' holiday from work after the funeral to give him time to sort out things and get his head around being a widower. However, the company had been very good and wouldn't hear of it. The chairman had told the managing director—MD—to tell Frank to take as much compassionate leave as he needed. When the MD spoke with Frank and relayed the chairman's message, Frank thanked him, adding that he was happy to take any business phone calls. Also, if anything came up, he could join meetings on the conference call link, explaining it would help him to keep in touch with what was going on whilst he was away from the office. The MD asked Frank the usual awkward questions people ask when someone close to them has died: How was Frank coping? How were the children coping with the loss of their mother? Whilst reassuring Frank that there was no hurry for him to return to work, the MD said he understood that Frank and the family had been through a very traumatic time. He told Frank to come back when he was good and ready. Frank thanked him again, said goodbye, and was grateful when he hung up the phone.

There wasn't that much that needed to be done other than paying the funeral expenses and sorting out the life insurance. He had reluctantly agreed that Eli could finish her term work at home instead of returning to university. But now that might help because Max needed to be looked after when Frank went back to work. Well at least that would help until the new term in September. It seemed like a good idea at the time to have Eli nearby so he could be around for her. So, it was also a good thing that he was home with her while he was temporarily off work.

Eli was holding up quite well, but he had heard her crying one night in her room after they had gone to bed. He was going to go in to see her but thought better of it. He raised it with her the next day when they were walking Max on the Common.

She told him that she did still get upset sometimes when she was alone and thought of her mum. She also confessed that she was afraid of the dark now and slept with her bedside light on. Frank's heart went out to her. He put his arm around her shoulder and told her how proud he was of the way she was coping. It was all part of the grieving process, and it was okay to cry and get upset sometimes.

Eli smiled and said, "The saddest thing, Dad, is that Mum's 'smell' is starting to disappear from around the house. The smell of our home was always so nice and reassuring every time I walked into the house. I always thought it was the smell of the house itself, but now I realise it was Mummy's individual smell, and it's fading day by day. It makes me so sad that it will disappear forever."

Frank hugged her close and said, "It might fade away, darling, but your mum's presence will always be in the house, and she will always be with you, wherever you are in this world. I'm certain of that. She loved you so much."

Tom called most nights to see if they were both okay, albeit only chatting for a few minutes, but at least he made the effort. Friday morning after they had walked Max, Sue called to collect Eli. They had arranged to go shopping and have lunch in the West End. Frank thanked Sue and said, "It's just what Eli needs. You're a star, Sue. Thank you so much."

Sue smiled and hugged Frank. She told him that she loved Eli's company because she kept her feeling young. Frank kissed Sue on the cheek and said that she wasn't to go spoiling Eli buying her any clothes or anything else like she usually did, explaining that, if Eli saw anything she liked, he had given her his Amex to pay for it—his treat.

Being alone gave him the chance to go through some of Gill's possessions in the bedroom. He had put it off a couple of times that week for fear of upsetting Eli. He wasn't sure if it was too soon. He went through her jewellery box. There were a few valuable items that were worth money—a bracelet he had bought Gill when Eli was born, a few pairs of gold earrings, a Rolex dress watch, her engagement and wedding rings. He had offered many times over the years to buy her new ones, more expensive ones. She wouldn't hear of it; she said hers weren't expensive by today's standards, but they were priceless to her and always would be. Gill wasn't really big into jewellery, not like Sue, who absolutely loved blinging it up.

He thought he would ask Eli if she wanted the bracelet, watch, and earrings and even her silver costume jewellery that Gill preferred to wear sometimes. He wouldn't have thought Tom would want any jewellery as keepsakes to remind him of his mum. Frank's mind went back to the question Tom had asked him when he called at the weekend. He thought, *If Tom did have money problems, he possibly might sell anything valuable instead of keeping it.*

He dismissed it from his mind feeling guilty for thinking that of his son. He would ask Tom what he would like of his mother's things to keep and remember her by.

He picked up Gill's phone out of the drawer; he had forgotten he had put it there with her other things when he came home without her from the Marsden on that fateful day. He sat on the edge of the bed and relived that awful afternoon in his head. He thought to himself, *It seems so long ago now!* He keyed in the month and year of her birth—her four-digit password. She had given it to him once when he wanted a number from her phone.

He would charge the phone up, wipe Gill's content from it, and give the phone to Eli. He smiled remembering she was always pestering her mum and him to upgrade her phone to the latest fashionable one. Eli was always saying, "My phone is so antiquated, and the camera on your iPhone is brilliant! Blah, blah, blah!" Frank thought she could have her mum's iPhone now; he was sure she would also appreciate it because it would be a keepsake.

He couldn't think what there was of Gill's that Tom might want. If he gave Eli getting her mum's iPhone and some jewellery, maybe he would like a piece of jewellery or her watch. Then, when he found the right girl and eventually married, he could give it her. Eli wouldn't mind, and she would be getting the rest of it. Tom always had the latest super-duper phone anyway, paid for by his company, much to the annoyance of Eli.

He plugged the phone into the charger and placed it on the bedside table. Max had joined him on the bed, and Frank scooted him off before he went downstairs to prepare a few things for the afternoon meeting with the office, which always took place promptly at three o'clock.

At around five thirty, Max ran down the hall to the front door barking when he heard Eli's voice as she shouted goodbye to Sue. He waited, wagging his tail, behind the front door. Frank looked out of the lounge window and caught a wave from Sue as she pulled away from the house into the traffic.

He opened the front door for Eli who was waddling down the path with two handfuls of clothes bags and a huge smile on her face.

"How much has this little lot cost me then?" asked Frank in his best fake annoyed voice.

Eli laughed and kissed him on the cheek as she struggled past him and Max with her shopping bags. She excitedly told him about all the shops they had visited and where she had bought her clothes, showing him each item as she made her way through the day's adventure.

He smiled and listened whilst he made them both a [cup] of tea as Eli chatted away about her shopping trip with S[ue]. He knew from experience that was what Gill did whenever Eli came back with some new clothes, and he had seen Gill go through exactly the same ritual with Eli when she and Sue had been on a shopping spree. He was just glad that his daughter was happy and that she'd had a great day out with Sue.

"I must text Sue and thank her again," he shouted as Eli and Max ran up the stairs to her bedroom to try on the clothes for Frank. He sat down with his cup of tea patiently waiting for the fashion show to start. Eli was shouting something down the stairs to him, but he couldn't make it out. He sat there with a smile on his face, just glad that she was in such a happy mood. Some days she seemed a lot better, but then she would have what she called her "sad days". On these days she found it unbearable knowing that she was never going to see her mum again. Frank felt guilty that he couldn't do anything about her "sad days", but he thought at least it was good that she was telling him about them. They could talk through her bad feelings. He was pleased that she appeared to be having more good days than sad days lately.

After dinner, Eli went upstairs to get ready to go out. She was going to a few bars in Clapham with her friends. Frank cleared away the dishes and the empty containers from the takeaway they had just enjoyed from their favourite Cantonese restaurant around the corner. Waving Eli off and telling her to take care for the third time, he sat down in the lounge with a glass of his favourite malt whisky. Looking around the lounge, he suddenly felt so lonely.

Why did it have to happen? Everything had been just so perfect. *Maybe that's why*, he thought to himself. Bad things happen to people every second of the day somewhere in the world. It's only when it happens to you or those close to you that it brings home just how fragile life can be.

As if he knew that Frank was feeling sad, Max came over to him and rested his head on Frank's lap. Frank smiled. Rubbing Max's head, he said, "It's just you and me tonight, old man, and it probably will be for many more nights to come, so I suppose we should get used to it." A bit worse for wear from the malt because he had drunk a bit more than he should have, he turned in for the night. As he lay in bed lost in his thoughts looking at the ceiling, Max was in his usual place on the floor at the bottom of the bed. If Eli had been home, Max would have slept with her as he always had since he was a puppy. The ping on Gill's mobile made him jump. Max let out a short, deep growl as they looked in the direction of the noise. Frank had forgotten he was charging up the phone. He reached over to the bedside cabinet, picked up the phone, pulled out the charger, and looked at the screen. It took him a few moments to focus his eyes and read the text. "What's all this then?" he said to Max. Puzzled he read the brief text again: "Hello, darling. I'm back. I've missed you. When are we going to meet up? xxx"

The message was identified by a mobile number rather than a name, so it wasn't from someone Gill had in her contacts. Frank swung his legs round out of bed and sat up on the edge of the mattress. Staring at the screen, he felt a bit dizzy. *That's the whisky*, he thought. After reading the short text again, he said to Max, who was sitting next to his feet, "Who the hell is it, Max? If it's a friend, I'm sure he or she would know about Gill's death. If not, we've missed notifying someone." He went over in his mind about telling all Gill's friends about what had happened. The only conclusion he could come to was that he must have missed telling someone of Gill's death. He thought back to the funeral and the wake. He was certain all her close friends were there and, indeed, some who weren't so close. Maybe he had missed someone from Gill's contacts list in her phone. Maybe it was a friend of Gill's he didn't know and she didn't have the details in her phone. That was probably the answer.

He read the text again and then once more. "I'm back" made him think it was from a friend who had been away somewhere for a while and possibly hadn't heard about Gill's death. No, everyone he and Gill knew had been told and had come to the funeral. He was certain of it. He decided the best way to solve the mystery was to reply. He thought it would be best to find out who it was before revealing the tragic news about Gill, so he sent a text back asking: "I'm sorry. Who is this?"

He got up and went to the loo and then decided he was wide awake now and wanted a coffee. Max followed him downstairs into the kitchen and flopped down on the cool tiles. Sipping his coffee while he sat at the breakfast bar, Frank stared at the mobile trying to think who on earth the message could be from. He was racking his brain.

It was more than possible that Gill had friends he hadn't met or didn't know about. After he had finished is coffee and still had received no reply to his text, he decided whoever it was had turned in for the night. He thought that was a good idea, and he said, "Come on, Max. Bedtime—again."

After he turned off the kitchen lights, they both trudged back up the stairs. Taking one last look at Gill's phone, Frank plugged it back into the charger. Then he turned off the bedside light and tried to go to sleep.

He woke just after eight as the bright sunlight was bordering the edges of the blinds. It was as if someone was shining a searchlight on the bedroom windows. It looked like it was going to be a hot, sunny day. He felt exhausted; he'd had a bad night's sleep. Always did when he had too much to drink. The whisky and also wondering who had sent the text to Gill the night before had combined to give him a restless night. Hauling himself out of bed, he checked the phone on the bedside cabinet for a new message. Nothing! After reading the original message again, he was still none the wiser. He put the phone down and went to the loo. He put on the towelling dressing gown that had been hanging on the back of the bathroom door. Max was waiting for him on the landing as he came out of the bathroom, running his fingers through his hair in an attempt to half tidy it up. Max jumped up and led the way downstairs.

Frank filled the kettle, flicked on the switch, and opened the back door to let Max out into the garden for his morning sniff around and pee. Breakfast consisted of two cups of coffee and two aspirins. He didn't fancy any food; he couldn't face it. He decided to get Max's walk out of the way early after he had read the newspaper and raised his caffeine levels with another cup of coffee.

He and Max left for the Common. On the way home,

he saw Eli walking back towards the house. He whistled and waved to her. When he caught her attention, she crossed the road onto the Common, and they walked back together. After the usual manic ritual with Max, she linked arms with her dad and told him about the night before, adding what a lovely day it was. She told him she was in a good mood, which lifted his spirits despite his throbbing headache. "Wish I felt the same," he said, feeling sorry for himself.

"Why? What's wrong, Daddy?" asked Eli. Concerned, she stopped and looked at Frank.

"Nothing to worry about, darling. I'm afraid it's self-inflicted. The malt went down a bit too well last night!" Frank replied guiltily.

"Well, it looks like you can't be trusted to be in the house on your own. You'll have to go around and stay at David and Sue's next time I'm out overnight!" she said mockingly

They looked at each other and burst out laughing. Frank put his arm around Eli and hugged her to him.

Closing the front door behind them, Frank unclipped Max's lead and hung it on the coat stand in the hall. The three of them went their separate ways. Max wandered into the kitchen heading for his water bowl as usual after his walk, Eli went upstairs to unpack her overnight bag and to get changed, and Frank took off his shoes and went up to the bedroom to check on Gill's phone. He walked to the bedside table, unlocked the phone with Gill's password, and saw another message had come through. Sitting down on the edge of the bed he opened the text page: "Oh, come on, don't be like that! I've not been away that long! I'll make it up to you when we get together. When can you get away? Can't wait to meet up, and I'll show you how much I've missed you. xxx"

Frank read the message again. Running his fingers across his forehead, he kept staring at the phone in his hand, trying to make sense of it. He was baffled. The message didn't sound as if it came from a friend; it sounded to intimate and not something a girlfriend would say. "When can you get away?" he said to himself. "Get away"? What did that mean? It sounded as if the person wanted Gill to sneak out for a meeting. And "show you how much I've missed you"? He felt a little lightheaded, and it wasn't the hangover! Startled, he dropped the phone on the bed just as Eli opened the door and walked into room with Max in tow. "Are you going deaf, Dad? I've been shouting you!"

Quickly standing up, he smiled replied, "I'm sorry, darling. What was it?"

"Are you all right? You look like you've seen a ghost!" said Eli with concern.

"I'm fine, thanks. Come on. Let's go downstairs and have a coffee." Smiling, Frank putting his arm around her waist and walked her out onto the landing, leaving the phone on the bed where he had dropped it.

"Just how much whisky did you drink last night, Daddy?" asked Eli, laughing.

All through the afternoon and evening he went over the texts in his mind. Eli had asked him twice if he was all right because he seemed so distant. He had hardly listened to a word she had said over dinner; he felt guilty he hadn't been good company. Eli had put it down to him maybe having a "sad" evening. *It hits you like that sometimes*, she told herself.

Frank couldn't get the texts out of his head. He kept coming up with different scenarios but kept returning to the same question: had Gill been having an affair? He kept telling himself he was wrong. She wouldn't do that. She wasn't like that. He would have known—wouldn't he? Yes of course he would. She wasn't secretive or overprotective with her phone. He knew her password for God's sake! She surely would have locked the damn thing if she had anything to hide and anything had been going on. Despite all the analysis as to why she wasn't having an affair, he kept asking himself the same question: *Then why don't you believe it?*

In the morning after another fitful night's sleep, he decided what to do next. Whoever sent the texts obviously didn't know what had happened to Gill. What if Frank just ignored the texts? Whoever sent them would keep on texting, and he would eventually phone Gill. From the content of the texts, it appeared Gill was cross with him—if it was a "him"—for going away. Frank decided "he" would probably be in touch again. He was confused by all the thoughts swirling around in his mind. He was becoming annoyed thinking of someone else in Gill's life. Who? Where had they met? How long had it been going on? What was "he" like? All these questions and doubts were driving him mad; that's why he had come to the conclusion that, for his own sanity, he had to know exactly what it was all about.

He was going to find out! He had the phone number. He wouldn't use Gill's phone; that would be a dead giveaway. He would call from the public phone on the edge of the Common. Eli was still in bed. He quietly got Max out of her bedroom without waking her. After a strong cup of coffee, he put on Max's collar and lead and left the house. Walking across the Common, he headed to the public phone box. He was planning his strategy with regard to what the was going to say. He didn't want the person to know who he was. He arrived at the phone box; it wasn't being used. Taking Gill's phone out of his pocket, he brought up the number. He took a deep breath and dialled the number. Straight away a man answered. "Hello! Mike the man here. What can I do for you?"

"I'm sorry, who is this? Is Gary there?" enquired Frank.

"Gary? This is South London Mercedes. There's no one here called Gary. I'm Mike Harrison, the owner. Can I help you?"

"No. That's okay. I must have the wrong number. Sorry," replied Frank. He ended the call, fumbling with the receiver as he tried to place it back on to the cradle. He breathed out heavily.

Looking out of the phone box window, he ran his fingers through his hair. He laughed out loud thinking how foolish that he was so nervous. His hands were shaking, and his heart was racing. So now he knew who the mystery texter was; it was "Mike the man"! He had seen the adverts for the dealership on television. He seemed to remember the advert boasted it was one of the biggest, if not the biggest, "Merc" dealership in London.

So, what do I do next? Crossing over onto the Common, Frank removed Max's lead and watched as Max ran off to play with a local Jack Russell pal.

Strolling along in the sun, he decided he would find out all he could about Mr Mike Harrison. For some reason, he felt quite pleased with himself. In a strange way, it was as if he was doing something about being taken for a fool. That was if Gill had been having an affair with this man. He still found it hard to believe that Gill, his lovely, adorable wife, would have cheated on him.

Chapter 15

THE DEBT

Tom took his first drugs when he was sixteen years old. He was on a sleepover with some school friends. One of them stole some weed from his older brother, just enough for two joints. Despite the badly made joints, the boys managed to smoke them and get high, giggling most of the night before finally falling asleep.

Tom wasn't a smoker. He had enjoyed the experience but not the taste; it had all seemed so daring to him and his pals at the time. The next time he smoked pot was at university. It was easy to get; everybody was using it. They had a Sunday night ritual: the house mates all had a joint each and had a few drinks while streaming the latest film on the internet.

By the time Tom finished uni, he was regularly smoking dope and had also tried coke at least half a dozen times. When he started work at the bank in the back office supporting the trading floor, he was amazed how many of the traders took coke. A few mates in other departments also used the drug. He had it a few times, mainly on nights out after work when some of the guys went for a few drinks and then onto a nightclub. When he was promoted onto the trading floor, his habit grew in line with his salary, matching the other traders who said they worked better with a couple of lines during the day. The standing joke between the traders was that the gents' on the trading floor was called the powder room!

Tom was always in control, or so he thought. One night, he even stopped Eli from trying coke at a party they were both at in a friend's flat in Chelsea. In the Uber on the way home, she was still pissed at him and called him a boring fart who was old before his time. Little did she know her big brother was anything but anti-drugs. It had been he who had supplied the coke to their friend at the party. He just didn't want to see his little sister taking drugs, even if she had tried them at uni. He also supplied coke to some of his work mates. At the last party in his flat, he had over three grands' worth in a bowl on the coffee table in his lounge for friends to dip into. It had been a good move not inviting Eli and any of her friends to that party.

Tom was a firm believer in the ethic work hard, play hard. Unfortunately for him, he had been playing a little too hard lately. He owed his supplier, Mattie Patterson, £10,000, and that was £10k he didn't have. He and Mattie got on very well. They sometimes enjoyed a drink together.

Tom gave him some insider information on which shares to buy from time to time. Mattie would respond when they next met with a couple of free bags as a thank you for the tip. Despite the share tips and the fact that Tom was also a very good customer, it was a dangerous situation to be in owing Mattie Patterson money.

Unusual for a dealer, Mattie had been patient with the debt, but it was probably because he knew Tom was good for it. Also, he and some of his friends had made good money from Tom's insider trading tips. But Mattie's patience had started to wear thin. He had lost his temper with Tom several times, and they had argued on the phone. The last time, Mattie had threatened him. To make matters worse, he had added a £5k penalty on to the £10k debt for being overdue, and Tom knew exactly what the next step would be—a good kicking or even worse if he didn't come up with the money soon.

CHAPTER 16

MATTIE PATTERSON

Mattie Patterson was born in Haringey, North London, the son of a Scottish mother, Peggy Patterson, and an Irish father, Tommy Mulligan—or so he had been told by his mum. He never knew his dad, who had walked out on his mum before Mattie was born, leaving his ex-girlfriend to bring up a young son all alone in a strange city. Heavily pregnant, she had left Glasgow with him, but then he had decided to move south to live and work in London. She had never been out of Glasgow before, and Tommy was her first boyfriend. Peggy's family, who were staunch Protestants, had thrown her out and disowned her for getting pregnant, and as if getting pregnant wasn't bad enough, she was pregnant to a Fenien. She had nowhere else to go but to tag along with the father of her unborn child, even though she knew he didn't really want her with him. They rented a grubby flat in North London above a betting shop; it was all they could afford.

Tommy Mulligan went about his business—whatever that was—and she got a job at a local Italian restaurant waiting on the tables. He would come home when he felt like it, sometimes not showing himself for days on end, and when he did, he always appeared well turned out in new clothes. She had a wretched life—pregnant, all alone most of the time, very little money, and frightened for the future. What would become of her and her baby? The restaurant owners where she worked were a family of Italians—the Bianchis. The place had a homely look about it with wooden tables covered in blue-check table clothes and surrounded by wooden high-back chairs. They served good, wholesome, tasty Italian food. It was very popular with the locals and always busy. They were good people. They took pity on Peggy and were very kind to her. They were the only friends she had in all the world. She worked long hours to earn as much as she could for when her baby made its entrance into this cruel world. She got very little money from Mulligan when he decided to come home.

One evening, about three months after they had moved to North London, Peggy got back home to the flat, exhausted after a long shift. Mulligan was waiting for her. He had his case packed and was sitting in the armchair, smoking. At least he had the decency to tell her he was leaving her rather than just vanishing without a word. He said he was going back to Ireland, casually adding that he had decided to go back to his wife and their four children. Despite hearing this, Peggy begged him to stay, saying she was so scared living there on her own.

He smiled at her pitiful whining, put his coat on, threw two twenty-pound notes on the table, and said he wouldn't be seeing her again. With that, he walked out of her life forever. She was devastated even though she had been expecting him to leave her for some time.

Frightened and all alone, she decided she would struggle on; she couldn't run back to her family in Scotland and beg for forgiveness. She knew what they would say and what they would do, and she wasn't going to let that happen. They would make her give up her half-Catholic baby for adoption rather than let him or her live in their Protestant home. She couldn't bear that; her baby was the only good thing she had in her miserable life. She would talk to the baby at night when she was all alone and Mulligan was out wherever he disappeared to. It made her feel safe that she would have someone to share her life with. At least they would always have each other.

As the birth got closer, she had to cut back on her work at the restaurant. The Bianchi's kept her on doing light work in the kitchen, preparing food, and sometimes working on the till. They were so good to her, especially Mama Bianchi, Chiara, who was a big woman. Peggy had seen black-and-white photos of the family from years ago, and Mama Bianchi had been a real stunner back then. Despite being a good five stone heavier than she'd been in her younger days, she still had a very pretty face.

Her family were from Napoli. They had come to London just after the war. She met and later married Matteo Bianchi in the early fifties. Matteo was now a tall, skinny man with a comb-over that didn't do a very good job of hiding his baldness.

Matteo and Chiara were always bickering, but it was always good natured; everyone could see the love they had for each other. Their "arguments" would always make

Peggy laugh and cheer her up even in her darkest times. She thought sometimes that Mama Bianchi would start one on purpose to make Peggy laugh and forget about her troubles at least for a little while. When Mama had enough and was bored with bickering, she would hit Matteo over the head with the tea towel. This would mess up his comb-over and result in a stream of Italian swear words directed at Mama Bianchi. She would respond by flicking the back of her fingers out from under her chin at Matteo. She would walk away smiling and wink at Peggy. They would both laugh at Matteo's livid reaction to this latest insult. The Bianchis had two grown-up sons, Lorenzo and Alessandro. Lorenzo lived in California and was doing very well working for some IT company, at least according to his mama.

Alessandro, the younger son, worked in the café, and the idea was that he would eventually own it when his parents finally decided to hang up the tea towels and pans and retire.

Peggy was the daughter Chiara and Matteo never had, and they had grown to love her since she had been working for them. They knew about the *bastardo* father of her baby who had mistreated her; they were glad when she told them he had finally left her. They said they were going to look after Peggy and invited her to move into their apartment over the café. They assured her it was big enough, and she would have her own lovely bedroom with enough room for the baby. Peggy wanted her own independence but knew, as she got closer to the due date, she would need to move in with them. Mama Bianchi saw how well Alessandro and Peggy got on together. Alessandro was always making her laugh, and they giggled and flirted together all the time.

He was a good-looking young man with dark eyes, thick black hair, and an olive complexion. They made a lovely couple and would often go to the local cinema together at weekends. Mama Bianchi tried matchmaking the couple many times but with no success. They appeared to be perfectly happy just being good friends. She told Matteo it was probably because Peggy was having another man's baby. Her son was very virtuous and wouldn't really like that, no matter what his feelings were for Peggy or how well they got on together. What Mama didn't know was that Peggy had promised Alessandro she would keep his secret safe from his parents. One night, after his mother's blatant efforts at matchmaking, he had confessed to Peggy that he was gay.

Two weeks before Peggy gave birth, she moved in with the Bianchi's, letting her flat go, happy to see the back of it and its bad memories. She had stopped working in the restaurant and was taking things easy on the strict instructions of Mama Bianchi.

She had the baby on 7 November, a lovely bouncing boy of eleven pounds, seven ounces. She decided to name him Mattie after Matteo. She didn't know how she would have survived without their kind help, and she wanted to show her gratitude. When Peggy explained to the proud "grandparents" that she was calling the baby Mattie in honour of Matteo and Mama, they cried so much it started Alessandro and Peggy crying as well.

Mama Bianchi and Matteo were like doting grandparents. They would take the baby out for walks in the buggy that they had bought for him; it was obvious that they loved having a baby in the family again.

Peggy would take baby Mattie with the Bianchi's to their Catholic church, and they looked just like all the other Italian families there every Sunday, chatting outside after the service. Peggy took the Catholic faith and became quite religious. She talked it over with Mama and Matteo and decided to have Mattie christened in their church.

The Bianchi's finally retired four years after Mattie was born. Matteo's health wasn't good, and he found running the restaurant too much of a strain for him. They were retiring to Southend and wanted Peggy and young Mattie to go with them, but Peggy had settled into North London life, and Mattie was due to start school. The Bianchis understood her reasons for wanting to stay in London. They gave her £1,000 to help her out with her new life without them. Alessandro told his parents that he had no desire to continue running the restaurant, so they sold it. After the sale, he left to travel around America with a friend. Peggy knew he wasn't going anywhere near America; he had moved in to a flat in Brighton with his boyfriend. She felt guilty about lying to Mama and Matteo, but what Peggy didn't know was that they both knew Alessandro was gay and had known for quite some time.

Peggy moved into a council flat in Brentwood Road, Tottenham, and got a job in a local dry cleaners' shop when Mattie started school at the local primary school. The £1,000 gift from the Bianchi's came in very useful but didn't last forever; eighteen months later, she started working an early-morning office cleaning job before going onto her day job at the dry cleaners.

Mattie's first brush with the law occurred when he was eight years old. He and three friends were caught breaking into cars on matchday near Spurs football ground. By the age of ten, Mattie was in an approved school, and two years later he was sent to a youth detention centre. It broke his mum's heart, living alone without her son, going to see him at weekends, then coming home to a lonely flat. She turned to the church. Her local Catholic church was St Francis de Sales on the High Street. She begged God to save her only child from the devil. Mattie saw the effect his actions had on his mum and promised her he would stay out of trouble when he was released. He went back to school and did behave himself for a while, but he and his three friends realised that there was money to made if they were clever enough and stayed under the police radar.

They got into drugs, running weed and coke, or "beak" as it was called on the streets, to punters dashing around on their mountain bikes during school holidays. When school holidays ended, they progressed to selling after school and at weekends. That's how he and his friends always had plenty of money.

A Saturday job in Tesco for a few pounds was for mugs. They earned good money without any trouble from the Old Bill, hidden in plain view. Mattie and his friends, at thirteen, were earning more than most of their dads and older working brothers.

Mattie loved his Mum; he knew how she had struggled for him. She was mum and dad to him, always had been. The only good thing to come out of his drug running for the local dealer was that she didn't have to work anymore. She'd had a hard life looking after him and had worked her arse off for him. It was his way of paying her back for the two jobs she'd worked so she could buy him things when he was a little boy.

He'd been a scrawny kid—no "meat" on his bones. Charlie Cotton Legs his mum used to call him, but that changed in his teen years. With good food and daily gym workouts, he grew into a strong, tough, muscly, good-looking six-footer with a shock of red hair and matching trim beard.

If there was any trouble, his mates always looked to Mattie, and he was more than willing to sort it out. He enjoyed his tough-guy reputation. He liked the respect that came with it from people in general, and the added bonus of the attention of the local girls who liked to be seen with him. They enjoyed his generosity; he and his friends were always splashing a bit of money around the neighbourhood. They had been told not to be silly with their cash; it was a sure way to attract the notice of the police.

Mattie's mum doted on him; he was always her little boy, no matter how big he had grown. She never asked where the money came from. She never pushed Mattie on the subject, but she knew he was up to no good. She would say to him each evening when he was going out, "You're not doing anything illegal are you? You promised you wouldn't get into any more trouble with the police, my darling."

His reply was always the same: "No, Ma. Wouldn't do anything like that. Those days are over."

Peggy would pray for his soul at Mass every day at St Francis de Sales, hoping God would have mercy on his soul. To try to help her prayers along, she would always make a generous deposit in the collection tray. Life had got easier for her thanks to Mattie, and in her eyes, he could do no wrong. It wasn't his fault he hadn't had a father to chastise him and keep him out of trouble when he was growing up like other boys. God only knows she had done her best, but a boy needs a father. All he had was that bastard Mulligan, whom he never knew. She heard the gossip about her son and his gang from the locals who wouldn't dare say anything to her face, but she had friends at church.

They would tell her what people were saying about Mattie and his gang. She heard the stories about the fights and the drugs. She worried so much. At least the police hadn't come knocking at her door. She would pray even harder to Saint Frances for Mattie's soul.

Mattie picked up the business of supplying drugs to customers, and he wanted to earn even more money than he was getting now. He saw the opportunity to branch out by getting young kids to work as mules distributing for him. He would take a cut of what they earned. He was taking more coke from the suppliers and making good money getting the kids to go out on the streets selling. It was easier than his team selling themselves. It was safer for them. Soon they had fifty kids out there selling for them. They had a good operation, and it was building. Mattie decided they could spread out further, so they recruited kids in Essex to work the streets there for them. In the beginning, Mattie and his gang would take a town each, build up a clientele, and then wait outside local schools to recruit kids who wanted to make easy money, just as they had started out.

CHAPTER 17

MEETING SAMMY BLOOM

Mattie Patterson's supplier was asked questions about the amount of "gear" he was moving, which brought Mattie to the attention of Sammy Bloom. Sammy was an old East End gangster who had started out as a seventeen-year-old enforcer working for Reggie and Ronnie Kray, who ran the criminal organisation known as the Firm. After the Kray twins' imprisonment, there were a lot of turf wars and killings for control of the rackets in the East End, with even the Richardson Gang from South London trying to muscle in on the legal and illegal businesses set up by the Krays. Sammy had a good head on his broad shoulders. He was more than just someone who could mete out violent beatings. If he hadn't turned to a life of crime, he would have made a successful businessman. However, as fate would have it, his best friends at school were the Lambrini brothers, Chas and James, so the die was cast.

It was the brothers who introduced Sammy to the Krays, and his gangster days began. Chas and James worked for the twins and were used to cleaning up the mess that Reggie and Ronnie left in their wake. This proved to be their downfall; they were both sentenced to life for disposing of the body of a local thug who was going around badmouthing the twins, which got back to Reggie, who went looking for him and stabbed him to death in a pub. Sammy saw the opportunity and also wanted some business, but his team wasn't big enough to stand up to some of the other gangs, so he used his head.

Sammy's business acumen saw the need to stop the violence that was attracting the close attention of the Met police, who, following their success with Reg and Ronnie, were eager to put the villains who weren't murdered by the gang wars behind bars. Sammy got the blessing from the twins to carve up the business between the three top firms, Sammy's being one of them, with the proviso that they kept the Richards on the south side of the river and the twins got a 40 per cent cut of all the profits from the businesses. Peace came to London and the East End once more. Good money was being made from protection, gambling, prostitution, and robberies again.

Sammy kept a low profile and didn't want any part of the celebrity status that Reggie and Ronnie enjoyed, which he believed had ultimately led to their downfall. His firm quietly went about their business, and times were good; the money just rolled on in. Needless violence only drew unwanted attention from the Old Bill and was ultimately bad for business.

He would remind the other firms of this if there was any conflict. He would arbitrate between the warring factions. He most often persuaded them to agree to a peaceful solution, so business and making money weren't interrupted. By the seventies, there was a new, bigger money maker, more profitable than all the other businesses put together: drugs!

The drug business boomed, growing from cannabis and acid (LSD) sold to the youngsters, to harder drugs like coke sold to the toffs who found it was the fashionable thing to snort at their elegant dinner parties. The markets just kept on growing and growing. With the high demand, profits soared. Sammy worked the drugs hard and reaped the huge rewards. His business brain, and muscle when needed, had given him the edge in the early days, and he was now the top dog in the London drug market. Most of the drugs sold in London and the south of England were supplied via Sammy's operation. He was a very wealthy and very powerful man.

Sammy had sent for Mattie. He wanted to meet with the young man who had managed to move 50 per cent more gear than the rest of his suppliers' mules. Sammy's man had made enquires locally about Mattie and passed on what he had been told about him back to the boss. Mattie turned up at the Rusty Nail Pub on the Mile End Road. It was a typical old-fashioned London boozer with a big coloured stained-glass window; bare floorboards; big wooden polished bar; and black wrought iron, old fashioned stools and tables. Sammy did his business in the snug at the rear of the pub. The snug was out of bounds to the public—well, strangers to be exact. The locals knew who used the room and would steer well clear of it during opening hours; it was always locked in the evenings. Sammy was paranoid about security and feared the Flying Squad would try to bug the room and put him behind bars.

Mattie got off to a bad start when he arrived at the boozer and asked for Sammy. Sammy's men always searched everyone going into the snug for a meeting with the boss. The swaggering, ginger-haired kid was no exception. They took the handgun that Mattie had tucked in the back of his jeans. One of the minders instinctively gave Mattie a smack around the back of his head for bringing a gun to a meeting with Sammy.

This prompted Mattie to turn and headbutt the six-foot-three muscle mountain. The ensuing mayhem ended only when Sammy came out of the snug to see what all the commotion was about. He was shocked at the heap of bodies rolling around on the floor as others tried to separate the fighting pair.

He shouted out above the din, "Hey! Hey! What the fucking hell is going on out here?" The sound of Sammy's voice quickly ended the rumpus.

"This little shit brought a shooter to the meeting, Sammy," said one of the heavies, trying to justify the carry on, pointing to Mattie, who was climbing back to his feet.

Sammy looked from Mattie's ripped sleeve hanging off his arm to his mess of red hair. Then he looked to his minder, who had a bloody hankie pressed to his nose. Then he looked to the upturned tables and stools. Sammy thought to himself, *So what I've heard about this little bastard is all true.*

"For fuck's sake, all of you just calm down!" shouted Sammy. He turned and walked back into the snug. Unobserved by any of his men, he broke out into a big grin.

"Ginger, get your arse in here now!" Sammy shouted over his shoulder at Mattie.

Mattie walked into the snug followed by two of Sammy's heavies. Mattie found out later that these guys always stood at the back of the room during Sammy's meetings.

There was a green carpet covering the floor of the snug. It was threadbare in places, and Mattie's feet stuck on it when he walked over it. The walls were papered with the sort of dark-brown flocked wallpaper evident in lots of old pubs around the East End; it probably had been very popular after World War Two. A long, green, creased leather sofa was against the right wall. Two matching armchairs stood opposite. A desk and chair were at the top end of the room. Everywhere stank of cigar smoke.

Mattie, despite hating being called Ginger, did as he was told and sat down on the sofa. One of the men standing near the door informed Sammy, "The kid's brought three lads with him. They're stood across the road. Do you want me to get rid of them?"

Pulling a chair around, so he could face Mattie, Sammy sat down and looked long and hard at the ginger-haired kid. Sucking on his teeth, he finally asked Mattie, "Are your friends over the road carrying, son?"

"Carrying? Carrying what?" replied Mattie with a quizzical look on his half-smiling face.

"Don't be fucking clever with me, son. Carrying? Guns! Fucking armed—that's what carrying means!" shouted Sammy, losing his patience with the shit of a kid who sat smiling at him.

Mattie looked Sammy in the eyes and thought to himself, *Don't push it anymore.* Slowly shaking his head, he calmly lied. "No. We have only one gun, and we thought

I should have it with me." Mattie thought to himself, *Carrying? This lot are fucking dinosaurs. I feel like I'm in one of the old black-and-white gangster movies Grandad Matteo used to watch.*

Sammy nodded his head thoughtfully, not taking his eyes off Mattie. He said to his minder, "No. Leave it. Let the fuckers stand out there in the rain."

Sammy was in his mid-sixties but still had a decent build despite his pot belly. He had big hands. His hair was practically white, thinning a little on top. His lined face was jowly. He still looked as if he could take care of himself though, not that he had to anymore, thanks to his army of gorillas. His expensive suit jacket was hung on the back of the chair near the desk. His dazzling white shirt was finished off with a red tie and black-and-white-striped braces. Sammy was very dapper in an old-fashioned sort of way. Mattie had already decided he liked old Sammy Bloom; he could learn a lot from him and hopefully end up as rich as him some day.

"Okay, Mattie. That's your name, isn't it? Tell me about this operation you and your three pals have set up." Sammy said, sitting back in the armchair.

Sammy listened and occasionally asked the odd question for clarification, but overall, he liked what he heard from the ginger-haired kid. Sammy thought to himself, *This kid hasn't just got balls, he's got brains too.* The kids' network was simple. They recruited young kids on street bikes to move the gear around their patch. The kids could get around in plain sight of the Old Bill without being stopped and searched. They were all safe from being ripped off because they worked for Mattie, and nobody was stupid enough to bring down the wrath of Mattie and his top boys. If any of the youngsters did get caught dealing, they knew they would be looked after if they kept their mouths shut about who they were working for. It was so simple that it was brilliant. Also, there were several layers of "faces" between the young dealers on the street and Mattie at the top. Sammy thought Mattie had a good network selling far and wide—North London and over into Essex. With their setup, he and his pals were not taking chances of getting lifted by the Old Bill.

Sammy stood up and lit his cigar again; it had gone out while he listened to Mattie. He blew a big thick cloud of blue smoke up into the air.

He watched as it hit the ceiling and spread across the top of the room like a nuclear mushroom cloud, then he turned to Mattie and said, "Okay, I like your style, kid. From now on, you buy your gear only from one of my boys—not your present supplier, who, by the way, is also supplied by my boys. The more you move, the more discount you'll get, and a bright kid like you don't need telling that you'll make more money, and you're under my protection if there's any trouble. You okay with that?"

Mattie smiled. That was what he'd been hoping to hear. They were in! They would soon be making big money! He replied, "Yes, sir, Mr Bloom. You won't regret it!"

The respectful reply wasn't lost on Sammy. He appreciated it but still thought to himself, *I need to keep an eye on you, Ginger. You're going to bring trouble to my door before you're much older. I can smell it.* Sammy smiled and replied, "Good! One more thing, kid: don't ever bring a gun to a meeting with me again. Is that understood?"

Mattie smiled back and said in a respectful tone, "I understand, Mr Bloom. It definitely won't happen again. I just wasn't sure what I was walking in to."

"Good. Now, before you go and join your three mates across the road, go and apologize on the way out to Big Tony in the bar for nutting him. I'll have a word with him, so it'll all be okay and won't be no bad feelings." Smiling, Sammy puffed on his cigar and opened the door to let Mattie out.

"Thanks again, Mr Bloom. You won't regret it," said Mattie again as he firmly shook the big man's hand.

As they walked back to the tube station, Mattie told his mates all about the meeting and the fight that had earned him a smack around the head. They all laughed, especially about his description of the gangsters and their old way of speaking. They teased him about the stink of cigar smoke on his clothes and in his hair, as well as the missing sleeve from his jacket. Mattie took it all in good spirit. It was an exciting time. They were climbing the ladder and were going to be in the money, better and bigger than they had been so far.

The boys went about their business with gusto. They were making good money, and times were good. The first problem occurred when their runners had some trouble with a gang in Essex who didn't like them coming onto their turf. Mattie and the boys were going to go up there and sort it out, but before it could get serious, Sammy Bloom stepped in.

He brought the Essex boys and Mattie to The Rusty Nail for a pow wow. It was all superficial; he had already sorted the problem with the boss in Essex, whom he supplied.

Mattie didn't like the outcome. Sammy told the two Essex boys that Mattie's boys wouldn't sell on their patch again. He lectured them that trouble only brought unwanted attention from the Old Bill. The Essex boys had a drink in the pub while Mattie, who was well pissed off with the decision, stayed in the snug for a lecture from Sammy.

"Sammy, they beat up four of my boys and nicked the gear off them. I need to teach them a lesson or we'll look a soft touch!" argued Mattie.

"Look, son, what we discussed just now is going to happen. You stay out of Essex. There's a bigger picture here, Mattie, and I'm not having you and your boys rocking the boat," replied Sammy, puffing away on his cigar. "Okay, you'll lose some revenue. I'll give you a slightly bigger patch in North London. You're making good money. If you start trouble, it will seriously affect your takings and, more importantly, mine. And we're not going to let that happen. Do you understand me? We don't want the Old Bill getting involved. That's no good to anyone!" preached Sammy, looking from Mattie to his two men, who were standing by the door.

Mattie got the message loud and clear: Do as you're told, or we'll deal with you and your boys, and you'll all end up badly hurt or dead. "Okay, Sammy. I suppose you're right. It does make sense. I don't want to cause problems. I appreciate the extra business," lied Mattie. He would happily go into the pub and shoot those two Essex bastards to teach them a lesson for fucking with him.

"Mattie, remember, don't trouble trouble until trouble

troubles you! That's always been my motto. That's how I've lived this long, okay, son?" said Sammy. He stood up, indicating that their conversation was over.

Mattie stood up and smiled at Sammy. "Sure thing, boss." Sammy gave him a hug and patted his back as one of the bodyguards opened the door to let Mattie out.

When Mattie returned to Tottenham, he had to pacify his boys who were itching for a fight. They wanted to go over to Essex for revenge. He explained what had happened and what he had been told by Sammy. "Look, we're doing fine.

We don't to want rock the boat. Our time will come; just trust me," promised Mattie as he looked each one of them in the eyes. He got nods of agreement as he looked at each one and moved on to the next.

Six months went by without any trouble. Everyone was selling more gear and making good money, but then it all kicked off, and this time it wasn't anything to do with Mattie. The Turks, who had been operating in North London and were spreading out further into the surrounding area, had made a move into Essex. Trouble was brewing. Sammy had told Mattie not to get involved when he complained about the Turks moving in on his area. Sammy said the situation was in hand and would be sorted very soon.

The following evening, two Essex boys were shot dead in Billericay. Things didn't look good; a war was looming. Mattie sent a message to Sammy saying he was happy to get involved. He saw an opportunity to grab back some of his patch that the Turks had taken. Sammy told Mattie and his boys to do nothing except to slow down the business until he heard from Sammy's men. Sammy's people and the Essex boys hit back at the Turks; four Turkish gangsters were ambushed in Essex on their way to deal with a "problem". They disappeared along with the car they were travelling in, never to be seen again. Two days later, two "warlords" flew into Stansted from Istanbul. They were met at the airport by two of their North London gang bosses and three minders. Unknown to them, their two cars were followed by Sammy's boys. On route to North London, they were stopped by an accident on the road they were travelling on. The men and the cars they in were never seen again. They became another story in East End folklore.

Rumour had it the Turks had been executed and buried in Epping Forest; the remaining Turkish gang leaders were told not to expect to see their men again, and they were given a further message when four Turkish restaurants they owned in North London were firebombed.

The Old Bill were all over the troubles like a cheap suit, especially after the shooting of the two Essex boys, but following the restaurant attacks, everything went quiet again, which was just what Sammy had ordered. The last thing the business needed was a continuation of a bloody war and more bodies on streets.

A meeting had been arranged at an Italian restaurant in Jamaica Road, and a peace plan was thrashed out between both parties. The Turks stayed out of Essex, and for that they could control all North London as far as the Essex border.

Also, Sammy would buy some of his drugs in bulk that the Turks were regularly smuggling into the country. Peace was restored, but for how long was anyone's guess. When Sammy explained to Mattie that he had to give up his patch in Tottenham, the news didn't go down well. As usual, hot-head Mattie wanted to have a shoot-out with the Turks, which Sammy wasn't going to allow. He gave Mattie the Camden patch, which extended down to the Thames, including the city. Mattie and his boys would make more money than they were making in Tottenham. They quickly did the sums and realised they had done well out of doing what they'd been ordered to do by Sammy. He had looked after them as he had promised.

Mattie and his boys moved down to Camden. Mattie bought a large terrace house just behind the market on Bayham Street; however, his mum refused to move from her flat and her beloved church in Tottenham. It concerned Mattie; he wanted her close by so he could look after her, but she was adamant she was staying put. Mattie still had good friends up in Tottenham who would watch out for her; they would make sure Peggy was well cared for. The local villains knew that, if they wanted to live, they had to make sure nothing happened to Peggy Patterson. Mattie's reputation was growing and spreading rapidly.

Mattie's first kill occurred late in his "drug life"; he was seventeen. He had set up a deal with a Midlands crew who had driven down from Solihull. The meet was at London Gateway Services on the M1. Not to be sniffed at, it was a tasty little deal worth £90K to Mattie and his boys. After the business was done, they changed cars and followed the Brummie crew back up the M1. They jumped them when they stopped at the Watford Gap services for a pee break and some food. They followed them into the toilets and took back the money and the gear that they had just sold them earlier. One of the Brummie crew started getting agitated. When he made a sudden move towards the waistband of his jeans, Mattie reacted quickly to defuse the situation. He shot him dead—one bullet through the left eye. After the initial shock and the deafening noise of the gun, everybody froze and looked at each other. Nobody moved. Seeing their friend dead on the floor with the back of his head running down the wall behind them stopped them thinking of fighting for their drugs. Mattie snapped at them, "Does any other fucker fancy dying today?" Nobody answered. He winked at the three shocked faces staring back at him and, smiling, said, "Take care driving back to Birmingham, now, won't you, boys?"

When news got to Sammy Bloom about what they had done, he got a call out to Mattie, who was told to get his arse in to The Rusty Nail pronto. "What the fuck do you think you are playing at?" screamed Sammy as two of his men walked Mattie into the snug.

Mattie had never seen Sammy so angry; it was so bad he didn't know if he would make it out of there alive. Mattie kept his mouth shut and just sat on the sofa. All he could think of was that he was supposed to be having dinner with his mum later, and he wasn't sure if she would be reading about his murder in the newspapers in the morning.

Sammy told him that the Birmingham gang naturally hadn't taken to kindly to being ripped off, and especially having one of their own knocked off, and rightly so. They were sending a team down to take revenge on Mattie and his boys. Luckily, they were trying to find another gang down there who would get involved in the fight. Sammy told Mattie that nobody would because Mattie and his boys were under the protection of Sammy Bloom. "Do you know what that means, you twat?" screamed Sammy as he paced up and down the snug chewing on his cigar. "That means they think I gave the nod to what you and your bunch of fucking cowboys did! Yes! They think I approved your stupid fucking ambush, you fucking idiot!" Sammy glared at Mattie and poked his chest with his thumb. *"Me,* you dumb fuck. We could have a war on our hands with half of the North because of your fucking stupidity and greed!"

Letting out a huge sigh, Sammy set off again pacing up and down the snug. Eventually he appeared to have burned up all his anger, and he started to calm down. His face wasn't blood red anymore. He finally sat down in an armchair. After looking at Mattie for a good minute or so, he finally said, "And there I was thinking you were a good un, a cut above the rest. Well, how wrong was I! What do you have to say for yourself, you fucking dumb shit?"

"Sammy, I'm so sorry. I didn't think it would cause you trouble. That would be a stupid thing to do—to piss you off! We wouldn't have taken a liberty with you after the way you've looked after us so well," pleaded Mattie, knowing that what he said in the next couple of minutes might just save his life. "What can we do to make it right, Sammy? Anything. You just tell me. You've been like a dad to me. I wouldn't do anything to cross you, Sammy. Surely you know that? I'll do anything to prove to you I really mean it," said Mattie, not taking his eyes off Sammy.

Sammy stared at Mattie long and hard, chewing on the end of his cigar, tapping his fingers on the arm of the chair. He finally said, "This is your lucky day, young Mattie. It's probably a big mistake, but I believe you, and because of that you live to fight another day, my son! Now, this is what's going to happen: I'm going to pay the Brummies' back the money you did them for along with giving them the gear you sold them and then pinched back. Also, to show them how sorry you are, I'm giving them a ten-grand sweetener for the family of the guy you shot dead." Getting to his feet, Sammy looked at his men who stood near the door. He took a few puffs of his cigar and then, turning to Mattie, he finished with, "And you, my son, are going to fucking pay me back every cent of it—by this Friday. Do you understand? The end of the week. Is that clear?"

"Definitely, Sammy. No worries. I think that's fair. Thank you so much. You won't regret it, Sammy, I promise you," lied Mattie. But there was a large measure of relief in his voice. At one stage, he'd really thought he was going to end up buried in Epping Forest with the fucking Turkish lot.

"Fucking right I won't regret it! Oh! And by the way, the geezer you killed? His old Nan is related to a member of the old South London Richards team. So, if I was you, I would stay on this side of the river, because, if they ever get you on their turf ... well ... Now get the fuck out of my boozer before I change my mind," said Sammy with a snarl.

After the Brummie business, Sammy kept Mattie at arm's length. Their relationship was never the same again. Sammy had his men keep an eye on Mattie's activities, just to make sure he was staying clear of unnecessary trouble. Mattie kept his nose clean and bided his time. He was making Sammy good money. That's all the boss was concerned with. Mattie knew he'd live if he was making money for Sammy's business.

Eighteen months later, Sammy was shot dead outside the side entrance of The Rusty Nail. His bodyguards "surprisingly" didn't see a thing. Normally, retribution and turf wars would break out, trouble would flare, people would die. Everything would get messy with gangs taking sides, but following Sammy's murder nothing happened.

Rumour had it that it was down to the Turks getting revenge. Even the Old Bill were investigating along those lines, but the faces in the know knew differently. Some of Sammy's top men had decided they wanted a bigger slice of the vast profits the business was bringing in.

Also, they felt Sammy was past his prime, and it was time for him to retire. Only Sammy would never have agreed to step down. They decided to bring Mattie in on the deal because they knew he had been unhappy with Sammy and had been biding his time. They could tell he was itching to get rid of Sammy, so why not use him to do it for them? Also, he could be trouble if they left him on the outside. So, it was either kill Mattie too or bring him in on the plan, on the proviso that he was the trigger man. He had to be the one to kill Sammy. Even though they all thought Sammy was over the hill and not making the money that was out there, they were still worried of the repercussions if the hit went tits up! Sammy could still call on some dangerous old loyal muscle if he managed to survive the attempt to top him.

Mattie saw it was a good opportunity to move up the ladder and also to make even more money. He had no qualms about killing Sammy. He hadn't forgiven Sammy for the cash he took off him and his boys after the Birmingham bust up. Also, he wasn't stupid. He had been brought in on the plan to get rid of Sammy. He didn't have an option; he was in or he was dead, simple as that! The few faces who could be trusted and needed to know were loosely brought in on the details. This was dangerous but essential so there could be a smooth transition business wise. The opinion that Sammy was past it appeared to be the opinion of quite a few within the trusted gangster fraternity.

Like most weeknights, at around 7.30, Sammy decided it was time to call it a day and go home. He told Big Tony Smith to bring the car round to the side door of the pub. As usual, Sammy would say his good nights and, on his way out, have a quick sociable chat to friends who were drinking in the pub. Sammy was texting his wife as he walked out onto the pavement. Looking up from his phone, he saw his three men with their backs to him standing at the front of the car talking. The group included Big Tony, who was the driver. He was just about to ask what the fuck was going on when a movement to his right caught his eye.

"Evening, Sammy, how you doing?" said Mattie, stepping out of the shadows. Sammy turned and saw Mattie walking towards him.

Mattie's heart was pounding. He tried to smile. As he got close to Sammy, he stopped walking. The two men were now facing each other, less than a metre of space between them. Sammy looked at Mattie and then at the gun Mattie was holding down by his side. Sammy didn't panic or try to run. He knew it would be futile to shout to his men. He knew what was going to happen.

He stood there looking straight into Mattie's eyes. He half smiled and said, with no emotion whatsoever in his strong voice, "So, it's going to be you, is it, kid? I should have had you fucking killed a couple of years ago. I always knew you'd be trouble."

Chapter 18

BUSINESS AS USUAL

The statements given by Sammy's bodyguards told of two foreign-looking "geezers" running up to Sammy outside the pub. One pointed a sawn-off shotgun at them, and because they were unarmed, they couldn't do anything; all they could do was watch. Meanwhile the other shorter man shot Sammy twice in the chest and then once in the head as he lay on the floor. Their statements concluded with a description of a car screeching to a brief halt near the two men. They jumped in, and the car sped away down the Mile End Road. It all happened so quickly they couldn't even remember the make of the car let alone the registration number. They were all in shock.

Mattie was haunted by the look of recognition and the half smile, half smirk on Sammy's face when he saw him step out of the shadows and walk up to him. Sammy had known exactly what was going to happen. In some strange way, it was if he had always known that it would be Mattie who would end his life! That look on Sammy's face never left Mattie, and for a long time afterwards, it would wake him up in the middle of the night in a cold sweat.

Following Sammy's murder, the police investigation got nowhere fast—no leads whatsoever and shit witness statements. They didn't manage to come up with any suspects apart from the two bogus foreigners. It didn't help either that nobody was prepared to speak about the murder, but then that always happened. They were used to the East End wall of silence. Some of Sammy's old friends who were still a threat and not happy when news got around that the old man had been topped were pacified with business opportunities that brought them good money. Sammy was given the big traditional East End funeral and a great send off. Then everyone quickly settled back down to business as usual.

Mattie's slice of the business included a share of the hard drugs that were brought into the UK and sold on around the country. He bought his weed from a South London gang called the Campbells; their gear was the best in the country, and because of that, Mattie was able to command a good price on the streets. Mattie also had his Camden turf, which ran down to the Thames taking in the city. It was very profitable. It ended just west of St Pauls. The area over the river on the Southbank and right up to Colliers Wood was run by the Brixton family, the Campbells.

Chapter 19

THE CAMPBELLS

The Campbell group consisted of five brothers: Kelvin, the eldest; Theo, the brains; Bruce and Oscar, the twins; and Billy, the baby of the family and most dangerous brother. They boasted of their Jamaican roots when in fact they'd all been born and bred in Balham. None of them had ever set foot on the Caribbean island they affectionately talked about as home. Their surname wasn't even Campbell. They chose that name because their old Grandpa, who was Jamaican, told them stories when they were youngsters of his life growing up in Kingston and his family in Montego Bay. He had once told them a little-known fact that the Jamaican phonebook had more Campbells listed than the whole of Scotland's phonebook. When they got into dealing and decided to move down to Brixton, they decided to take the name Campbell. This helped their standing with the other gangs in the early days when they first started to expand their business. There were endless boasts of their army of Yardie relations they could call on in a turf war, not that they needed it—they were ruthless and very soon became feared and respected by many of the other gangs.

Mattie had done business with them a lot in the past and had good relationships with all the brothers. Why not? There was plenty of money to be made for all of them, especially with the quality of the weed they were bringing into the country. Mattie's motto was that it was better to have them on the inside pissing out than on the outside pissing in.

Mattie sat in the Campbells' shitty lounge smoking a spiff. It helped relax him a little. Not that he felt threatened by the brothers. He trusted them. Well … as much as anybody could be trusted in their line of business. He knew they weren't stupid enough to take him on. There hadn't been any trouble between the local gangs for a good few years, and everyone was happy to keep it that way. He just fucking hated Brixton, especially coming to the Campbells' house. For all their money, they lived like fucking pigs. In fact, in truth, Mattie didn't like coming south of the river. He always felt uneasy when he crossed the river. The North Bank was home, after all. Always had been and always would be.

I must have a fucking good shower when I get home, and throw away these clothes, he thought to himself as he sat on the threadbare, stained sofa.

Looking around the tatty, stale, stinking lounge, especially the old grey flocked wallpaper peeling off the walls, he thought, *How can anybody live like this?* But he had to admit that, without a doubt, they did have the best shit in London. The Moroccan Gold he was smoking was blowing his fucking head off. After confirming that the next shipment was coming in at the end of the week, Mattie handed over a big brown holdall bursting with £150k in twenty- and fifty-pound notes to Kelvin, the eldest of the brothers. This was payment for his share of the consignment.

Kelvin tossed the holdall on to the floor where it bounced off the leg of the filthy coffee table, scattering some of empty lager bottles and dark-brown-stained coffee mugs that looked as if they had been there for months. Theo picked up the bag and gave Kelvin a withering look. He was the money man of the brothers. He looked after all their money, laundering it and investing it in property at home and abroad. He was not a normal Campbell brother. He was wasn't a fighter like the rest of them; he had the brains of a top accountant. A very shrewd and respected man was Theo.

On occasion, Mattie would have a couple of drinks with Tom Quinn when he was up in Camden. Tom would give him inside tips on shares that were due to rocket. Mattie would make a killing on these tips, and he'd pass the tips on to Kelvin, who also made plenty. The brothers were very grateful for the extra cash-earning information Mattie passed on to them. As far as Mattie was concerned, they owed him one.

"Anything else we can do for you, man?" asked Kelvin, eyeing Mattie and wondering. *He doesn't really want to be here. Even the joint isn't calming him down. What is it with him coming over of the river?*

"As it happens, there is, my old son," replied Mattie, handing him a recent photo of Tom Quinn doing a deal with two of his boys in a side street near his bank. "This guy owes me. He lives on your patch in Clapham. I'm going to sort it, but I don't want any of your boys supplying him in the meantime—at least not until I get my dues."

With a quick glance at the photo, Kelvin handed it to young Billy. His "boys" looked after Clapham. Billy was a nasty bastard, and everybody on their patch knew him and feared him, not only for being a Campbell, but also for his mood swings. One minute he could be joking, and then in a second, he would turn nasty for no reason whatsoever. His hero was Jason Bourne. He loved the Bourne trilogy and thought of himself as "an asset"—an agent with the power to kill covertly.

What went in Billy's favour was his schoolboy looks. Although he was twenty, he could pass for a fifteen-year-old, and his young looks had got him out of trouble on many occasions.

Smiling at Mattie, Kelvin asked, "Okay. No problem. Do you want us to sort him for you?"

"No thanks. I prefer to keep it inhouse. At least my boys won't get carried away and top the fucker." Mattie laughed and stood up, ready to go, at least pleased with himself that he hadn't touched anything in the fleapit of a fucking place. "I want my money. I don't want him dead—not yet anyway!"

Kelvin, as always, walked him out to his car, smiling and nodding to Mattie's boys who sat in the front, not recognising them as "regular faces." He had a good look at them and filed their faces away for future reference, something he always did when new faces turned up with a rival boss. "You never know when it might save your life," he always told his brothers. Resting his hand on Mattie's

Wandsworth Common

shoulder he said, "We'll get the gear to you on Saturday morning. Always a pleasure doing business with you, Mattie."

Climbing into the back seat, Mattie smiled and replied in a kinder tone, "And you, my son."

Kelvin closed the back door and waved the car away down the street, relieved at how the meet had gone. He could never be sure with Mattie, the only guy in the business that Kelvin was wary of. He knew Mattie was clever, violent, and calculating—a very dangerous mix.

"Get me out of this shithole and back across the river sharpish!" snapped Mattie to the driver. "Also, I want that cunt Tom Quinn done this week. I know he's been a good punter over the years, and we've had a few beers together, but I've had enough of his shit. He's got too big for his boots. He needs to be taught some respect. Who the fuck does he think he is shouting back down the phone at me? I don't give a shit if his mum has just died, okay? Get Scottish Archie to come and see me tomorrow morning to sort it."

His driver Chas replied, "Sure, boss. I'll get Archie over first thing tomorrow. No problem. You chill now. We're about to go over the river." Chas hated it when they had to go across the river; he knew it agitated the boss big time, and that was dangerous for everyone!

Mattie's mood lightened as the car crossed Blackfriars Bridge and headed up Farringdon towards Kings Cross and then home to Camden. He sat back and began to enjoy the effects of the Moroccan Gold he had just smoked. As calm washed over his body, his mind drifted away.

Chapter 20

WHO IS HE?

It was two days since the last text, and Frank had been busy finding out about Mr Mike Harrison. It had been easy enough. People are happy to put their lives online. Through social media, they are willing to tell the world all about themselves. It's there for anyone who cares to read it. It was something that never ceased to amaze Frank. He soon discovered that Mike Harrison owned the second-biggest Mercedes dealership in London. Also, he was married to a woman called Penny, and they had two young daughters. They lived in Wimbledon opposite the Common on Parkside. He looked at lots of holiday snaps—California, Barbados, Thailand, South Africa—all the usual happy family snaps posted on Instagram.

Frank hired an investigator to find out what wasn't on social media. This proved very interesting and showed a different picture than the one painted on the internet. The report consisted of the following:

Harrison is originally from the East End and grew up with his parents in Rotherhithe. After leaving school, he was a member of an East End gang, who followed Millwall Football Club. He got into trouble and served time in prison for grievous bodily harm (GBH) at a football match. After he was released, he started selling second-hand cars. It appears the start-up money came from his uncle, who was an East End gangster. Harrison did well with the car pitch and then progressed to having a successful pitch on the Mile End Road, then a sports car showroom in Bethnal Green. What very few people knew was that his second-hand car showroom wasn't as successful as it appeared. It was used for laundering money for his uncle's dodgy business deals, but young Mike did very well out of it.

He started making "legit" money when he got the Mercedes dealership, although it looks like he still continues to pass some of his uncle's dirty money through the business. With his cut and the Merc sales, he's never looked back.

The investigator said that was all he could find out; it wasn't healthy sniffing around the East End trying to find out about one of their own as he soon found out. He wrapped up his on-the-ground investigation when he was punched in the face by one of two very dubious looking men. They told him, as he lay on the pavement holding his broken nose, that they didn't want to see him in the area again. They wanted to know who had hired him to ask questions about Mike Harrison. The investigator later told Frank it was only a police car stopping to see what was going on that saved him from a good kicking and not having to give them Frank's name.

Frank thanked him for his work and his discretion. The report was very thorough and useful. He felt sorry for the man standing there with two black eyes and a white plaster across the bridge of his nose. Frank paid the bill plus an additional £200 for his "extra" trouble.

CHAPTER 21

THE REALISATION ABOUT GILL

Frank had just finished dinner and was helping Eli clear the table when he heard the ping from Gill's mobile in his pocket. "Just going to the loo!" he said over his shoulder to Eli as he walked out of the kitchen.

"Anything to get out of wiping the dishes," shouted Eli after him, laughing.

In the toilet Frank, stared at the mobile. It was *him* again. If he had been in any doubt about Gill's relationship with this shit of a man, it was perfectly clear now. He read: "Come on. I've been punished long enough now for going away. When are we getting together? I've got a big hard-on waiting just for you. xxx"

Frank entered a response: "Well, the best thing you can do is stick it up your arse." His finger hoovered over the send button. Looking down at the screen, he stopped himself. Staring at his phone, he deleted his reply. For the first time in his life, he hated another human being! What should he do now? He couldn't confront Gill about it and find out what the hell was going on and tell her just what he thought of her. What did he think of her? He still found it hard to believe that she had cheated on him. He hated her "boyfriend", and he didn't even know him for God's sake! Reading the texts, it appeared that Gill had not wanted him to go away on a family holiday. That must be why Harrison thought she was giving him a "hard time".

He needed to talk to somebody about all this nonsense. It was driving him insane. He was still grieving over the death of his wife, and now he had this to deal with "what a fucking joke." He thought to himself, *As if losing my wife isn't bad enough, I now find out I didn't really know her at all, even after all the years we spent together.*

He spent the rest of the evening watching TV, cuddled up with Eli on the sofa. She asked him several times if he was okay and if he wanted to talk about anything. He had to try to cheer up for her. She had been through it too. He tried to put the thoughts of the affair out of his head. *She obviously thinks I'm upset over Gill*, he thought. *If only she knew the truth.* At least she appeared to be holding up well. The burning question he kept asking himself was why? Why would Gill want someone else?

She obviously loved him. Anyone could see that. And she adored the children. Their life was good. Their sex life was fine. Family always came first, so why would she risk it all to have an affair? She wouldn't do that … but she had. How can a person live with someone for twenty-odd years and not really know her? Or had he just missed all the signs? How could she have an affair and keep everyone from knowing what was going on? Then a light went on in his head—Sue! She and Gill were like sisters. Gill would have confided in Sue for sure; after all, that's what women do, isn't it? He would confront Sue and find out what she knew about all this! Did David know? Had they all been having a bloody good laugh at him behind his back all these years? He was sure David wouldn't have known. He was a good friend, and Sue wouldn't have betrayed Gill's confidence, not even with her own husband. She would have been worried he might tell Frank. He would ask David outright when they met next; he would know if David was telling him the truth. After all, he had the element of surprise. David and Sue wouldn't know he'd found out about the affair.

By the time he climbed into bed, he had decided he was going to phone Harrison in the morning, tell him about Gill's death, and put an end to the bastard's text messages once and for all. After he received the first text, several times he had decided to phone him, but had always backed down. This time, he told himself to man up and do it.

Placing his breakfast dishes in the sink, Frank walked into the lounge and picked up Gill's phone. He checked that it had charged during the night. In the hall he picked up the lead and called Max. "Come on, boy. Let's go walkies."

Closing the front door quietly behind them so as not to wake Eli, Frank led the dog across the road and onto the Common. It was a bright sunny Saturday morning. The usual array of dogwalkers and joggers were out and about already. Safely away from the road, he slipped off Max's lead so he could have a play and a run around. He went over in his mind what he was going to say to Harrison. Then he revised it, changing words. What about tone and expressions. Should he be calm? Angry? Threatening? He looked at his watch. It was 10.45. *He'll be at work now in the showroom. This is it,* he said to himself. He walked to a park bench and sat down, surprised how calm he was. The only problem was that he wasn't sure how long he could remain cool and calm. Up to now, when he had thought of phoning the bastard and confronting him, he would break out in a sweat. Taking a deep breath, he pressed call on Gill's phone.

"Good morning, darling! So, you've finally forgiven me and called at long last!" Harrison said. Smiling, he closed his office door and sat down at his desk.

"Good morning to you to, *darling*," replied Frank sarcastically. He continued, breaking the short silence, "This is Frank Quinn—"

"I know who you are," interrupted Harrison. "So, to what do I owe the pleasure of this call?"

Harrison's calm attitude annoyed Frank, but he did his best to remain calm too. "I've called to put you straight, arsehole!" he replied.

"You put me straight? Don't make me laugh, you fucking wimp!" teased Harrison.

"I would like nothing more than to put you straight on your arse," responded Frank. As he jumped up from the bench, he realised he was shouting and gaining the attention of two women who were walking past with a German shepherd. They gave him a dirty look and muttered something to each other. Frank was uncomfortable. He couldn't ever remember calling anybody an arsehole before in his entire life, but it seemed appropriate for the areshole he was now talking to on Gill's phone. Sitting down, he took a deep breath. He settled back into his new "tough guy" role that he had been rehearsing. Then he dropped the bombshell on the unsuspecting boyfriend: "Gill died while you were away. That's what I'm putting you straight on, arsehole."

Harrisons loud laugh down the line wasn't the reaction Frank had expected. Neither was his reply: "You fucking liar! Do you think I'm stupid?"

The reaction knocked Frank off track for a few moments. In his rehearsals, he hadn't expected that reply to the devasting news. Leaning back on the bench, he said threateningly, "I know all about you and Gill and a lot more about you than you can imagine, arsehole. Does your wife, Penny, know? Perhaps I should tell her what you've been up to!"

That had the desired effect. He had found Harrison's Achilles' heel. Harrison screamed down the phone, "You go near my family and I'll kill you! Do you fucking understand me?"

Without another word, Frank ended the call. He felt so relieved. It wasn't his nature to be nasty and rude, even to someone like Harrison who was the height of arrogance.

He looked up at the sky and breathed out heavily. He sat there for a few minutes gathering his thoughts. As he rubbed his forehead, he realised his hands were shaking. Clearing his head, he went over the call in his mind. He realised he had hit a nerve when he threatened to tell Harrison's wife. The man's reaction was worth noting for future reference.

He decided he disliked Harrison even more now that he had spoken to him. As he started to calm down, he was strangely excited by the phone call. He felt that he had got one over on the cocky bastard. He realised Max was sitting next to him on the bench looking up at him. Smiling, he stroked his trusty friend. "Come on, buddy. Let's go home and see if Eli's up yet." They started off walking back across the Common.

"Well, that went well, Max," he said sarcastically, but he did feel as if a weight had been lifted. He felt that he was finally in charge of the situation for the first time since he suspected the affair. He had finally spoken to Harrison. Now he decided he wanted to see him in person.

What was Gill's attraction to the man? He had seen photos of him and his family on Instagram. Okay ... he could see that some women would find him appealing. He wasn't bad looking—thick blonde hair, probably a six-footer and reasonably well-built. But that wasn't Gill's kind of man. He stopped walking. He realised the irony of what he had just said to himself. It showed what he knew. She'd obviously been attracted to Harrison. They'd had an affair! At least his hands had stopped shaking.

"Come on, Max," he said smiling and walking on again feeling pleased with himself about how the morning had gone.

His phone rang, interrupting his thoughts. It was David. "How you doing, Frank? Do you fancy some company this afternoon? We can watch the rugby and have a couple of beers. Sue's arranged to take Eli for lunch and then shopping in town before Eli meets up with friends."

Frank jumped at the offer only because it would give him the chance to raise the question of Gill's affair. "Sounds good to me. What time are you coming over?"

"Sue will drop me off at twelve thirty if that's okay

with you, and she'll collect Eli at the same time." David ended the call.

When he walked into the hall, Eli shouted through from the kitchen, "Morning, Dad. Fancy a coffee?"

Max bounded down the highly polished wooden floor in the hall to greet Eli in the kitchen. Frank hung the lead and collar up on the coat stand and followed him into the kitchen. Kissing Eli on the forehead, he smiled and sat down next to her. "Did you sleep well? I believe you and Sue are going out for lunch."

Smiling back, she handed him his coffee. "Yes, I did, and yes, I am. Will you be okay on your own tonight? I'm going straight out with friends after we've been shopping." He explained about David's phone call and assured her he would be fine. Since the funeral, she'd taken it upon herself to care for him and fuss over him now Gill wasn't here to do it.

He was sitting in the lounge when he saw Sue's car pull up outside the house. She and Dave both climbed out and walked up the path. He put down the newspaper and opened the door just as they were about to ring the bell. "Come in," he said. "Eli's ready." He kissed Sue on the cheek.

Walking into lounge, Sue smiled sympathetically and asked, "How are you bearing up, Frank?"

As David slumped down on the sofa, Frank smiled back and assured her he was all right, but behind the words, he was thinking to himself, *You knew all about Harrison, didn't you?*

Eli came bounding down the stairs and burst into the lounge. Kissing and hugging Sue and David, she announced,

"I'm ready! Shall we go?" After kissing her dad and asking him again if he would be okay on his own in the evening, Eli and Sue left, slamming the front door behind them.

"I'll get us a couple of beers," announced Frank, and he walked out of the lounge.

"The match starts at two," shouted David after him.

"Good. I want to ask you something first."

Frank came back into the lounge and handed his friend a beer before sitting back in his chair.

"Fire away, my friend. Ask anything you like," said David in a light-hearted mood. He took a long, noisy slurp of his beer.

Frank took a deep breath and thought, *Probably best if I just come straight out with it.* "Did you know Gill was having an affair?"

Even before David replied, Frank knew the answer when he saw the look of shock and horror on his friend's face as his question sank in. David blurted out in shock at what he had just been asked. "What! Who? Your Gill? Are you fucking joking me? Gill? An affair? Never! Never in a million years!"

David sat there in total disbelief, never taking his eyes off Frank, who had stood up and was walking around the lounge. Frank started to tell his friend about the recent events following the funeral—the text messages, discovering who Harrison was and what he did for a living, that morning's phone call with him, and the threat that ended the call. When he had finished, he looked at David, who was still staring at Frank open-mouthed, beer in hand. There was a long silence as they stared at each other.

"Well … any comment?" asked Frank.

Gathering his wits and trying to take in everything he had just been told, David shook his head. "Are you sure, Frank, really? Are you sure you're not mistaken?" It was David's turn to stand up now. He walked over and stood in the bay of the window, turning to look at Frank.

"I'm afraid so, buddy. I've not lost the plot and dreamt all this up. I haven't, really. But at times I feel as if I have lost my mind. It really is driving me mad." Frank sighed and took a long drink of his beer.

"Bloody hell, Frank. I'm so sorry. I don't know what to say. I've known Gill and you for years. I knew her really well." He corrected himself: "At least I thought I did. She was the last person I'd have thought would have an affair."

"Tell me about it," said Frank. "I still find it hard to believe, I can tell you." He shook his head slowly as he ran his fingers across his forehead.

"How long had it been going on?" asked David.

"I don't know, to be honest." Frank shrugged.

"You look like shit. Is there anything I can do to help?" David offered, sitting back down. He was really concerned about his old friend. The news about the affair on top of grieving for Gill and trying to get the children through It all was taking its toll on him.

"Yes, there is actually. I would like to speak with Sue about it and get all the details, if you don't mind?" Frank blurted out.

"What?" shouted David, jumping up out of his chair. "What makes you think she knows anything about all this?" he asked defensively. He paused, looking at the half smile on Frank's face. He sat down again, took a mouthful of beer, and ran his tongue across his bottom lip. He had answered his own question. "Yeah, you're right. She would know; they were so close. Sue would know about it for sure."

They both sat there in silence drinking their beers, lost in their own thoughts, Frank stood up and asked, "Another one?"

"After your revelations, I'll need more than one, Frank. I think you should keep them coming all afternoon."

They never did get watch the rugby. Instead Frank explained in detail what had happened after the funeral, showing David the texts on Gill's phone.

"He sounds a bit of a nasty piece of work, Frank, from what you've told me about him and the phone call. What do you intend to do next?" asked David, surprised that, after what must have been six or seven bottles of beer, he felt as sober as a judge.

"I'm thinking of messing up his perfect life like he has mine. I'll tell his wife all about their affair when, hopefully, I get all the details from Sue!" Frank walked into the kitchen and went into the fridge for more beers.

"Let me text Sue. We're supposed to be out tonight at the Richardson's for dinner. I'll tell her to cancel, and I'll say that I'm keeping you company because you're on a bit of a downer! I didn't really fancy going anyway," said David, accepting the beer from Frank. He put the down beer on the worktop, pulled his phone out of his pocket, and sat down at the breakfast bar. After texting Sue, he went back to their conversation, asking Frank, "Do you really think it's a good idea stirring up trouble for Harrison, Frank? Especially after he's threatened to harm you if you go near his family!"

"Why should he get away scot-free? I don't think that's fair, do you?" snapped Frank slamming the fridge door.

David was shocked at Frank's sudden anger. He couldn't remember him ever saying a cross word to or about anyone, let alone raising his voice to him. Trying to take the heat of the situation, he said in a sympathetic tone, "I don't know, Frank. I suppose it's easy for me to say. I haven't been through what you have—losing my wife and then finding out she had been playing around. But I just can't see what you will gain by causing trouble for him. Maybe you should just get on with your life after everything you've been through these past few weeks. Also, what you've already told me you've found out about him, and then today's telephone conversation, he does seem like a bit of a nasty bastard."

David's words appeared to work. Frank calmed down a bit. Sitting back on a seat and breathing out heavily, he shrugged his shoulders and asked David, "Maybe I'll have a think about it. Will you speak to Sue about it tonight or tomorrow morning? I want to know the truth about the affair. So please tell her no bullshit. That wouldn't be fair, and it would only piss me off big time."

"I will, promise! She mentioned to me earlier that Eli was out for the weekend, so why don't you come around to ours for lunch tomorrow?" suggested David, taking a big swig from his fresh bottle of beer. *It's started to take effect now*, he thought. *I feel pissed.*

"Okay. Sounds good. Though I doubt she'll feel like cooking after you tell her what I want to discuss." Frank laughed and bent down to give Max a few treats.

They took their beers back into the lounge and settled

down to an evening of getting very drunk and putting the world to rights, just as they usually did when they had a heavy session. Frank sat down and stroked Max, who had followed them, hoping for some more treats. The dog rested his head on Frank's lap. Frank said to his trusty pal, "The game's afoot, Max. Things are moving at a pace now. We'll get to the bottom of all this shit! it's time for the good guys to strike back." Looking over at David, he raised his beer in a toast, and they both laughed.

David said with a measure of concern in his voice, "I hope you know what you're doing, Frank. I don't think it would be a good idea to stir up a shitload of trouble for yourself, especially with everything you, Tom, and Eli have been through recently!"

Frank smiled and nodded at his drunken friend, but he had already decided what he was going to do next. Despite David's advice, he was going to get revenge and cause big problems in Harrison's life.

CHAPTER 22

SUNDAY LUNCH

Frank stood on David and Sue's doorstep, ready to go home. David looked concerned and asked, in a sympathetic voice, "Do you want me to come with you for a walk on the Common? We can talk, or we can just walk. Your call."

Frank smiled and replied in a kind tone, "No. I'm fine, thanks. I just need to digest everything that Sue's told me. It was a hell of a lot to take in all at once."

The friends hugged each other, and David promised he would call Frank on Monday evening to see how he was. He added, "Please don't do anything stupid regarding Harrison now that you know all the facts."

Frank thanked his friend again and then led Max down the path and across the road on to the Common.

It hadn't been a pleasant Sunday lunch; they had hardly eaten any food. Frank suspected that it was David who had cooked the roast lamb meal. Sue was visibly upset and was drinking when Frank walked into the house. He'd smiled and hugged her close to him.

Sue thought she was going to be sick with fright. Frank

took off Max's lead and sat down, smiling again at Sue. Once they were all settled with a glass of wine each. Frank had calmly asked Sue to tell him what she knew about the affair.

When David had rolled in at 11.30 the night before swaying from side to side with all the drink and told her about his time with Frank, she was shocked and had burst into tears. The tears got far worse when he told her Frank was coming around for Sunday lunch to hear what she could tell him about Gill's affair with Harrison. When she finally managed to stop crying, she told David she didn't want to do it, but David argued that she owed it to Frank. She had cried herself to sleep.

She wasn't sure she could get through the afternoon; she hadn't slept much during the night, worrying about speaking to Frank about Gill. She had drunk a couple of glasses of wine before Frank arrived to and calm her nerves. At first it was difficult talking to both men about her best friend's secret affair. The fact that Gill was no longer alive didn't make it any easier; in fact, it possibly made it worse. Sue felt as if she was betraying their friendship and her friend's memory; it wasn't an easy thing to do.

She remembered what David had told her the night before after rolling in drunk and dropping the bombshell on her. He repeated it again on Sunday morning. He had advised her to think hard about what she was going to say. He believed she should tell the truth.

She started at the very beginning. Gill had met Harrison at their gym, and then Sue and Gill had bumped into him in Wimbledon Village when they were shopping after visiting Sue's parents. She explained that there appeared to be an instant connection between the two of them. Harrison was a real charmer. She found it so very difficult saying this to Frank.

Sue felt as if she had betrayed Frank, and that upset her even more. She had always liked him. What was there not to like? He was always the gentleman and had been a genuine friend to both her and David over the years.

She carried on, saying that Gill agreed to meet Harrison for an innocent lunch in Clapham on a day that coincided with one of Frank's business trips to the States, and the pair of them ended up in bed. She didn't really want to tell Frank that they sometimes made love in the Quinn family home. There was nothing to be gained by him knowing that. She had decided she owed him the truth about the affair, but not all the hurtful details. She added, truthfully, that a lot of times the couple took a room in a hotel in town.

Frank and David sat there in complete silence as the story unfolded. Sue reiterated quite a few times that Gill and Harrison had stopped seeing each other several times, once for over a year, but then they always seemed to get back together again.

She added that Gill really loved Frank and that she always felt guilty about cheating on him, even though that fact seemed pointless after what she had just been telling them both. The impassive look on Frank's face worried her; she had never seen him like that before. The Frank she knew had always carried his heart on his sleeve. He was somehow different now. It wasn't contempt or disgust; it was a lack of emotional reaction at what she was telling him. This was not what she expected. She had thought he would get upset and might even cry! All he seemed to be feeling was total indifference. It was as if she was talking about one of their friends and not his wife. Nothing she had told him so far appeared to have shocked or hurt him.

She had to pause several times to take a drink to refresh her dry mouth. What she was doing was one of the hardest things she had ever had to do. She just wanted it all to be over as quickly as possible. She started to cry. Frank declined David's offer of another glass of wine. He just sat stroking Max's head as he waited for Sue to compose herself and carry on with the story. She explained that Harrison had gone away on business and a family holiday to South Africa for over six weeks. It was whilst he was away that Gillian had died, so he wouldn't have known about it when he came back. Sue sighed heavily as she came to end of her story. She dabbed her red eyes with her handkerchief. She looked at Frank and then at David, who gave her a discreet, well-done nod. They all sat in silence for a minute or two. Sue felt uncomfortable with the silence. Not wanting to make eye contact, she just looked down at her hands. She was clutching a handkerchief.

It was Frank who finally broke the silence. Clearing his throat, he thanked Sue for her honesty, adding that there was one question she hadn't answered. "You said, Sue, that on several occasions, they had stopped seeing each other, and once for something like a year, so that left me wondering … just how long had their affair been going on?"

Sue's answer shocked them both. David, who was also hearing the story for the first time, blurted, "Fucking hell, Sue! What? About six months after they moved down here from the north! Christ, that's like twenty odd years—that's not a love affair, that's a bloody secret life!"

David's outburst upset Sue all over again, and she started to cry again, but his comments exactly reflected what Frank was thinking.

As they walked across the Common, Frank slipped Max's lead to give him a run. As he watched the dog, he tried to take in everything that Sue had told him. He thought, *Christ! The more I find out about it all, the worse it just seems to get!* Surely there wasn't anything else to find out that could make the whole sordid thing any worse. All kind of thoughts were going through his mind. He wondered why Gill had stayed with him all these years when she was also seeing Harrison. It appeared that she must have loved both men in her life. That didn't make sense to him, but then again, none of it did.

Maybe she stayed with him because of Tom and Eli. She loved them both deeply, and she also knew just how much he loved his children. Taking them away would have destroyed him. The fact that he was abroad so much probably made it easier for Gill to live her double life.

He just couldn't get his head around any of it. How can a person love two people in that way? She obviously loved Harrison if she'd stayed with him for so long. That wasn't just a physical relationship—not for twenty years.

He gave up trying to fathom it all out. Sue's declaration really had a big help. Now it appeared that he had all the facts. Even if he couldn't understand Gill's reasons for betraying him, the facts him helped to crystallise exactly what his next move was going to be. He would start tomorrow.

Chapter 23

A TRIP TO CLAPHAM

On Monday morning, Frank let Max out into the back garden before he made breakfast for himself and Eli. After clearing up the dishes, he walked Max on the Common whilst Eli got on with some course work for uni. He told her he had an appointment in the city later in the afternoon. He left home at 4.30 and made his way down to Clapham. Despite the fact that it was only a few miles away, he arrived across the road from the South London Mercedes Dealership forty-five minutes later. Parking across the road at the head of a side street, he had a clear view of the showrooms. He could see what looked to be a few members of staff and the odd customer.

He climbed out of the Range Rover, locked it, and walked a short distance down the road, stopping at the Costa Coffee. He took a seat at one of the tables outside that gave him a decent view of the showrooms. He was sure he caught a glimpse of Harrison shaking hands with a man whom he took to be a customer. The man followed Harrison into what appeared to be his office. Finishing his coffee, Frank crossed the road and walked up past the showroom. Parked on the side of the forecourt was a top-of-the-range Merc Sports with a private plate: MH 1. *It has to be* his, thought Frank. It was typical of the flash bastard, but then again, he did own a Mercedes dealership.

Back in his car, Frank waited patiently. Finally, at 7.20, out *he* came, immaculately dressed in a dark-blue business suit. He was probably just as smart and perfect as when he left for work that morning. He climbed into MH 1 and started up the engine. Frank waited until he had pulled out into traffic and slowly followed two cars behind. He was in luck. It looked as if Harrison was heading towards home in Wimbledon. Up Putney Hill, Frank lost sight of the silver Mercedes sports but assumed he was heading up towards the A3. On the green light, he caught up with the traffic and could see Harrison's Merc four cars in front. Harrison turned off the roundabout towards Wimbledon Village and the Common. Frank was one car behind now as they sped down Parkside towards the village. He saw the Mercedes slow, indicate, and turn left, stopping at a set of high, black wrought iron gates. They opened, and Harrison's car pulled into the drive as Frank drove past. Parking up on the next left turn, he waited several minutes and then walked back by Harrison's house but on the Common side of the road. His car was parked on the drive next to a Mercedes 4x4 with a plate PH 12, which Frank assumed was his wife's car.

It was a grand modern house, one that he, Gill, David, and Sue used to call a footballer's house. Nonetheless, it was impressive. Frank made a note of the number of the house. Having seen enough, he decided to head back home to see Eli.

Chapter 24

A SERIOUS WARNING

When Frank was on his way home, Eli phoned. She was crying hysterically. Frank pulled into a parking space and finally managed to calm her down. From what he could make out, she was saying something about Tom. Finally getting a grip of herself, she told him the police had telephoned. Tom had been attacked when he was on his way home after having a few drinks with friends after work. He had been taken in St Georges Hospital.

"You stay at home, Eli," Frank told her. "I'll go and see what's happened, and I'll be in touch soon, I promise, my darling."

"I want to come too," Eli said, sobbing.

"Please, Eli. Just do has I ask. Everything will be okay. I'll be in touch as soon as I've seen Tom," pleaded Frank.

He wasn't too far away from the hospital; it was on the route he was taking to reach home from Wimbledon. After parking up, he went to reception where he was directed to the ward Tom was on. The ward nurse told him that Tom had been admitted after coming into A&E. He was stable and asleep, and if Frank waited, she would see if the doctor could spare him a few minutes. Ten minutes later, a doctor appeared and spoke with the nurse. They both looked over in Frank's direction, and then the doctor walked over to Frank. Smiling, he held out his hand and introduced himself.

"Thank you for seeing me, Doctor," said Frank, standing and shaking hands with the doctor. "How is he?"

"Let's sit down." The young doctor smiled reassuringly.

Frank couldn't believe how young he looked. With his pimples and shock of ginger hair, if he had been wearing a school uniform, he would easily have passed for a six former. *It just means I'm getting older*, thought Frank to himself.

"Your son was checked out thoroughly when he was brought in," the young doctor explained, maintaining eye contact with Frank. "The police have spoken with him briefly, but they have not taken a statement. I didn't think he was up to it. From what I could hear, he was the victim of a random attack outside a bar in the city. Does he work down in the city?" he enquired.

"Yes, he works there in the financial sector," replied Frank.

"Okay. Well, despite his size, I'm afraid he took a bit of a beating from the two men who attacked him. He's not a pretty sight presently. He's got a lot of bruising to his face, which will go down in time. He's also got three broken ribs and a fracture of his left wrist, and he's lost a few teeth! But he's a strong young man. We've done a scan, and there are no other problems to report. He should make a full recovery. We'll keep him in for observation for the time being, just to be on the safe side."

Frank thanked the young man again for taking the time to see him. He went to Tom's room and spent ten minutes at his son's bedside looking at Tom's bruised and swollen face. He thought to himself, *Shit! Life just keeps getting better and better! What have you got yourself into, young Thomas?*

Frank sighed heavily. It broke his heart to see his son like this. As big as he was, Tom was still Frank's little boy—always would be. Something bad was going on in Tom's life. Frank was determined he was going to get to the bottom of it. *Here's another problem to add to the growing list*, he thought. Then his mind quickly turned to poor Eli. She'd been so upset. He decided it was best to go home and be with her. Frank was worried about his daughter. *She's had a rough time the poor thing, what with her mum and now this nonsense with Tom.* He stood up, gently rubbed Tom's arm, and left for home.

His key in the front door alerted Max, who began to bark a greeting as he came skidding up the hall across the wooden floor to greet him. The dog was quickly followed by Eli, who fell into her Dad's arms, sobbing. "How is he, Daddy? What happened? Who did this to him?" She blurted out her words between sobs, her head buried in her dads' shoulder.

"Hey! Come on now! One question at a time please," he replied, purposely smiling and trying to make light of the situation for her sake. He walked Eli down the hall and into the lounge. He said, "Why don't you pour me a well-earned drink. I'll get changed quickly, and I will bring you up to speed with what I know. But, Eli, darling, he's going to be fine. Trust me. I spoke with the doctor. He'll be out in a day or so." He kissed her on the forehead, turned, and headed upstairs.

His words appeared to have reassured Eli; she had started to calm down. When Frank returned, she was sitting on the sofa with Max lying across her as usual. Frank slumped down into his favourite chair. After taking a slurp from the tumbler Eli had given him, he let out a large sigh. He felt a bit better. He finally started to relax. He had changed into a tee shirt and jeans, ideal for another warm evening.

"Why would somebody do that to Tom, Daddy? Everybody he knows likes him. I can't ever remember him having an argument with anybody, let alone a fight!"

Frank relayed everything he had been told by the doctor. Eli had even managed a giggle and a smile when he told her about the pimply young doctor who was a double for a young Ron Weasley in the early Harry Potter films. He left out the detail of Tom's badly swollen bruised face and tried to play down the injuries. He realised that, with all the nonsense about Harrison and Gill, he had neglected poor Eli at a time when she needed him most.

"Do you and Tom talk, darling?" asked Frank, pouring himself another large whisky.

"Yes. Of course we do," Eli replied, looking up from tickling Max.

"No, I mean really talk—about what's happening in your lives … problems and serious stuff?" asked Frank, sitting back down. "There's something going on in Tom's life—some kind of trouble he's got himself in that I think has led to this attack tonight. I've had a feeling all is not right with him for some time now!"

Eli looked over at her dad. She was shocked and started crying again. "Why? What trouble do you think he's in, Daddy? He's never talked to me about any problems—honestly."

Frank moved Max out of the way and sat down beside her. He put his arm around her, and she buried her face into his shoulder again. He assured her everything would be okay. Whatever problems Tom had, Frank would make sure they solved them so he wouldn't get hurt again.

They sat quietly for a while, Frank enjoying his malt, Eli enjoying feeling so safe cuddled into her father. Frank broke the silence and asked, "How are you coping, darling, without your mum? What with your studies and me being busy with one thing and another, we've not really had time to talk very much about you."

She straightened up. As she pushed her hair back off her face with both hands, her gaze wandered to the window and out to the Common across the road. Her voice was a gentle whisper. "I miss her so much, Daddy. I still can't believe she's not here and that I'll never see her again! I still pick up her smell around the house, but it's fading now, and that makes me so sad. The other day I came home from shopping with Sue and shouted down the hall, 'I'm home, Mum!'" She looked into Frank's face and smiled a tearful smile. His face quivered with emotion as he pulled her closer.

She continued, "It's so easy to forget she's gone. I try so hard because I know she wouldn't want me to be sad. I know it's not been that long, but it's not getting any easier, and I thought it would with time."

Frank hugged her tightly, kissed her on the forehead, and replied, "You've been so brave, and I'm so proud of you. It will get easier, but it will take a while. It's still early days yet. Your mum will be looking down on you. She would be so very proud at how strong you've been!"

"I don't feel like I've been strong, Dad." Eli sighed.

They sat there together in silence for a few minutes, enjoying the quiet and each other's company.

Finally sitting up, Eli rubbed her eyes and ran her fingers through her hair. She asked, "Shall I let Max out in the back garden for five minutes?"

"Sure, I suppose so." Frank smiled. "The poor thing will want a pee. What do you fancy for dinner?"

Frank convinced Eli not to go with him to the hospital with him the next day. It hadn't been easy. She was adamant that she wanted to visit her brother. Frank said he had to get to the bottom of Tom's troubles, and he didn't think Tom would open up in front of Eli. Also, he would be out of hospital soon. There was also another reason—he didn't want her to see her brother in the state he was in. He would prefer her to see him when he was looking a little bit less battered. Seeing him now would only upset her, and she'd been through enough.

When he arrived at the ward, he could see Tom sitting up against his pillow talking to a police officer. Approaching the bed, Frank heard the officer saying to Tom, "If you can remember anything else, no matter how trivial, don't hesitate to call the number I've given you."

Okay, I will. Thanks," replied Tom. He made eye

contact with his dad, who was standing directly behind the policeman's chair now. "This is Constable Ivell, Dad. He's just been taking a statement about last night."

The policeman stood up, turned, and shook hands with Frank. "Pleased to meet you, sir. PC Ivell ... Les Ivell." The young officer smiled.

Frank instinctively smiled back and shook hands, once again shocked at just how young the police officer was. He looked even younger than the doctor he'd spoken with last night. It was beginning to depress him. Was he really getting that old?

"Any arrests yet?" Frank enquired, knowing the answer.

"Not yet, I'm afraid, but hopefully soon. We're trying to get a look at the CCTV on the street to try to identify your son's attackers." He spoke in a very official sort of voice. Frank smiled again and discreetly looked the young PC up and down as the officer turned to wrap it up with Tom. Frank moved towards the bed ready to ask Tom how he felt.

"Well, I'll leave you two in peace now," said the young PC. He said his goodbyes and left.

Frank sat down on the chair at the side of the bed that had been vacated by the young policeman. He spoke first, asking Tom, "What hurts the most, son—face, ribs, arm, or your pride?"

Tom tried to manage a smile. "Everything hurts, to be honest, Dad. Especially my pride!"

Frank looked at his son's swollen, bruised face, sighed, and asked, "What's going on, Tom? Whatever it is, it must be a big problem for this to happen to you. They did a good job on you, son!" Tom looked shocked at his father's assessment of the situation. He started to reply, but Frank cut in. "Surprised are we, Tom, that I'm not has daft as I look? I hate violence and have always stayed clear of it all my life, but even I know when someone's been given a warning like you were given last night. Whatever it is, I'm here for you, and I promise I will sort it out. You owe it to Eli and me to tell me, especially after what we've all been through recently. Eli is so upset again about this business, Tom, and I don't like that. I know you don't either."

"I'm sorry, Dad. I don't want either of you to be upset because of me. I've been so bloody stupid!"

"Come on. Out with it! What have you done? I assume it's to do with the arguments you've been having on the telephone?"

"Yes, it is. I owe a serious guy money that I haven't got!" confessed Tom. He wasn't sure what hurt most—speaking with his face so bashed up or confessing to his dad what an idiot he had been!

Frank was surprised by Tom's willingness to open up straight away. He thought to himself, *Well that was easier than expected*. He looked long and hard at his son. Taking a deep breath he replied, "Why do you owe the money? Gambling? Drugs? Which one is it?"

Looking down at the bed, not wanting to make eye contact with his dad, Tom replied, "It's for drugs." He'd always hated disappointing his dad, who had worked so hard through the years to give him and his sister the best start in life that they could possibly have.

"Okay, now that we know what the problem is, we can deal with it," said Frank. "How much do you owe this 'serious guy' and how do I get in touch with him to sort it out?"

Tom was relieved he had finally told his dad. Clearing his throat he replied, "Fifteen grand. But I don't want you to get involved with him, and I don't think he would like it either." He was surprised his dad's face didn't show any sign of shock or emotion.

Frank replied, "I think this guy won't mind me getting involved. He just wants his money. What he's done to you makes that pretty obvious. I'm sure he won't mind your dad getting involved."

Tom quickly added, "I promise I will pay you back, Dad—every penny, even if it takes me a couple of years."

Frank nodded. He glanced around and said in a whisper, "I bloody well know you will. I'm doing this because I don't want you getting another beating or, God forbid, anything worse!" After looking around the ward again, he turned back to Tom and asked in a hushed voice, "Are you an addict?"

Tom shook his head and was genuinely shocked at the question "No! It was just recreational. Honest, Dad. And I promise I will never touch the stuff again."

Frank looked into his son's swollen face and bloodshot eyes and thought to himself, *If only it was that easy.* But that was a conversation for a later date. He replied, "I certainly hope not, son. I really do."

Tom explained who Mattie Patterson was and described his business deals. He also told his dad how to get in touch with the dealer but emphasised he should not mention money, drugs, or anything like that over the phone even though the dealer used a "burner". He was just to say he was Tom's dad. That would be enough for the drug dealer to recognize whom he was speaking to. "A burner, Dad—"

Tom was shocked when Frank cut in. "I know perfectly well what a burner is—it's an untraceable mobile phone, Tom."

"Dad, I can't emphasize enough just how dangerous these people are," pleaded Tom. "I really think it would be better if you left it to me to sort out. I can call him in a few days when I'm feeling better. I really think he might not want you getting involved even though you are my dad."

"Whether he or you like it or not, Tom, I am involved. You're my son I'll be okay. Don't worry. I've had lots of tough meetings in my time. I'll be very careful." Frank looked down at his mobile phone at the drug dealer's number he had just typed in.

Tom's voice quivered with emotion as he replied, "Dad, I don't think you understand the sort of people you will be dealing with. I'm sure you've had plenty of difficult meetings, but those people are nothing like these guys. If they didn't like what you're saying, they will stand up and shot you in the head!" Tom studied his dad's face. All he saw was determination—no fear or concern, just a determination to protect his son.

Frank smiled and replied, "I told you not to worry about me, son. I'll be careful. I don't intend to make this situation any worse than it is already is. Trust me."

Tom's face was aching after all the talking, first with the police officer and then with his dad. He was worn out, but he felt relieved after telling his dad his troubles despite the shame of how stupid he had been.

"You get some rest now, son. The nurse told me that they hope to let you go home tomorrow. I think it would do you good to come home and rest for a couple of days with us. Call me, and I'll come and get you when you are discharged." Standing up to go, he kissed his son on the forehead.

Tom nodded. "Thanks again, Dad. I'm so sorry to put you through all this."

Frank fastened his jacket and said reassuringly, "Don't worry. Like I said, I'll sort it out."

Tom smiled meekly and replied, "Thanks, Dad. Please be careful." Watching his dad walk away down the ward, Tom's face quivered with emotion. He just hoped that his stupidity wasn't going to get his dad killed!

Chapter 25

FACE-TO-FACE CONFRONTATION

As he drove back to Wandsworth, Frank felt relieved that Tom had come clean and told him what the problem was. He was a bit surprised how quickly he had offered up what was wrong. Since he was a young boy, Tom had always kept any problems to himself and just dealt with them. Frank had thought he would have to drag the situation out of him. *He must really be worried to just to come out with it like that.* Frank decided he would phone this Mattie Patterson in the morning—not from his mobile, but from a public phone box. That would be safer. He didn't want a drug dealer having his telephone number. His mind wandered and he wondered what Eli was cooking for dinner. His mood had lifted now that he finally knew Tom's problem. Even though it was a drug debt, which was a real shock, at least now he could help his son and hopefully put this problem behind them.

When he opened the front door, Max came bounding

down the hall to greet him, followed by Eli who hugged him and kissed him on the cheek. "How's Tom, Dad?"

"Good. He's on the mend," he replied, taking off his jacket and hanging it in the closet in the hall.

"You've got a friend from the office waiting for in the lounge," Eli said with a smile. "He's called round to see how you are."

"Oh, okay. Are you preparing dinner?" asked Frank

"Yes. It will be about forty-five minutes," she shouted over her shoulder as she disappeared into the kitchen, Max clicking his way behind her.

As Frank opened the door and walked into the lounge, he was stopped dead in his tracks, not believing what he was seeing. His mouth dropped open in shock. Standing before him in front of the fireplace as if her owned the place was Mike Harrison, one hand holding a wine glass and the other hand in his trouser pocket. He had a bloody big smirk on his face. Trying hard to compose himself, Frank quickly closed the lounge door and turned back to face his wife's lover. In a voice just above a whisper so Eli wouldn't hear, he said, "What the fuck are you doing here?" Before Harrison could offer a reply, Frank hissed at him, "You've got a fucking nerve coming around to my home!"

Harrison just beamed a cocky smile. Placing his wine glass on the coffee table he looked around the lounge and replied, "It's been a while since I was last here, Frankie boy! I thought I would pay you a personal visit to find out why you followed me home the other night."

"I want you to leave now. Right *now! Go!*" said Frank, trying hard not to lose his composure and his temper.

Harrison's smile dropped from his face, and he took a

menacing step towards Frank. He was slightly taller and had a much bigger build, Frank tensed, worried that Eli was going to walk in any minute.

"I told you when you phoned me not to try to cause trouble for me with my family, so you decide to follow me home? What for? Why?" Harrison growled, his face starting to redden with anger.

All Frank could think of was Eli in the kitchen; otherwise, he would have gladly taken a swing at the cocky bastard who stood in front of him. "Fuck off. You'll find out soon enough. Now get out of my house!" replied Frank in a quiet firm voice.

Harrison caught Frank off guard. He shot forward, grabbed Frank by the throat, and pushed him backwards onto the sofa. Using his knee to pin Frank down, his put his face an inch away from Frank's. He whispered threateningly, "I've already told you once. Don't fuck with me. You'll see soon enough what a big mistake you've made ignoring my warning." After aggressively pushing Frank's head further back into the sofa, he stood up, stepped back, and ran his fingers through hair to get it back into place. Then he calmly fastened his suit jacket.

Frank struggled to get to his feet. He had been surprised by Harrison's speed and strength, but his concern was still for Eli in the kitchen. "Go!" said Frank as firmly as he could without shouting, pointing at the lounge door.

Harrison just smiled. He straightened his tie and brushed Frank's shoulder with his own as he walked out of the lounge. Frank followed him down the hall as Harrison sauntered to the front door. The man turned and looked Frank up and down with utter contempt. He smirked and said, "Thank Eli for me for the drink. She's a lovely girl. I can see a lot of her mum in her. Nothing of you, though, arsehole, but then again, she wouldn't look anything like you, would she? Because she's not *your* daughter."

Harrison laughed before he finally walked out of the house, closing the front door behind him. Frank watched as he disappeared down the path.

Frank stood frozen to the spot in the hall, staring at the front door. Harrison's parting words about Eli screamed out in Frank's head. He struggled to catch his breath; he thought he was having a heart attack. He tried to calm himself. He tidied up his hair with his fingers, and he walked back into the lounge. Harrison's words and smirking face assaulting Frank's senses. His hands shook as he poured himself a whisky. Sitting down before his legs gave way, he took a large gulp of whisky and sat staring at the fireplace. He put his tumbler down next to the wine glass. He looked at the empty glass left there by Harrison and felt sick. Surely what Harrison had just said couldn't be true? It couldn't be that Frank wasn't Eli's father, and that bastard was? No! No, it couldn't be!

Frank couldn't think straight. The image of Gill and Harrison with baby Eli when he was away in America working was too sickening to even think about. Is that why they continued to see each other for all those years—because Harrison was Eli's dad? And that's why Gill wouldn't—or couldn't—end the affair? It was all beginning to come together now. Every fact he learned was another piece of the jigsaw puzzle.

Frank sat there running his fingers across his forehead trying to take in what had just happened and, more importantly, what had just been said. His mind was whirling at Harrison's parting comments. He thought, *I could have a blood test to prove that Eli is my daughter.* No, he wasn't thinking straight! How could he do that? Eli had been through so much these past weeks. Something like that would surely push her over the edge—losing her mum, Tom's attack, and then finding out her dad wasn't Frank but her mum's long-time lover! No, completely out of the question. She must never know.

For fuck's sake, Frank thought, *what is happening to our lives? Things just keep getting worse! I've just got to the bottom of Tom's problem and am about to sort it, and another problem comes up.* He sat there for a few minutes quietly thinking.

Frank decided he was right. Eli must never find out, even if it was the truth. She couldn't cope with something like that, especially now. She needed time to grieve and get back to some normality. He would speak to Sue to see if she if she knew. Maybe Gill had confided in her about it when she fell pregnant with Eli.

When Eli walked in, smiling, Frank nearly jumped out of his skin. His mind had been miles away. "Oh, has your work friend gone, Dad?" she asked glancing around the lounge, quickly adding, "Dad, are you all right? You look like you've seen a ghost. What's wrong? What's happened?" She walked over to Frank and sat down next to him on the arm of his chair.

"No! I'm fine thanks, darling. Really, I am," lied Frank, forcing a smile. Looking at his daughter's worried face, he kissed her cheek.

"Did your friend say something to upset or concern you, Dad? You seem shocked. Is your job okay?" Eli asked

"Yes, of course my job is okay, you silly thing. And no, he didn't say anything to upset me. Nothing at all, darling, but promise me, if he ever comes back and I'm not home, don't let him into the house."

Eli looked even more worried now. "Why? What's going on, Daddy?"

He smiled again trying to reassure her, thinking that really hadn't been the right time to say that to her. *You dope!* "Nothing to worry about and nothing sinister, my darling. It's just that he isn't really a friend, and I don't trust him or even like him, to be honest with you. That's all. Not many people at the office do like him. He's only happy when he's causing problems. I'm not that friendly with him, and I don't know why he bothered to call. He's not a nice person!" Frank said, mixing truth with lies. Thinking he was digging himself into a hole, Frank changed the subject. Trying to lift the mood he asked, "Anyway, how's dinner coming along? What are we having? I might have to nip round to David and Sue's for a little while later. I'll take Max with me for his evening walk … save you a job of taking him."

Eli smiled. Standing, she replied, "Supper will be ready in about ten minutes. It's my homemade cottage pie. I know you love it. Are you hungry?"

"I always have room for a plateful of your cottage pie, darling!" Frank smiled, feeling sick at what had just happened.

Frank sat in the lounge drinking his whisky and wondering what Harrison meant when he said, "You've made a mistake ignoring my warning." Was he planning something? What could he do? It was probably just the cocky bastard's bravado.

Tom and Eli would be home, so he could keep an eye on them in case Harrison tried to approach them and tell them about his affair with their mum or something shitty like that.

Over dinner, Eli asked about Tom and his problem. Frank wasn't sure if she could take the truth but naively decided it would be a good deterrent if she ever thought of dabbling in drugs. Eli sat there in stunned silence as her dad explained the problem that had led to her brother being beaten up. Frank had judged it completely wrong again. Eli burst into tears. She couldn't eat the rest of her dinner as she cried for about ten minutes. Frank was furious with himself. *What was I thinking? I am so bloody stupid! I've just given Eli something else to worry herself sick about.*

They sat in the lounge, Frank cuddling her. She was so fragile as a result of everything that had happened recently. He hadn't realised just how fragile she actually was until now, and he wasn't helping. He should have said it was a random attack on Tom. Why had he decided to tell her the truth about Tom? he really was a bloody fool at times.

She finally fell asleep on the sofa. Frank covered her with a throw and went into the kitchen to clean up the dinner plates. He wondered if he should leave her alone while he visited David and Sue later. He was cross with himself for being honest with her. He should have realised it would only upset and worry her that Tom might still be in danger. He decided to call Sue instead of leaving Eli alone. David answered the phone. After the initial small talk about how things were going, Frank explained about

Tom getting attacked outside a bar near his office. He didn't go into the details about why Tom had been attacked; he had decided he would keep that within the family, at least for now. He made a mental note to tell Eli and Tom when he came home not to mention why it had happened to Sue or David next time they met them.

David was shocked and said how sorry he was to hear what had happened to Tom. "Bloody hell, Frank, you're having a tough time of it at the moment, aren't you? In fact, you all are, for God s sake!"

"Tell me about. It's just one thing after another. Whatever happened to good news, David?" asked Frank dejectedly. "Is Sue there?" enquired Frank now that he had updated his friend about Tom's attack.

"Yes. Do you want to speak to her?"

"If it's not inconvenient, yes please. Something else has come up now, and I need to ask her what she knows about it." Making sure Eli was still fast asleep on the sofa, he walked into the kitchen and closed the door after him.

"Why? What's happened now, Frank?" asked David after shouting Sue over to the phone.

"I'll go through it with both of you," replied Frank.

Sue's voice came on the line. "Hi, Frank. What on earth's happened to Tom? David just said something … Tom's in hospital and he's been attacked?" She was very close to both Tom and Eli and was upset to hear about what happened

Frank quickly went over the attack again, stating again that he didn't know what it was all about. He went on and explained that Tom was coming out of hospital the next day and would be staying at home with him and Eli for a few days convalescing.

"That's terrible! He's such a nice young man. Why would anybody pick a fight with him, the bastards? Can I call round when he's home to see him and Eli? Is that's okay, Frank?" pleaded Sue.

Frank smiled into the phone and replied, "Yes, of course it is, Sue. You don't have to ask. You know that. I know that David told you to leave us to grieve for Gill, but I think Eli really needs you at the moment. I'm worried about her."

"How is she, Frank? I've spoken to her on the phone a few times. She's trying so hard to be brave. It breaks my heart, it really does. She's so sad." Sue spoke with real concern for her goddaughter.

"To be honest, Sue, that's the reason I called. Can you put me on speaker phone so David can hear this too?" He heard Sue shout out for David. Then she came back and told Frank he wouldn't be long; he had just nipped to the loo.

Frank listened as Sue explained that she was pleased that he wanted to speak to her. She hadn't been sure if he would bear a grudge over her revelations about Gill on that horrible Sunday afternoon. Frank promised her he didn't blame her for Gill's affair and understood that Gill would have confided in her; after all, that's what best friends do. Sue was genuinely relieved and got a little emotional as only Sue could do. Thankfully they were joined by David before she started to weep.

"Now I've got you both on the voice box," Frank began, "Sue, I'm afraid what I need to ask you is about Gill and Harrison again." He could hear Sue let out a big sigh. Frank updated them on what had happened with

Harrison, explaining how he had followed Harrison home from his showroom and, unbeknownst to Frank, Harrison had spotted him. David and Sue were both shocked when Frank told them that Harrison had been at the house earlier when he got back from visiting Tom in hospital.

Before he could tell them how he'd been attacked by Harrison and then threatened with what he was capable of, David cut him short by shouting out, "For fuck's sake, Frank, why on earth did you follow him home? From what you've learned about him, and your telephone conversation, we knew he sounded a real nasty bastard. I warned you!"

"Do you think he's had Tom beaten up as a warning to you, Frank?" asked Sue, her voice shaking with emotion.

"No, I don't think so, Sue. If he had, he wouldn't have come around to the house to threaten me. Also, he's such an arrogant bastard, he would have boasted about it," lied Frank.

David and Sue both agreed and fell silent as Frank continued with the events of earlier that evening. Frank explained Harrison's parting words about Eli. There was complete, stunned silence on the phone. Frank finally asked the sixty-four-thousand-dollar question. "Do you know if he's telling the truth, Sue? Is it possible? Could Eli be his daughter? If you do know, please be honest and tell me. I really need to know."

There was silence on the end of the line. Finally, Sue's tearful voice answered. "I honestly don't know, Frank. Truly I don't. Gill never said anything to me about him being the father. She never gave me any indication that he *could* have been."

"But it could be possible, Sue, yes?" asked Frank, feeling

a bit guilty about pushing it when it was clearly upsetting Sue so much. He could hear Sue sobbing on the end of the phone. He waited for her to compose herself and hopefully answer his question. "Oh, Frank, I suppose it could be possible. They were seeing each other then I think. But I'm sure he's just being a real bastard and trying to hurt you. I'm sure Gill would have confided me if what he's saying were true." He heard her start sobbing again.

"Okay. Thanks, Sue. I'm sorry to upset you all over again, but I needed to ask. I hope you understand?" said Frank genuinely sorry for making her so upset.

David's voice came over the phone. He had taken the call off speaker, so it was just the two of them on the line now. "What are you going to do about all this, Frank?"

"Nothing. Nothing at all. What can I do? Eli is so fragile at the moment, what with losing her mum and Tom getting beaten up. I don't want her upset anymore. I'm not sure how much more she can take. She's close to the breaking point." Frank sighed and paused for a few seconds before continuing to explain his dilemma. "I can't even go to the police and tell them that Harrison came to my house and physically assaulted me. Anyway, it would only be my word against his. If I reported the incident, he would make sure Eli found out about his claim to being her dad. She'd find out about her mum's affair with him, and I can't let that happen, David."

"That's true, Frank. It's a bloody awful situation to be in, but like you say, you have to protect Eli. When you say you're not doing anything else, does that include Harrison too?" enquired David. Before Frank could answer he carried on. "You have to leave things with him alone now, Frank.

No good will come of it. Having a go at him—and God knows he deserves it ... well, you're better leaving things alone now and staying well clear of him."

Frank cut in and angrily replied, "That's easy for you to say, David, but you would feel differently if it was you!"

David replied sympathetically, "I know. That's very true, but you have to be logical about it all, Frank, and try to leave emotion out of it. Bloody hell, he knows where you live! He could go around to your house anytime or purposely encounter Eli and tell her about the affair and announce he's her real dad. You can't be with her all the time. Don't forget, Frank, you're going back to work soon. You've got to let it go for all your sakes and especially for yourself, Frank; otherwise, all this nonsense will drive you insane."

"Shit. I'm sorry, David. Of course that's true. I never thought about that. It hadn't occurred to me. Everything is just so fucked up. It's been coming at me from all sides," replied Frank wearily. "Listen, I'll have to go. I want to check on Eli. She's asleep in the lounge. Please, not a word, obviously," Frank pleaded.

"Of course. Sue and I won't say anything about this to anybody—rest assured. Think about what I've just said to you, Frank. Take care, my old friend. If there's anything I can do, you know I'm here for you. We both are," replied David.

Frank thanked him again and hung up. He walked into the lounge to check on Eli and found her still fast asleep on the sofa with Max. Max looked up at Frank has he tiptoed over to the sideboard and quietly poured himself a large scotch. He needed it. He sat down in his chair and lovingly looked at Eli. He really hated Harrison—not just for the affair with Gill, but also for coming around to the house, roughing him up, and most of all saying what he did about Eli. Even if it wasn't true, that made it worse. It was a shitty thing to say to another person

Thinking that Harrison could be Eli's father made him feel physically sick. *For fuck's sake, Gill, what did I ever do to you to deserve all this?* he said to himself. He had been a good, caring, loving husband, a good provider, a good father. Yes, he was away in the States with his job quite often, but that went with the job, and he was bloody well paid for it. Gill never used to complain about him being away. *But then she wouldn't, would she?* he thought, taking a gulp of his scotch. She was jumping into bed with Harrison as soon as he left.

Frank's northern upbringing encouraged him to believe that he was never the victim. His parents instilled that into him and his siblings. It was a northern trait not to ever feel self-pity. Whatever happened, his parents would always say, "There's other people worse off." It was best to just get on with life and deal with whatever the problem was.

As he thought about everything that had happened since Gill's death, he decided he didn't deserve any of it. But it just kept coming his way. His life kept taking bad turns, and none of it was down to him. Because it wasn't his fault, he couldn't stop it. All he could bloody well do was meet it head on and deal with it. It wasn't anything to do with revenge, but it was all about being a father and protecting Eli and Tom and then hopefully finally getting their lives back to normal—back to the way it used to be before all this nonsense started!

The following morning the main to-do events on the

day's agenda were, one, to phone the drug dealer to arrange a meeting, and, two, go to the hospital and collect Tom and bring him back home. Frank showered, dressed, and had breakfast.

He left Eli asleep in bed. He thought it was the best place for her; she certainly needed the rest. Putting Max's lead on, he quietly pulled the front closed as he left the house. He crossed the road onto the Common. Letting Max off the lead, he walked along thinking what he was going to say to Mattie Patterson on the call. He remembered what Tom had said about not saying anything about drugs or the attack. He wasn't to use any surnames. That was all simple enough. After the call, he would make plans to get the money together. He should have it all in three or four days. He just hoped this Mattie Patterson was a patient man!

Calling Max over to him, Frank clipped the lead on and walked towards the parade of shops and restaurants that bordered the Common. Nobody was using the phone box. He took a deep breath and dialled the phone number Tom had given him; a deep voice immediately answered with just a curt, "What?"

"My son, Tom, gave me your number. I want to sort out this misunderstanding."

There was a pause then the voice replied, "There wasn't any misunderstanding. He should have settled up when he was told."

Frank took another deep breath and replied, "Understood. Can we meet up to settle things?"

"Did Tom tell you what was involved?" the voice asked.

Frank replied, "Yes, he did. I'll bring it with me."

"Good man. Thursday morning. Noon. At The Dark

Angel, Camden High Street. Bring it in a brown leather holdall."

The phone went dead. Frank stood there looking down at the receiver in his shaking hand. He said to himself, *Well, that was short and sweet.* He was just glad it was over. It seemed to have gone okay. *I've just got to get through Thursday now*, he thought. *And what the hell is the dark angel?*

Max snapped him out of his thoughts by jumping up at him. Frank smiled, patted Max's head, and said, "Okay, fella, let's go." He was relieved he had got the call over and done with.

As he walked back to the house, he made a couple of calls on his mobile. One was to arrange an appointment with his accountant to get the money together. The other call was to David at the office to see how things were going at work and to remind him that he needed a bit more time off work.

David said, "That's no problem, Frank. You've had a lot going on these past few weeks. A few directors asked after you. I told them about Tom, and they send their regards."

Frank closed the front door behind him, took Max's lead off, and replied, "I know, but I've got to come back sometime David. Won't be long now. Just a few things to settle and I'll be back in the saddle." Hearing Eli walking about upstairs, Frank said his goodbyes to David and ended the call. "Morning, darling. Would you like something to eat?" Frank shouted up the stairs.

Eli appeared at the top of the stairs in her PJ's and shouted down, "Morning, Daddy. No. Just some coffee if that's okay. What time are you going for Tom?"

"I'm waiting for him to get discharged. He said he

would ring. As soon as he does, I'll nip down and get him," shouted Frank from the kitchen as he retrieved the coffee pods from the cupboard.

Frank asked Eli if she had slept well. They chatted over a coffee as they sat at the breakfast bar in the kitchen. Frank's mind wandered. He thought, *I hope Tom's face isn't too bad now and the swelling's gone down*. He was worried Eli would be upset seeing her brother all bashed up. Looking at her, he thought how pale and drawn she looked. He couldn't help thinking, *Is she my daughter or that dirty bastard Harrison's?* He felt guilty thinking about it in front of her. He was her dad, and she would always be his daughter.

Frank's phone pinged. It was Tom texting to say he was allowed out and was ready to come home. Frank gave Eli the good news, pleased to see her face light up. Finishing his coffee, he went to the sink and rinsed out his cup. He picked up his car keys, kissed Eli on the forehead, and left for the hospital.

On the way home, Tom asked his Dad if he had spoken with Mattie Patterson. Frank filled him in on the short conversation they'd had that morning—word for word. He told Tom he thought it had gone okay.

Tom said he wanted to go to meet him on Thursday and pay him the money, but Frank shot him down, telling him he didn't want him to go near Patterson again.

They travelled in silence for a while until Frank broke the silence. "By the way, I told Eli the truth about the attack. However, Sue and David don't know why you were attacked. I want to keep it that way, okay?" Tom looked over at his Dad with a pained expression on his bruised face. "What?" asked his dad.

"Sure. I won't mention the problem to David and Sue. I just wish you hadn't told Eli though. How is she?"

"How do you expect her to be!" snapped Frank. "She's very fragile because of what she's been through recently what with your mum and now you," Frank replied in a harsh tone.

Tom looked out of the window and muttered sheepishly, "Sorry. I just wish you hadn't told her. I can't see the benefit in her knowing."

Frank's attitude and tone softened. He admitted he had made a big mistake telling Eli. "It seemed like a good idea at the time. You know—honesty being the best policy. But I really upset her. I didn't realise just how fragile she is, Tom. She needs a lot of love and care. I'm glad you're going to be home for a while. It will do her good to spend some time with you"

"I'll look after her, Dad. Losing Mum probably hit her more than it did you and me, and God knows how bad it was for us," replied Tom looking out of the passenger window.

They travelled the rest of the way in silence. When they pulled up outside the house, Eli came to the door, struggling to keep Max in check as he tried to get out to the car to greet Tom. She hugged Tom and clung on to him has they walked down the hall into the lounge. Frank parked the car, and when he joined them in the lounge, Eli was drying her eyes. Seeing her bruised and battered brother, whom she adored, had broken her heart.

"Come on now, Eli. He's not as bad as he looks. And just think, you get to mother him for a week before he goes back to his own place," said Frank, trying to lift the mood.

They all laughed, and she snuggled into Tom with Max jealously cuddling into her.

They had a relaxed family dinner that Eli had lovingly prepared while Frank had gone to collect Tom. She was a really good cook; she had been taught well by Gill. The mood was pleasant and happy, which made Frank smile after all the shit he'd experienced these past few weeks.

Thank goodness Tom and Eli weren't privy to most of it. It was good to see them both laughing and joking as Tom mercilessly teased Eli as usual. Frank wistfully glanced at the empty chair at the opposite end of the table where Gill used to sit. He got up and left the table and went int the kitchen. He opened another bottle of wine. It was so good hearing the pair of them laughing in the dining room. He thought, *Tom being home for the week is probably just what Eli needs at the moment to lift her spirits.*

He walked back into the room followed by the ever-faithful Max, who was very excited that the family were all together again. Frank topped up everyone's wine glass and sat back down. His thoughts drifted to Thursday's meeting in Campden and what, if anything, he was going to do about Harrison. He really hated that bastard! *First things first, though*, thought Frank. *Let's get the Campden meeting out of the way.*

Frank left the house while Tom and Eli both were still asleep in bed. He smiled to himself thinking about the night before. It had been good to have them back together again, and they had probably drunk far too much wine. But what the hell—they all deserved a good time. He filled up the car at the local garage and then stopped off to buy a brown leather holdall for the meeting, as per the drug dealer's instructions. He would be collecting the money from the family accountant on Wednesday. When he got back home, Tom and Eli were in the kitchen, both still in their pyjamas, enjoying a cooked breakfast. It smelled absolutely delicious.

Eli jumped up and kissed Frank has he walked into the kitchen. She greeted him with a cheery, "Good morning, Daddy. I've done you some breakfast. Sit down. I'll get it out of the oven for you."

Frank did as he was told, smiling at Eli who seemed to relishing her lady-of-the house role, fussing over the two men in her life. He thought, *It will do her good having Tom here.* Turning to Tom he asked, "Did you sleep okay?"

"Like a log. Thanks, Dad. I think all the wine we drank helped a lot though."

Placing the plate down on the table in front of Frank, Eli turned to Tom and asked, "Are you up to coming on the Common with me to walk Max? It will do you good to get some fresh air, although your face might frighten some of the other dogwalkers!"

"Cheeky bugger! Of course I'll come with you. You're not allowed to cross the main road on your own anyway," retaliated Tom, winking at Frank while Eli let out a fake loud laugh and stroked Max who, had excitedly jumped up at her on hearing the word *walk* and his name mentioned in the same sentence.

As the siblings walked Max, Eli had chance to speak to Tom about the attack and to ask him how long he had been taking drugs. Also, how he had managed to get into such debt. It wasn't an easy conversation for Tom. He knew Eli had always been proud of him. She had looked up to her big brother, and he felt he had let her down badly. He didn't mention that their whiter-than-white dad had a meeting at the end of the week with the drug gang to pay off his debt. Frank had told Tom on the way home from the hospital that he mustn't mention anything about the meeting to Eli. He didn't want her to worry and get upset about anything else. Tom promised, and when he saw Eli, he realised why his dad was so worried about her. She had lost a lot of weight and looked ill. She looked drawn and quite nervous. He changed the subject, asking her about her course work and how she was coping being away from her friends at uni.

When they got back home, Sue was in the lounge chatting with their dad. They both stopped talking when Tom and Eli walked into the room. Sue jumped up off the sofa and gave Eli a big hug and kissed her on the cheek. Her smile disappeared when she saw Tom behind Eli. "Oh, my darling, what did they do to you?" She hugged and kissed Tom gently, afraid she would squeeze him too hard and hurt him.

Frank said, "He's looking a bit better than when I first saw him in hospital a couple of days ago. The swelling's gone down and the bruising isn't as bad now."

Trying to cheer up Tom, Sue looked at his bruised face up close and replied, "You're still the most handsome man I know. Much better looking than your dad and Uncle David. Isn't that the truth, Eli?"

"No! My dad and Uncle David have always been far better looking," Eli taunted, and they all laughed.

After Sue had left, they had a nice chilled evening in front of the TV with a takeaway from their favourite local restaurant across the Common. Tom hadn't wanted to go over to the restaurant to eat because of the way he looked.

Frank never said a word, but he was pleased they had decided to eat at home. He didn't think it was right for Tom to sit in a restaurant looking as if he'd just gone twelve rounds with Mike Tyson.

Frank looked at his children cuddled up with a throw over them on the opposite sofa. They were watching TV. Max lay sprawled out on the rug in front of the sofa. Frank smiled. He was content with his glass of scotch in his hand. It was nice having them both back home in Wandsworth again. *Just like the good old days*, he thought. *Except Gill is missing. But Tom and Eli seemed to be bearing up.*

Chapter 26

REVENGE

The next morning, Frank was first up as usual. He gently opened Eli's bedroom door to let Max out. Frank looked over at Eli. She was still fast asleep, which Frank was pleased about. She needed to rest. He quietly closed the door. Max followed Frank down the stairs and into the kitchen. Frank opened the blinds to let the sunlight in. After he let Max out in the back garden for his morning pee, he made himself a coffee. Walking to the front door, he picked up the newspaper off the mat and went into the lounge to enjoy his first of many morning mugs of coffee. He enjoyed the relaxing start to the day, especially several coffees and a healthy breakfast and reading the paper. He was enjoying it while it lasted; he knew it had to come to an end once he went back to work.

Walking over to the kitchen sink, Frank rinsed out his coffee cup and placed it on the drainer. He walked to the back door and called out for Max. Then he walked back to the sink and stared to fill it with hot water for washing his breakfast dish and coffee cup. He looked out of the window, glancing up at the clear blue sky. His gaze went to the garden where he saw Max lying on the lawn shaking violently. Frank knocked over a stool and nearly fell as he ran out of the back door as fast as he could. He ran down the garden to where Max lay having some kind of violent fit.

Hours later, Frank closed the front door behind him. He walk down the hall, hung up his jacket, and walked on into the kitchen. His mind was racing. He tossed his car keys onto the breakfast bar and jumped with fright when Tom's head appeared from behind the open fridge door. "Good morning, Dad!"

"God!" You gave me a start," blurted out Frank. "I didn't see you there. You nearly gave me a heart attack!"

"So it seems. Would you like a coffee? I'm just about to make some fresh." Tom laughed as he got a bottle of milk out of the fridge. "You're out early. Where have you been?" added Tom as he took two mugs out of the cupboard.

"Where's Eli? Still in bed?" asked Frank, closing the kitchen door.

"Yeah," replied Tom. "Is everything okay, Dad?"

"No, it's not, Tom. Not at all, son. I've had to rush Max round to the vet's. I found him in the garden. He was having some kind of a fit this morning after I let him out for a pee!" Frank sat down on a stool at the breakfast bar.

"Bloody hell! He was fine last night. Is he okay? Where is he now?" asked Tom.

"He's at the vet's. They're not sure if he'll live!" replied Frank worried at the effect it would have on Eli if Max did die.

"What! Are you being serious, Dad? He's *got* to live!"

said Tom, shocked at the possibility that they could lose Max.

He joined his dad on a stool at the breakfast bar. Frank had a pained expression on his face. He rubbed his forehead with his fingers as he told Tom about finding Max lying on the garden shaking with white froth coming out of his mouth. "I found a few pieces of chocolate at the bottom of the garden near where Max lay. I took them with me to the vet's. They can't say for sure, but it's possible Max might have been poisoned. They're going to have the chocolate analysed."

"What? I don't believe it! Poisoned! Why would they say that, Dad? Who on earth would do something like that?" asked Tom in complete disbelief.

"What about your 'friend' Mattie from Camden, Tom?" asked Frank, looking at Tom who looked shocked at the question.

"What? No, he wouldn't do something like that. Too subtle for him. He would just shoot a guy, not poison his dog!" said Tom, pushing his hair back off his forehead with his fingers. "And why would he anyway? You've spoken to him, and you're to meet him on Thursday to sort out the money! There's no need to do something like this. Apart from that, it's just not his style," said Tom, certain he was right about Mattie Patterson.

"Are you certain about that, Tom? He had you half beaten to a pulp." But before Tom could reply, Frank saw reason in Tom's answer and added, "No. You're probably right. There's no need to do anything else now. It doesn't make sense that he'd do something like this now we've agreed to pay him."

"Are you going to speak to the police—to see if they can do anything?" asked Tom, who had walked over to the window. He was looking down at the bottom of the garden.

"I don't know. Let's see if poor Max pulls through first," replied Frank thinking, *If it wasn't the drug dealer, and it probably wasn't, I know a real nasty fucker who would do something like this!*

"I'll check there's no more chunks of chocolate down at the bottom of the garden," said Frank, adding, "When Eli gets up, we'll just tell her Max took ill. We mustn't say anything about poisoning. I don't want her to get paranoid after what happened to you. God knows how she's going to get over it if Max dies."

"Okay, Dad. I was going to go back to my flat to pick up a few clothes and things, but I'll stay here with her instead," replied Tom, knowing Eli would need him if Max didn't get better.

"No, you need to sort yourself out. But If you could wait until Eli gets up, that would be a big help. Actually, if you could take her with you, it might help take her mind off Max. Otherwise, she'll just sit around fret," replied Frank.

At the bottom of the garden, a door led out onto the street behind their house. Frank hurried up the side road, looking behind to check that Tom hadn't followed him. He made his way up the Main Road to the public phone on the edge of the common. He dialled Harrison's number, "Good morning, Frank—"

Frank cut in and didn't let him finish his greeting. "You've poisoned my dog, you fucking, evil bastard!"

Harrison laughed that cringing laugh of his. "I warned

you, didn't I, dickhead? I told you you'd regret it if you fucked with me. Big time. And now you know."

Frank exploded, furious that the bastard didn't even deny it. "If I ever see you again, I swear I will fucking kill you, you evil piece of shit!" Ending the call, Frank couldn't believe how anybody could do harm to a defenceless animal. He regretted saying that he would kill Harrison, even though at the time he'd meant it!

Frank made his way back to the house. As he walked up the garden to the house, his phone rang. He glared at the screen, thinking it was Harrison phoning him back, but he recognised it was the vet calling. He took a moment to calm down. Taking a deep breath, he answered the call. "Hello. Frank Quinn here." He stood in the garden looking up at the sky, worried about what the vet was going to say to him!

"Okay. I understand. Thank you. Yes, please. If you would let me know and the cost, I'll sort out payment. Thank you again." Frank pressed the end button on the phone and stood there looking down at his mobile in his hand. His eyes filled with tears.

He looked up to see Tom standing in front of him. "Are you okay, Dad? Who was that on the phone?"

"It was the vet. They've had to put Max down. Whatever it was, it caused his kidneys to fail. The poor little fellow was in agony. Shit! Eli's going to be devastated," replied Frank, his voice breaking with emotion.

Tom puffed out his cheeks and rubbed his mouth with his fingers. He started to quietly cry. The two men stood there in the garden in silence, both upset at the news and lost in their own thoughts about their little faithful pal,

Max. It was Tom who broke the silence. "The house will seem empty without Max padding around the place! He was a big part of the family."

Frank smiled, rubbed his eyes, and replied, "I'm going to have to go out for while, Tom. If Eli gets up before I'm back, will you be okay to break the news to her about Max? Please be careful what you say. Don't forget what we agreed to tell her. I'll only be about an hour or so." Frank patted Tom's shoulder affectionately and walked back into the house. Grabbing his coat in the hall, he headed for the front door.

"Is anything wrong? Anything that you're not telling us about, Dad?" asked Tom following his dad up the hall to the front door.

Tom's question stopped Frank in his tracks. He turned to face his tearful son. "No, not at all. Why do you ask?"

"Where are you going now? You never said anything about having to go out. Also, it's not like you leaving me to tell Eli about Max, especially knowing how fragile she is at the moment! All this business about Max possibly being poisoned … why would somebody throw poisoned chocolate over our garden wall to kill our dog? Why won't you tell me what's going on, Dad? Tom was relieved that he had finally got these questions off his chest. Once he'd started, he hadn't been able to stop. It had just all come out.

Frank looked shocked at Tom's accusations. "There's nothing going on, Tom, I promise you. I just need to go back to the accountant's to make sure all's good for the money on Thursday. That's all, and if you are worried about telling Eli, I'll do it when I get back. Just tell her Max is out with me."

"No, I don't mind telling Eli about Max. It's just that you've seemed preoccupied recently. Eli's mentioned it to me, and I've noticed it too," said Tom, studying his dad's face and finding it hard to believe his dad's reassurances.

"I'm a little surprised you're asking me questions like this, son. I've arranged to meet up with a drug dealer and pay off your drug debt on Thursday, to hopefully stop him having you killed. Now there's a sentence I never thought I would ever say, Tom. Also, with everything we've been through recently, yes, I am preoccupied. As a parent, I have the worry about the well-being of both Eli and you. We've all been through an awful time, Tom." Frank felt so guilty at what he'd just said to his son.

"I'm sorry, Dad. Maybe *preoccupied* was the wrong word. You just seem troubled, and I want to help if I can. I know you've got to be strong for me and Eli, and I'm sorry about the trouble I've caused you by being so stupid. Also, I really don't mind telling Eli if she's up before you get back," said Tom looking flushed and guilty down at the floor

Later, in the phone box, Frank stared at the number he had brought up on his mobile. He looked up and out across the Common, then he took a deep breath and waited for a minute. He finally decided what he wanted to do. He dialled the number on the public phone!

After the phone call, Frank got back into his car and drove off towards the accountant's offices in Wimbledon.

As Frank walked back to his car after his meeting with his accountant, his mobile rang. it was David. "Hi, Frank. Where are you? Are you okay? Sue's just been on to me. She's had a phone call from Eli, who was sobbing her eyes out. She said Max is dead. What's going on? Is it true? Sue arranged to go around to yours to be with Eli, and she's going to take her out later if Eli's up to it, the poor thing."

"Yes, it's true. Max is dead. It happened this morning. I've had a couple of important things to do, but I'm on my way home now. Tom's with Eli at the moment. I asked him to tell her if she got up before I got home," replied Frank as he started up his car and pulled out of the carpark.

"I can't believe it. Poor old Max, and especially now after everything you've all been through. What caused it?" asked David.

"The vet thinks Max was poisoned, and I know now that he was. I told Tom to tell Eli he had taken ill and not to say anything about poison! I don't want Eli to be more upset than she already is," explained Frank.

"What the fuck, Frank! *Poisoned*? What do you mean, poisoned? Deliberately? And by whom? And how do you know when the vet's not sure? Who would do something like that to a dog?" asked David, pausing to catch his breath, realising he had just thrown a barrage of questions at Frank.

"*Harrison*. It was that evil fucker Harrison, David," replied Frank in a calm voice.

"What! How can you be so sure about that without any evidence? You need to take a step back, Frank. You're becoming bloody obsessed with this guy!" said David, voicing his opinion strongly, worried about his friend's state of mind.

"Because he admitted it, David. I knew it was him. I rang him this morning when I got back from the vet's! He laughed down the phone about it and said he had warned me not fuck with him," confessed Frank.

David jumped up from his desk, shocked at what he

had just been told. Closing his office door with his foot, he shouted down the phone, "Frank, this is getting fucking ridiculous. It's got to stop! I told you what I thought of him. Why don't you understand that this guy is a nutcase? Killing poor old Max just proves it! What are you going to do? Are you going to report it to the police?"

"No. I don't want them involved, and besides what would I say to Tom and Eli? "Your mum's lover—oh, and by the way, possibly your real father, Eli—murdered Max as a warning to me not to mess with him!" Frank sighed.

"Shit, Frank! I know you want to protect Tom and Eli from the truth, but who's going to protect you from that raving lunatic? Okay, he's got you over a barrel, and I understand you don't want Tom and Eli to find out about the affair that Gill had with him. But, Frank, if you are not going to the police about him, you've got to walk away and leave it alone now ... surely!

This just proves what I've been saying all along. If he can kill a poor, innocent dog, he is capable of anything," said David, exasperated at his best friends' stubbornness. He sat down again behind his desk and took a long deep breath.

"Yes, I know. You're right, David. I really don't want Eli hurt anymore. I know I've said it before, but I just don't know how much more stress she can take. She's going to end up a complete wreck," admitted Frank as he pulled up at home and turned off the engine.

"Sue's picking Eli up in a little while," said David. "They're going over to Wimbledon Village for a meal and a good talk. She wants to try to cheer Eli up. I'll speak to you later, Frank. Please think about what I've advised you," said David. He listened to the silence on the end of phone, patiently waiting for Frank's reply.

"Okay, I'm home now. I'll speak to you later, David. Thanks for the call." With that, Frank ended the call, and after locking the car door, he walked up the path to the front door.

As he opened the door, Eli ran down the stairs in tears and threw herself into her dads' arms. Frank hugged her tightly and gently kissed her forehead. "I thought he was out with you until Tom told me what happened. It's so quiet without him already, Daddy. What will we do without him around to cheer us up?" She began to sob again.

"I know, my darling. We're all going to miss him terribly. Come on. Let's go into the lounge. You're going out with Sue later, aren't you? You need to calm down before she arrives. You will upset her too if she she's you like this," warned Frank. With his arm around her shoulders, he guided her into the lounge. "At least the vet said he didn't suffer, so no matter how much we are going to miss him, it was probably for the best," Frank lied.

They sat there in the lounge just cuddling and talking for half an hour. Eli had stopped crying and was finally calm. They were chatting about Max and his funny little ways; she even managed a few smiles at her dad's tales about things Max used to get up to when Frank walked on the Common with him.

The doorbell rang. It was Sue. Eli wiped her eyes on the hem of her top and ran upstairs to fix her make-up while Frank walked up the hall to open the front door.

She shouted down to her dad, "Tell Sue I won't be long. I'm just getting changed."

Sue smiled sympathetically at Frank when he opened the front door. She gave him a big hug, and they walked down the hall into the lounge. "I just spoke to David before I came over here. He told me what really happened to Max," announced Sue.

"Shush!" said Frank, quickly glancing up the stairs and closing the lounge door. "Eli doesn't know. I told Tom to say that Max was ill when I got up, and I took him straight to the vet's."

"Sorry. Don't worry, Frank, I won't say anything to Eli," promised Sue. Then she asked, "What are you going to do about it?"

"I know what I would like to do to that bastard, Sue," replied Frank through gritted teeth. They both looked out of the bay window and stopped talking when they saw Tom walking up the path with a holdall.

"I'm back now!" shouted Tom to no one in particular has he threw his bag down at the bottom of the stairs and walked into the lounge. "Hi, Sue. I thought that was your car on the road. How are you?" Tom smiled and kissed her on the cheek as she pulled him towards her and hugged him.

"I'm fine thanks, darling. I'm so sorry about poor old Max, Tom," replied Sue letting Tom go from her bear hug.

"I know. Who would do something like that?" he replied in a hushed voice looking straight at his dad.

Frank could feel his face flushing under Tom's suspicious gaze. "Let's change the subject now," said Frank in a low voice. "I can hear Eli on the stairs, and she's only just stopped crying."

Chapter 27

THE CAMDEN MEETING

Thursday came around too quickly for Frank. He was nervous, although not as nervous as Tom apparently. When Tom walked into the kitchen, it was obvious from his face and his messed-up hair that he hadn't had a good night's sleep. "Good morning. I wish you would let me do this Dad. I don't like you getting mixed up with this sort of people," pleaded Tom.

Frank poured himself a coffee. Looking at Tom he replied, "I don't like the idea of you being mixed up with these people either, Tom, but you are where we are, and because of that, I *am* mixed up in it. Besides, you've got to look after Eli while I'm out. Try to keep her happy. She's been quite good, all things considered."

"I'm really sorry, Dad. I don't know how many times I can say this … but this guy is dangerous!" Tom spoke in a quiet voice in case Eli was up.

"Don't worry, son, and don't keep apologising. I'll be okay. I know what to do and what not to do—and what to say and what not to say. We've been over it all many times." Frank smiled.

The tube seemed to take ages getting across town and up to Camden. Walking up Camden High Street, Frank finally saw the store known as The Dark Angel on the opposite side of the road. He couldn't miss it really. There was foot-high lettering across the front of the shop. Underneath that was a life-size model of the naked Dark Angel of Camden stretched out in a crucifixion pose, scanty black ribbons protecting her modesty.

It must have been ten years since Frank had last been in Campden and on the High Street. He was fascinated by the young people shopping and just hanging. He wondered at the way they were dressed. The area was still as he remembered it—buzzing and so diverse. It was like a time warp. Goths, bikers, punks with their pink spiked hair, and plenty of tourists. Everyone was shopping and taking photographs of the people all around them, and the amazing buildings. The artistic shop fronts were just as bizarre as the locals! To the left of The Dark Angel was a shopfront decorated with a fifteen-foot plimsoll and a large black scorpion. To the right, a huge Chinese dragon took up the top half of the shop front.

It was an eatery. As Frank approached, he recognised Mattie Patterson from the description Tom had given him. Anyone could spot his shock of red hair from a mile away. He was sitting with three men at an outside table. All were smoking and drinking coffee. They were chatting and laughing, ignoring all those in the strange, fashionable world that was Camden go about their business. There was an empty chair to the right of Mattie, which Frank assumed was for him. Taking a deep breath and clearing his throat, Frank crossed the road and walked up to Mattie's table. He spoke directly to his son's supplier: "Hi. I'm Tom's dad. We spoke on the phone earlier in the week."

Only Mattie acknowledged Frank's existence in their company. The other three men didn't even look up; they just carried on talking as if he wasn't there. "Well, hello, Tom's dad. Take a seat," replied Mattie, pushing the empty chair out from the table with his foot. "So, you want to discuss some business with me. Before we start, do you want a drink?" asked Mattie, giving Frank a big false smile.

"Yes. A white coffee, if that's okay," replied Frank, trying to sound relaxed. But his heart was beating so fast he thought it was going to burst out of his chest. Sitting down, he had placed the grown holdall containing the money next to him on the floor between himself and Mattie Patterson.

Mattie looked over at one of the men, who promptly got up and walked inside to get Frank's coffee. Looking back at Frank Mattie said, "Before we talk business, Tom's dad, I need you to do this for me: Take the holdall inside. One of my guys is waiting for you. He will take the money out and stuff your bag so it doesn't look as if it's been emptied. Then he'll give it back to you. It's just for show for the Old Bill across the road at the first-floor window taking photos of us all, you included. So, I wouldn't turn around if you don't want to end up in the Serious Crime Squads album."

Frank's immediate reaction was to turn and look across at the first-floor window, but Mattie stopped him by putting his hand on Frank's shoulder and assuring him, saying, "Relax, Tom's dad. It's okay. It's safe. Just chill. They know who we are and what we do for a living, and we know they're here and what they are doing. They've been onto us for a long time but can't nail us for anything, and we want to keep it that way. Now fuck off inside. It's safe there. We own the place. Don't worry. And when you come back, you can tell me what I can do for you."

When it was over, Frank sat on the tube on the way back to Wandsworth. He was glad the meeting was over. He had been so worried over not knowing how it would go.

But it had gone better than he had expected. The news that they were being photographed and probably videoed by the Serious Crime Squad unnerved Frank a lot, though. He had just started to calm down when Mattie had told him they were under surveillance. That had started him off again. He was expecting a heavy hand on his shoulder any minute telling him he was "nicked." *You've been watching too many cop films*, he told himself, and he smiled. Mattie had realised he was unnerved by what he had said, and had assured him he was safe. He explained that the police had been watching him and his men on and off for many months, hoping to build up a drug case against them, which didn't seem to concern Mattie or his men in the slightest.

Forgetting what they did for a living, also what they had done to Tom, Frank was kind of taken with Mattie Patterson. He was easy to talk to, very confident, and not threatening at all. It made him smile that Mattie called him Tom's dad all the time, never once asking him what his name was. Frank snapped himself out of his reverie and reminded himself that the man sold misery that killed people. Also, because of his trade, he was almost certainly a killer. He began to doubt that had he done the right thing getting involved with these people. One thing that really worried him was that Mattie wouldn't give any assurances that Tom wouldn't come to any further harm in the future. He would only say, "Don't worry about it. I like Tom."

Frank had told Mattie that Tom had promised his dad that his drug-taking days were over, but Mattie didn't seem at all convinced. Maybe he knew Tom better than Frank did? *Anyway, we are where we are*, thought Frank. He ticked off several problems from the list that he kept in his head. *Hopefully we can start getting our family life back on track.*

As Frank walked back from the tube station, his mobile went off. It was the vet, who explained to Frank that the chocolate he had brought in with Max had been laced with the drug phencyclidine, otherwise known as PCP or angel dust. Max had eaten a few pieces, and that had been the cause of his pet's fit. The drug had caused kidney failure.

Frank lied and told the vet that he had reported the incident to the police and that a gang of teenagers had been hanging around the neighbourhood. He suggested they could have drugged the dog. He thanked the vet for the call and told him he would be in to pay the bill first thing in the morning.

What the fuck was Harrison doing with PCP? Frank thought. *Maybe he does drugs.* The drug problem appeared to be rife lately; Frank thought it was probably worse than he'd realised. Drug use was something that had never interested him and Gill. *Or so I thought*, he corrected himself. *Who knows? When Gill was with Harrison doing their steamy business, they might have been taking drugs!* Strange that he could think of them together now, and it didn't bother him. When he first found out about the affair, thinking about them and visualising the two of them together made him feel sick. He couldn't bear to think about the two of them in bed together. Now he didn't think about it—not so much. Their affair had thrown up too many problems in Frank's life since he found out about it. He was more focused on dealing with those problems than he was on their shitty relationship.

When he opened the front door, for a moment, he expected Max to come bounding down the hall to greet him. His half smile turned into a frown when he remembered Max was gone—forever.

Tom came out of the kitchen. He looked relieved to see his dad home safe and sound. "How did it go, Dad? I tried to ring you, but your phone was busy."

"Yes. I was on to the vet," replied Frank, struggling to take off his coat. Once Tom confirmed Eli was out with her friends, Frank explained that the vet had told him it was PCP that had killed Max. "He said it was probably youngsters taking drugs, and they'd done it for a sick joke."

Tom said, if he ever caught them at the back of their house, he would kick the shit out of them, but presently he was more interested in the meeting with Mattie Patterson. "So, how did it go in Camden, Dad?" asked Tom again.

"It went as well as can be expected, I think. I paid him. He wasn't alone. There were some other men with him. Funny, they were all so laid back, as if they did meetings like that every day," explained Frank kicking off his shoes and leaving them where they landed for the time being. "Actually, that was a daft thing to say. I suppose they really *do* things like that every day. I was very nervous at first, but strangely, I started to relax in his company. You must promise me, Tom, that you won't have anything more to do with them," pleaded Frank.

"Of course. I said I wouldn't, Dad. Why do you say that now?" asked Tom.

"Despite the fact that I gave him the money, he wouldn't give me any guarantees that you wouldn't come to any harm in the future. I hope we can trust him, Tom. Also, did you know they are under surveillance by the Serious Crime Squad? They seemed to think it was all a joke. I must be honest—that scared the hell out of me. Mattie told me about it just after I had managed to calm myself down after approaching them," explained Frank, pouring two large whiskies and handing one to Tom.

"Don't worry, Dad. I've told you I've learned my lesson. I wouldn't put you and Eli through anymore worry and heartache again. I promise," Tom assured his dad. He took a sip of the whisky and added, "Thanks again, Dad. I'll pay you back every penny. I promise."

"Okay. But for now, I'll settle for a few stiff belts of my favourite malt." Frank smiled and raised his glass to Tom.

The next morning, Frank was walking back across the common. He had been to the vet's to pay Max's bill. He still couldn't believe Max was dead. It was a lovely summer day. Mums and dads were out in the sunshine playing with their kids. People were relaxing and reading as they sat in their deckchairs. Frank was envious of the dog walkers, who were out in force. It seemed so strange that he didn't have happy Max bounding along beside him. Feeling sad, he thought to himself, *Another thing that was normal in our life is now gone forever.*

Frank walked along the Common lost in his thoughts.

He was going over everything in his mind that had happened since Gill had passed away. Surely, people don't live their lives like that, do they? All the drama, the problems, the deceit? It was all so alien to him. He wished that he could turn back the clock to when their lives were so simple and so perfect. But now he now he had found out that their perfect lives hadn't been so perfect after all. Gill had her secret life that was unknown to her family. Then there was Tom, a young man with successful career—and a secret drug-taking life! Then there was perfect Eli who was the innocent one out them of all. But she possibly had a father she didn't know about. A "father" who had killed her dog just to make a point to the father she knew and loved! What a mess everything was! What a God-almighty bloody mess!

When he got home, Eli was busy doing course work. She had kept her word and was working hard, ignoring the distractions of friends wanting her to do lunch and go clothes shopping as her girlfriends always appeared to want to do.

Tom had moved back to his flat and was nearly ready to return to his job now that his face was more or less presentable again. Frank just hoped that he was good to his word about not getting in touch with the Camden drug gang again. Hopefully, things could finally start getting back to some kind of normality.

CHAPTER 28

A JOB FOR THE CAMPBELLS

Mattie was in a bad mood as he sat in the passenger seat of the Range Rover. They had just pulled up outside the Campbells' shitty house on their shitty street in shitty Brixton. His hatred had escalated as they drove across the river. Though that wasn't the cause of his bad mood, it didn't help. They had endured the journey in silence. His men knew to keep quiet for self-preservation when he was in one of these moods. Standing at the front door were Kelvin and Theo Campbell, waiting to greet him as usual. They were relieved to hear Mattie tell the driver and the other two men to stay in the car as he climbed out and slammed the door.

He never usually came mob-handed; normally it was just him, his driver, and sometimes one other. *Maybe they have a bit of business elsewhere afterwards*, Kelvin thought to himself. "How you doing, man? This is an unexpected visit. We weren't due to meet for a few weeks." Kelvin smiled and bumped fists with Mattie.

"I'm good, bro. Good to see you again," lied Mattie,

thinking he had never once seen the Campbells' spotter. The spotter had surely texted or phoned Kelvin to let him know that his visitors were about to arrive, so he could be waiting at the door to greet him. Even though Mattie scanned the people, the kids, the faces, when they were nearly at the Campbells', he'd never been able to spot the little fucker. *I will one day*, he thought. *There's only one route in to where they live, and that's off the main road, so it shouldn't be that difficult.*

Mattie followed Kelvin and Theo into the lounge. Even though they had a couple of windows open to let in the fresh summer air, Matie breathed in the familiar stale smell. It turned his stomach. The other three brothers—Billy, Bruce, and Oscar—were all there. They stood up and greeted Mattie warmly. Mattie declined a "smoke" but accepted their offer of a bottle of beer.

"So, what brings you to our door, man?" asked Kelvin. "Don't get me wrong—not that we're not pleased to see you, Mattie," he added quickly.

"Can't I just come and see how my old friends the Campbells are doing?" Mattie laughed as he carefully sat down on the shitty sofa.

They caught up on what was happening in their respective businesses. There hadn't been any major problems. Money was rolling in. There were no issues to share other than a few mules getting busted, which didn't prove too costly. Also, the arrests reassured the public that the Old Bill were tackling the drugs problem on the streets, which everyone knew was a load of old bollocks. The men discussed the quality of the last shipment and the gossip that was going on in the Campbells' manor.

Finishing up, Mattie said, "I've got a bit of business for you that I would like doing."

Now we get to why you are really here, thought Kelvin to himself. He looked at a photo Mattie had just handed him.

"He lives on your patch. I want him topped," said Mattie. He finished his bottle of beer.

"The usual fee?" asked Theo, glancing over Kelvin's shoulder at the details and photo Mattie had handed over.

"Definitely. But there's something else. I want Billy to do it, if that's cool with you lot. I don't want any fuck ups, and Billy's a top geezer at jobs like this."

Kelvin looked over at Billy's young smiling face. The youngest brother's chest swelled with pride at the compliment just paid to him from the big man from Clapham. He said, "Happy to sort it for you, Mattie."

"You'll do for me, my son." Mattie nodded and added, "There's a message I want you to give him just before you do him so he knows what it's all about and who it's from."

"Consider it done, Mattie." Billy smiled, already going over his "strategy" in his warped mind. Young Billy took his business very seriously. He often fantasised about being a Mafia hitman or an "asset" like the character in the Jason Bourne movies. He'd watch the "target" for days to see what his routine was and then come up with the best plan for doing him. It never failed to amaze him how people follow the same routines day in day out without ever altering it in the slightest way. They were like robots. That made it so easy for them to get robbed or attacked, or in this case, murdered. Kelvin had always drummed it into them how important it was to change the way they went about their daily routines. Especially in their line of business, random behaviour would possibly keep them alive.

Kelvin walked Mattie out to his car and waved him off as usual. He wasn't sure about the bit of business they had picked up from the visit. Going back into the lounge, he looked over at Billy and then at his brothers. Sitting down in his chair, he finally said to Billy, "Don't fuck up this job Mattie wants you to do. It's obviously personal. What did he wanted the guy to hear before you did him?"

Reflecting on Billy's reply, Kelvin carried on. "It's definitely personal. Listen, Billy, we don't want any trouble with him, you understand me? Mattie asked for you, and you've agreed, so if there are any fuckups, as far as he's concerned, you're in the frame. You understand that, don't you? And we wouldn't let that happen to you, bro. So we would have a big problem with him and probably end up going to war with his lot."

"Course I do, bro." Billy smiled. "I'm not fucking stupid, and I'm also a pro!"

Kelvin stood up, laughed, and grabbed Billy in a playful headlock. "Do you hear that, my brothers? Young'un here's a professional! A professional what? I've no fucking idea."

Chapter 29

A RELAXING WEEKEND

Frank wanted to spend some time with Eli over the weekend. He was hoping she didn't have any plans. On Saturday morning, she came downstairs in her pyjamas and joined him in the lounge, sitting down on the sofa. She looked as cute as a button. He smiled, walked over to her, and sat down. He gave her a kiss on the forehead and a big hug.

"Morning, Daddy," she said, hugging him back. She felt so safe in his arms—just as she had felt when she was a little girl.

"Morning, my darling. What are you doing this weekend? Any plans? asked Frank, kissing her forehead again.

"Nothing really. I don't want to go out with the girls. I would only start thinking of Max and get upset again and spoil the evening. I can't help it. I keep thinking of him all the time," replied Eli, feeling herself getting upset again as she talked about Max.

"I know, darling. You're bound to. So do I. It's so sad.

Let's have a nice weekend together, just you and me. Shall we go to the cinema tonight? I'll see if there's anything good on." Frank was trying to take her mind off Max.

"Do you know what I would really like to do tonight, Dad? Have a takeaway and then watch a good film snuggled up on the sofa under the throw." Eli smiled, quite happy to have a lazy Saturday night at home.

"Then that's what we will do, my princess. Job done," replied Frank reassuringly. "Now, let me make you some breakfast. What would you like to eat now we've agreed on a chilled weekend?" Frank beamed at her as he got up and walked towards the lounge door.

It was good spending a relaxing weekend with Eli. She certainly needed some TLC after everything the poor darling had been through lately. He had spoken to Tom, and all appeared good with him. He had gone out in Clapham with some friends. Frank couldn't help once again running through his meeting with Mattie. It concerned him, and he wasn't sure if he had done the right thing getting involved with the drug dealer and his Camden gang.

Over the weekend, Frank also thought long and hard about Harrison. He finally decided he was going to let his wife know what a shit she was married to. Frank read over the letter he had written to Penny Harrison after Eli had gone to bed. After reading it one more time, he was happy with the content. He sealed the envelope, ready for posting Monday morning. It explained who he was and exposed her husband's long affair with Gill. He had decided he wouldn't mention about the bastard killing the family dog. He would keep that one up his sleeve, possibly for use later if needs must. He included photos of the texts and screengrabs that Harrison had sent showing his mobile number.

He had thought about going to the family home to tell Harrison's wife everything. He also thought of trying to catch her dropping the children off at school. He decided against confronting her. It would only spook her, and he probably wouldn't even get chance explain who he was or tell her everything. Having a stranger walk up to her and start talking about her husband's sex life was definitely a no-go. She would be frightened and not listen to a word he said.

Frank wanted her to hear the full story and have all the facts. Seeing it all laid out in a letter was the best option. He didn't feel good about posting the letter. He felt guilty for the upset he was going to cause her. After all, she was the innocent party. But he had decided it was only what Harrison deserved.

Chapter 30

THE RECON

Billy followed his "target" from his home down to his workplace on a stolen scooter with fake number plates, which he had borrowed from one of his local runners. He always got a buzz out of doing the "recce" before a hit. In his head, it made him feel like an "asset" on the big screen. He felt very professional—a glamourous, trained killer instead of the dirty little drug dealing killer that he really was, someone who didn't give a shit about the heartache or devastation he left in his wake. Happy with the information he had on the target, he set about his morning's work. He sat in the café across the road and ordered a full breakfast.

He had a clear view of the exit. If the guy came out to go anywhere, he would see him and could quickly follow him. He was looking for a pattern in the guy's behaviour so he could decide where and when the deed would be done. The guy came out at lunchtime with another man, possibly a client. They crossed the road and went into a glass-fronted restaurant three doors away. Billy sat outside the café having lunch and another coffee. He watched them get a table and order a bottle of wine and some food. They left the restaurant an hour and half later. They stood outside the restaurant talking. Then they finally shook hands, and the target went back to work. The "client" walked off down the road.

Billy returned to the café just before six o'clock and relieved one of his runners who had been watching the target. He'd given the local runner strict instructions: If the guy came out, he was to follow him and phone Billy immediately with the details. Ordering another coffee, Billy sat and waited for his man to appear at the end of the business day. Billy's mind wandered to Mattie. He thought this guy must have really done some serious shit for Mattie to want him to know what he was being killed for just before it happened. He idly dismissed the thought. It was none of his business, anyway. The guy obviously deserved it. Billy was just being paid to do a job, and that was the end of it as far as he was concerned, but Mattie could be a nasty bastard when he was pissed about something.

Despite Mattie's friendly, laid-back nature, which usually put strangers who met him at ease, there was a nasty side to him. When he was pissed off about something, people did well to get out of his way rapidly.

Billy had watched him at their house many times, and he had seen that Mattie was the only man who made Kelvin nervous. Billy knew that, if his big brother was wary of Mattie—and Kelvin was a hard bastard—then he damn well should be wary too.

At 6.30 in the evening, the target came out of the building. His working day was over, hopefully. Billy followed the guy all the way back to his home, which he was happy about. It had been a long day, and he didn't fancy tailing him to a bar or restaurant, which could take up another hour or two of the evening. *Same again tomorrow*, Billy thought to himself. *And hopefully I'll have the "where" "when"*. The "how" Billy had already decided, but he didn't have a lot of time left to come up with the "where".

Chapter 31

HELLO, MRS HARRISON

Eli answered the phone. It was Tom ringing to see how they were. "What have you been up to, Eli?"

"I've been doing more course work. I promised Dad, and despite the lovely weather, I've been hard at it. What have you been up to?" replied Eli as she sat on the bottom step of the stairs playing with a pen that she had found on the table next to the phone.

"Just got in from work. A few of the guys went for a drink after work, but I couldn't be bothered. Thought I would come home and have an early dinner and maybe watch the big match on TV. Is Dad there, Eli? I'd like a quick word with him if he is." Tom struggled to take off his suit jacket and finally threw it onto the chair.

Blowing him a kiss down the phone, Eli walked into the lounge. She handed the cordless to her dad telling him, "It's Tom. Can you keep him on? I want to speak to him again after you've finished with him."

"Hello, son. How's your day gone?" asked Frank, nodding to Eli as she walked back to the kitchen.

"Not bad, thanks, Dad. how's yours gone?"

"Good thanks, son. Any sign of your friends' people from Camden today?"

"No, Dad. They don't work in the office. I wasn't expecting to see or hear from them, and I haven't done," replied Tom, annoyed that his dad had asked him that.

"Sorry, Tom. I'm not trying to rub your nose in it. I'm just concerned that's all. Nothing more than that!" Frank apologised when he picked up on Tom's annoyance.

"I know, Dad, but seriously, don't worry. Everything's okay now, I promise Please don't bring it up again," pleaded Tom.

"Okay, son, if you say so. You know him better than I do. Again, not rubbing your nose in it, honestly!" Frank had his own agenda with regard to asking about Mattie Patterson. He heard Tom laugh sarcastically on the other end of the phone. They said their goodbyes, and Frank walked into the kitchen and handed the phone back to Eli.

Frank poured himself a generous measure of his favourite malt. Taking a sip, he stood looking out of the lounge window onto the Common. It was a busy evening thanks to the lovely warm weather. Everyone was enjoying the Common—children playing ball games, young lovers lying on the grass or walking hand in hand, the usual faces walking their dogs. He thought about poor old Max and what that bastard had done to him. It was all just so bloody pointless, but it just gave Frank more resolve to deal with the lunatic.

He sat down on the sofa. Once again, his mind went back to the meeting in Camden with Mattie. It had been troubling him, and as much as he tried, he couldn't get it out of his head. He felt he was doing the right thing letting Harrison's wife know about the affair instead of his origin emotional plan.

Frank was up and out early the next morning. He had posted the letter to Harrison's wife. He didn't feel guilty about the trouble it would cause his wife's lover, but he did feel for the man's wife. He had called into the local shops for some groceries on the way back home. He hadn't quite got the hang of having to make sure there was food in the house. Gill had obviously looked after all that and the running of the home. A few times he'd started to cook something for dinner only to find the fridge bare. Eli had taken on the role of "housekeeper", and very good she was at it too, but she was really busy with her course work. He thought he would do the shopping and cook her a nice dinner.

He'd had an update on business from David late in the afternoon, following the weekly board meeting. David told him they were all glad to hear that Frank was returning to work the following Monday. "It's about time you did a bit of work again, you lazy bastard," teased David.

"You're right, as usual," confirmed Frank. "I've got to get back in the saddle sometime, and I feel I'm ready now!"

"What's happening with Harrison? Anything new after poor old Max?" asked David pensively.

"No," lied Frank.

"Good. He's nothing but trouble, and you're best leaving things alone now. Just concentrate getting on with your life and getting things back to normal for Tom and, especially, poor Eli. God knows you all deserve some normality after what you've been through recently," said

David, relieved at Frank's answer to his question about leaving Harrison alone.

"That's what I intend to do, David!" lied Frank again. They ended the conversation after arranging to meet up at the gym at the weekend for a catchup on work over a few drinks in the bar before Frank returned to the office on Monday morning.

The next morning, Frank was shattered as he sat having some cereal and a coffee in the kitchen. He'd had a really bad night's sleep. The Camden meeting was still heavy on his mind. Also, the letter to Harrison's wife would land on their doormat today. That kept popping up in his thoughts as well. He had a few jobs to do that would take up most of the morning if he could work up the energy to get dressed. He was planning to go to the gym in the afternoon, although he wasn't sure it was such a good idea after his lack of sleep.

After doing his jobs, he did make it to the gym and had a decent workout. He went into the spa afterwards, which was just what his knackered body needed. He came to the decision in the sauna after a long deliberation that he was going to call Mattie Patterson later when he got home.

"Hi, Dad! How was the gym? Did you work up a good sweat?" teased Eli, shouting down the hall when she heard the front close.

"Yes, thanks, darling. Couldn't be bothered doing too much, but I worked up a good sweat in the sauna and steam room afterwards, which was really good." Frank laughed as he walked into the kitchen and put his gym gear and towel into the washing machine.

"Good! I've finished my coursework, I'm pleased to announce!" declared Eli, as Frank joined her in the lounge.

"Excellent! You've worked so hard. I'm proud of you. Fingers crossed for your grades," said Frank, kissing her on the forehead.

"Would you like a coffee, Dad? I'm having one," said Eli getting up and heading into the kitchen.

"No thanks. I've just got to nip across the Common on an errand. Shouldn't be too long," said Frank, and he got up and headed up the stairs. Putting his sports bag in the bottom of the wardrobe, he went over to the bedside table drawer and found the piece of paper with Mattie Patterson's telephone number scrawled on it. After the Camden meeting, he thought it wise to delete Mattie's number from the notes app on his phone when he had got back home, but not before he had made a note of it under the initials MP on a piece of paper.

"You won't be too long will you, Daddy? I'll be starting to prepare dinner soon," shouted Eli up the stairs from the hall.

"No. Shouldn't be too long, and we'll have a bottle of wine with dinner to celebrate the end of your course work," came the reply from her dad's bedroom.

"Sounds good to me, Dad," said Eli approvingly before she went back into the kitchen.

Frank closed the front door behind him. He walked down the path and crossed the road on to the Common. He headed over towards the south side to where the public phone box stood on the opposite side of the road.

He had gone over things so many times in his head, and he had decided he was doing the right thing making the call to Mattie Patterson. It wasn't just for his own peace of mind; he knew deep down it was the right thing to do.

The Common was busy. There was no reason he should have paid any attention to the man striding across the Common behind him heading in the same direction. Even if he had noticed the man, Frank wouldn't have thought anything of it. He certainly wouldn't have felt threatened in any way. The man had been watching the house for some time from his position on the Common. He had seen Frank return from the gym a short time earlier and had thought about going to the house. Then when he saw Frank come out again shortly afterwards and cross the road on to the Common, he was pleased he had hesitated. He thought to himself, *Perfect. Just perfect.*

Frank felt someone close behind him. He turned slightly and glanced over his shoulder. He gasped when he recognised the face beneath the pulled-down baseball cap and above the hunched shoulders. Frank was about to turn and speak when he felt the knife stab into his lower back. Instead of uttering words, Frank screamed out in pain. His whole body shook as if he was having a fit. He lurched forward in one bizarre movement. His brain tried to work out what had just happened. The attacker was so close to Frank now that, from a distance, the two of them would have looked like one person.

The attacker had anticipated Frank's attempt to move away from him. He grabbed the back of Frank's collar and pulled him close towards him. His right arm swung back and then forcefully forward. The blade went in hard again an inch or so below the first wound, penetrating deeper in to Frank's back.

Wandsworth Common

Frank screamed again, louder this time. His body shook violently. His arms flailed wildly. His legs gave way. The attacker let go of his grip on his victim's collar. Frank collapsed falling face down on the ground. The attacker stepped over Frank's body and carried on walking. Although quickening his step, he made sure not to break out in a run. He didn't want to draw attention to himself. Once away from Frank, he slowed his walk slightly, never once looking back in the direction of the attack.

The attacker walked on heading towards the main road. He could see the side street bordering the Common where he had parked up. All the time, he still listened for any shouts aimed at him from someone on the Common who might have witnessed what he had just done. There were no signs of any panic or cries for help from passers-by. Everything seemed to be normal, just as it had been when he first walked onto the Common. People were enjoying the sunshine. Children were laughing as they played with each other. There was no commotion at all coming from behind him as far as he could make out.

The attack had been over in a about twenty seconds. The attacker reached the main road and waited for a gap in the traffic. He crossed over. Still there were no shouts of "Stop!" from behind him. He had waited until Frank was at a reasonably "quiet" part of the Common before he made his move. He had hoped that nobody was close enough to witness what was actually happening. It had all gone off like a dream. His face broke out in a big smile.

Frank managed to turn over. He lay motionless on the grass, looking up at the sky. Anybody looking over his way would have thought he was lying there enjoying the balmy early-evening weather.

The pain was unbearable. By the time he had realised he was in danger, it had been too late to protect himself. The attack was already happening, and then it had been over so quickly.

In between his gasps for air, Frank stared up at the clear blue sky. He said in a hushed voice, "It's too late to change anything now, Gill. I was trying to do the right thing. I truly was. Please believe that. I'm so sorry."

Chapter 32

THE DAY OF RECKONING

Tom had finished work and was in the wine bar with a couple of friends from the office when he got the call from Sue. "Tom, is that you?" Before he could answer, she continued in a tearful voice, "Your dad's been attacked on the Common, Tom. Come home." She started to sob.

Placing his finger to his ear to try to drown out some of the background noise, Tom quickly walked towards the door. "Sue, I can hardly hear you. Just a second," he said as he pushed the bar door open. Stepping outside, Tom said, "Now that's better, Sue. What was it you said about Dad?"

"He's been attacked on the Common. Thank God somebody found him and called an ambulance. It doesn't look good, Tom. I'm at the hospital with Eli," repeated Sue sobbing down the phone.

"Sue, please calm down. Which hospital is he in? Where have they taken him?" Tom was already hailing a passing cab. He jumped in before Sue could reply.

Sue continued, "We're at St Georges, Tom. We don't know if he's still alive. They won't tell us anything. Eli's in a terrible state. The police phoned her, and she immediately phoned me. We're both here now, and David is on his way."

"Okay, Sue. Take care of Eli. I'm in a cab now and on my way there!" As he hung up, he shouted to the cabbie, "St Georges hospital as quickly as possible please!"

In the cab on the way to the hospital, Tom sat looking out of the taxi window. He thought, *What the hell's going on? I've had a feeling something wasn't right for a while, and this just proved I was right. What with Max being poisoned and now this, why is all this shit happening? Did Dad upset Mattie Patterson when they met up?* His mind was racing. *If it wasn't Mattie, who could it be? Surely Dad hasn't pissed anybody off so much that they would kill his dog and then try to kill him. Was it a random mugging?* Tom thought and then dismissed that as a bit too much of a coincidence after poor old Max. *What if it was Mattie? If it was, we couldn't do anything about it, and we certainly couldn't tell the police. We would all end up dead.*

Tom shook his head, racking his brains. *It doesn't sound like Mattie's work. He doesn't do warnings. If it had been him, Dad would be dead now! So that leaves the question, if it wasn't Mattie, or random, then who was it?* He just couldn't see his dad having any enemies. He was such a nice guy. Everybody liked him. He wasn't the kind of man to cause anybody trouble.

Chapter 33
A PROBLEM SOLVED

Harrison walked through the front doors of the showroom; he said hello to a potential customer and shook his hand. Turning to his salesman, he told him to look after the customer and give him a good deal. He delivered the directive in his usual loud, brash manner. The salesman played along as usual and said he would do, winking at his boss when the customer turned and smiled at his wife.

Smiling, Harrison walked away and went into his office. He threw his briefcase down at the side of his desk. Thankfully, the showroom was busy. No one had noticed him sneak into his office through the back doors ten minutes earlier. He had gone straight to his en suite bathroom where he had checked his clothes for any blood, scrubbed his hands, and washed his face. Checking himself over again in the mirror, he'd combed his hair and then smiled at what he had just got away with. It couldn't have gone any better if he had precision planned it.

After cleaning himself up, he had walked back around the side of the building and into the showroom through the main doors for all to see. He sat down at his desk in the privacy of his office. He took out the brandy bottle and crystal tumbler from the cabinet where he kept his drinks. He pushed himself back in his big, black, leather chair and put his feet up on the desk. He took a gulp of the Grey Goose he had just poured himself. It felt good going down—relaxing. Looking up at the ceiling, he smiled broadly again.

Less than an hour earlier, Harrison had walked back to his car where he had parked it. His heart had been pounding, and his breath had been coming in short, nervous gasps. Opening the boot of his Mercedes, he'd looked back across the road onto the Common where the trees were. No one was heading over in his direction or even looking his way. Everything on the Common appeared to be normal. There was no commotion where he had left that pussy Quinn wallowing in his own blood. He smiled because he knew that meant nobody had seen him do what he had done. There were no witnesses!

He had removed the dark-blue boiler suit he had worn over his shirt and suit trousers together with the surgical gloves and baseball cap. He'd placed them all in a black bin liner and closed the boot. Once in the car he'd run his fingers through his hair and looked in his rear-view mirror to check his face for any blood. He'd been clean.

He'd started up the engine of the A class Merc that he had borrowed from stock. He would get old Alf, who prepared all the second-hand cars for sale, to give it a good clean tomorrow just to be on the safe side. He'd checked his rear-view mirror once again, indicated, and gently pulled away from the curb. Driving down the side road, he'd joined the main road, turned right, and headed back in the direction of Clapham and the showroom

He would burn the contents of the bin liner in the workshop when the staff had finished and left for the day. Then he would lose the knife down a drain around Putney when he was heading home to try to pacify his stupid bitch of a wife and convince her not to leave him again. He smiled and thought, *It's all a fucking game. She'll be back even if she does me "for good!" this time.* She always came back after finding out about his little flings. She had left him only twice. The other times he had talked her into staying. It was the money and the lifestyle—she enjoyed them too much to throw it all away on a divorce. Also, she was frightened of him and his evil temper. She knew he would eventually make her pay for trying to take his girls way from him. It was at times like this that he wished Gill had left that pussy of a husband of hers and moved in with him. Christ! He had begged her to enough times.

He took another gulp of his Grey Goose and mentally went over the day's events. He had received a phone call earlier in the day from his wife demanding to know about this "long-standing affair" with a woman named Gill Quinn. That's what had sent him off in a rage to Wandsworth Common. He didn't need this shit now, especially with all the work he had on. He had told that fucking Quinn not to mess with him, so what did the fucker do? Send his wife a letter. Why hadn't Quinn believed him? Was he fucking stupid? *Why are goodie two shoes like Quinn so weak and straight that they always try to do the right thing?* Well, he would sort the bastard out once and for all this time. He didn't need aggravation like this in his life, especially when it distracted him from doing business.

Tom eventually found Sue and Eli. The hospital was huge with a parade of shops in the main hallway. Eli saw him walking down the corridor and ran to him. She collapsed into his arms, sobbing. Sue was also crying. He put his arms around both of them and pulled them into his chest. "Do we know how he is yet?" Tom asked, but neither of them answered. "Come on. Let's all sit down," he said, and he guided Eli and Sue back to the seats.

As they sat down, Sue dried her eyes and said, "A policewoman's been sitting with us. She's just gone to get us some coffee. She should be back soon. We haven't had an update yet about your dad, Tom."

"Here she is now, Tom," said Eli, looking down the corridor.

Tom looked up. The policewoman was walking towards them carrying a holder full of coffees. When she got to where they were sitting, Tom stood and introduced himself. He declined the offer of the officer's coffee. She explained that a detective had just arrived and would speak to them shortly. "Okay. Thank you." Tom smiled.

As Tom sat back down with Eli and Sue, the policewoman waved to a man and walked up the corridor to meet him. Tom assumed he was the detective she had mentioned. He turned to Sue. "Do you know what's going on, Sue? Something is definitely not right. Dad has been on edge and preoccupied with something for quite a while now. Then Max, and now this with Dad. Something's not right, but he wouldn't say anything when I asked him."

"He's been through lot recently, darling. It's bound to

have an effect on him. I don't know of any problems apart from your poor mum passing away and then you being attacked. I really don't know what today is about. Why would someone attack your dad?" Sue feeling guilty lying. She was certain it had been Harrison.

The policewoman came back with the tall chap, who was wearing a suit and carrying a folder under his arm. The detective introduced himself as DSI Harper—Roger Harper. He asked who Sue was. When she explained that she was a close family friend, he took Tom and Eli into a side room further up the corridor. He explained that their dad had been stabbed in an attempted robbery on the Common. A dog walker had found him lying on the grass. He'd been bleeding from a stab wound in his lower back and was drifting in and out of consciousness. As the detective addressed them, Eli quietly sobbed again as she pictured her dad bleeding helplessly. Tom was trying his best to comfort her while listening to the details that the detective was telling him about the attack.

"I've spoken with the doctor," Detective Harper continued. "Your dad's in the operating theatre. He's lost quite a lot of blood. It's too early to say if he will survive." He glanced from Tom to Eli, concerned that his feedback was upsetting the victim's daughter even more. He asked Eli, "Would you prefer to sit with your friend outside while I'll talk to your brother?"

Eli took a deep breath, wiped her eyes with a hankie, and replied, "No. I'll be okay thanks."

"Do either of you know of any trouble or problems your dad might have had with anybody lately?" asked the detective, looking from Tom to Eli. True to her word,

Eli had replaced quietly sobbing with sniffing and then blowing her nose quite loudly.

Tom replied that they had no idea who could have attacked their dad, adding he was a popular man who didn't have any enemies that they were aware of. The detective asked a few more questions about their dad. Eli told him her dad had gone out shortly before the attack, telling her he was just going on an errand and wouldn't be long, so she had started preparing dinner. That was the last time she had seen him. When the detective asked where their mother was, he seemed genuinely sorry when Tom explained about their mum's death.

"Okay. Thanks," said the detective. "But if you do think of anything that might help later, please give me a call. Until then, I'll leave you in peace." He turned to Tom and said, "It might be a good idea if you could get the doctor to give your sister something." He smiled sympathetically at Eli as he handed Tom a card containing his contact details.

Tom thanked him, feeling as guilty as hell that he hadn't mentioned anything about Max being poisoned. He wasn't sure he should let the police know about that. He needed to speak to his dad before saying too much to the police. Maybe his dad could establish what this was all about. If Tom had mentioned what had happened to Max, he was certain it would have got the police digging into the family issues, including Tom's attack. It was all too dodgy. Also, Eli was there, and she hadn't been told the truth about Max, on the instructions of his dad.

Maybe his dad's attack was a case of being in the wrong place at the wrong time. His dad would always use that expression when he told him and Eli to be careful when they were going out. "You could just be in the wrong place at the wrong time," he would preach to them. No, Tom thought, he had done the right thing saying very little to the police, especially if his dad was in some kind of trouble over something he had done. At least he could speak with his dad and hopefully find out what the hell had happened. That was, if he pulled through. Tom physically shuddered.

Tom and Eli followed the detective out of the side room, back out into the corridor. Again, they said goodbye and then sat down with Sue, who pulled Eli to her and cuddled her.

"I assume we can wait here for news of how he's doing?" Tom asked the policewoman. After smiling at Sue, Eli had calmed down, but she was so pale and looked ill.

"I'll get a nurse to come and sort you out. Don't worry. I'm sure she'll find you somewhere a bit more comfortable to wait until the doctor comes to see you," said the policewoman encouragingly.

Chapter 34

WIMBLEDON PARKSIDE

Harrison sat in traffic. He was in the one-way system in Wandsworth on his way home. He wasn't looking forward to the evening he was going to have with his wife, Penny. It was all so fucking tiresome. He had stayed late at the showroom to sort things out. Also, he wasn't in a hurry to go home to her shit either. It was already starting to go dark, which helped as he pulled over in a side street in Putney. Checking nobody was about, he got out of the car and walked round to the gutter. He dropped the knife down the drain, hearing a slight splash. At least everything had gone okay as he cleared up evidence after the staff had all headed off home. All the evidence had now gone or had been destroyed. His alibi was well sorted with his pal who lived in Jamaica Road. No problems. So far so good.

He was certain Quinn had recognised him just before he was stabbed. If he was still alive, he must have kept his mouth shut; otherwise, Harrison would have had a visit from the Old Bill by now. There hadn't been any breaking news on the radio about a murder on Wandsworth Common, so if Quinn had recognised him, he was being sensible and keeping stum. He must have finally realised that nobody fucked with Mike Harrison. *The pussy!* Harrison thought to himself, and he smirked.

Along Wimbledon Parkside, he slowed and indicated before he turned in to the gates of his drive. He stopped and took a deep breath. He wasn't looking forward to going in knowing that stupid cow was inside waiting for him. Anyway, he had it all worked out in his head what he was going to say to her. He pressed the fob to open the gates, but nothing happened. He stared at the gates. He looked down at his hand and pressed the fob again. Nothing. He shouted, "Open up for fuck's sake!" It was then he was aware of a black kid on a mountain bike standing next to the driver's window staring in at him. He waved his hand, gesturing backwards over his shoulder and shouted to the kid, "Go around the back of the car. I'm waiting for the gates. Anyway, you shouldn't be riding on the fucking pavement!"

The kid didn't move. He just gave Harrison a look that was half smile and half smirk. He said something that Harrison couldn't understand. Harrison thought, *I'm not in the mood for this little fucking gob shit. Nope! Not tonight, smart arse.* He muttered "The little bastard!" Then he lowered the driver's window. His face was starting to flush with anger as he shouted, "What did you just say to me, you little shit?"

The black kid just gave him a big toothy smile and said, "This is for the *dog!*"

Harrison didn't see the gun until it came up into view above his driver's side door. By then, it was too late to do anything. It happened so quickly. Harrison only managed to get out a quizzical "What?" Then there was a flash together with a loud noise from the black kid's hand.

The bullet went through the centre of Harrison's forehead. Blood and parts of his skull hit the passenger window and slipped down onto the front seat, onto the back seats, and into the passenger well. His blood started to drip from the roof of the Mercedes. The dashboard was also splattered with the deep red, sickly sweet-smelling liquid.

The upper half of Harrisons body had been angled towards the driver's window. The force of the bullet had sent his head backwards where it stopped in the gap between the two front headrests. Now he appeared to be staring at the roof of the car. His mouth was open, and there was a look of utter shock on what was left of his bloodied face.

Billy looked up and down the road. It was all clear. There was nothing to concern him. He threw two £10 bags of blow down into the pocket of the driver's door, careful not to get any blood on his hand. He took one last look at his handiwork before pushing the bike backwards away from the side of the car. He turned and cycled across the road back onto Wimbledon Common. Waiting for him were two of his young runners. They had been waiting patiently where Billy had left his car.

Without exchanging a word, Billy handed the bike to one of the kids and dropped the gun in to a brown paper bag that the other kid was holding open for him. Again, without a word said, they nodded to Billy. He smiled and nodded back at them. They rode off in different directions into the darkness of the Common. Billy stood and watched them disappear into the blackness before he walked over

Wandsworth Common

to his car. He started up his BMW M3, lit up a joint, and drove back to the main road. He waited for a car to go past. Before pulling out, he looked over to the right where Harrison's car was still parked at the gates that Billy had disabled ten minutes earlier. Turning left, he drove along Wimbledon Parkway on to the main roundabout over the A3. He headed down the hill towards the one-way system in Wandsworth, up past Clapham Common, and then home to Brixton. He was pleased with how the evening had gone. He was enjoying his smoke and thought to himself, *Job well done. Jason fucking Bourne couldn't have done better!*

CHAPTER 35

THE AFTERMATH

Harrison's murder was reported in the newspapers and on the local television news reports and London radio stations the following day. The shooting of a successful businessman outside his home was unusual in the present day of teenage gang murders by stabbings and the occasional shooting in the inner city. A few days later, when the story had all but disappeared from the media, they picked up on the letter Frank had sent to Harrison's wife. News of it kickstarted interest in the murder all over again. The story was back in the nationals again. What intrigued the media, and indeed the police, was fact that Frank had been attacked earlier on the same evening that Harrison had been murdered. It all seemed like too much of a coincidence. First the news of the attacks had come out and it had been followed by the news of the affair. The murdered man had been having an affair with the wife of the man who'd been stabbed on Wandsworth Common. It was a good, juicy, middle-class scandal. With the lack of other interesting news at that time, the papers wouldn't let it drop. Even the Sunday redtops ran double-page spreads on the attacks, the story, the families, and the theories. They kept the story running so everyone could read all the details about Harrison and Gill. It was terrible for Tom and Eli having their lives laid bare for everyone to read about—from Frank's fellow directors to Tom and Eli's friends and old friends in Leeds and South London. Frank was oblivious to all the publicity as he lay recovering from the operation that had saved his life.

In the media coverage, Harrison hadn't come out of it looking too good. It was revealed for all to know that he'd been born and raised in the East End. His uncle was the old gangster Sammy Bloom, who had worked for the Krays in his younger days and had been murdered a couple of years previously on the Mile End Road. Harrison had been sent to borstal in his teen years for football gang violence, drug dealing, and extortion. He had made a lot of business enemies over the years on his climb up the social ladder, who were more than happy to talk to the media about him. All were interviewed by the police in connection with the murder, but to no avail. The police didn't appear any nearer to catching the killer. Old girlfriends also came out of the woodwork with tales of Harrison's nasty temper and kinky sex preferences. Friends of his poor wife told stories of domestic violence and mental bullying, saying she should have left him years ago.

On the other hand, the police investigations showed Frank to be an upstanding, law-abiding citizen, a devoted husband, and a loving family man, despite his wife's affair with a successful businessman. The family lived in Wandsworth. He was a company director in a top insurance firm in the city, recently widowed with two grown children. But his letter to Harrison's wife tied him to the murdered man and possibly to the murder itself.

When Frank was finally strong enough, he was interviewed by the police about the attack on him on the Common. He had developed an infection and lost a kidney, which had further delayed the police speaking to him. During the interview, he told them that he had been attacked from behind and he didn't have any idea who the attacker was. He had wanted to keep a distance between himself and Harrison. He had just felt a terrible pain and started to pass out. Unfortunately he was unable to give the police any description of the assailant whatsoever. Amazingly, although the Common was busy that evening, there were not eyewitnesses to the incident.

At first, Frank was of great interest to the police regarding the murder of Harrison outside his home in Wimbledon. The distraught Mrs Harrison produced the letter that she had received on the morning of the shooting from Frank about the affair. Without any other leads, the letter made Frank the number-one suspect as far as the police were concerned, but their extensive investigations had hit a brick wall.

The investigating officers thought it was case solved and wanted to speak to Frank straight away. To their frustration, they soon discovered that he had a cast iron alibi—even though they didn't realise it was courtesy of Harrison. He had been in hospital at the time of the murder. In fact, he'd been having lifesaving surgery! He'd been the victim of a vicious robbery.

Frank had been interviewed on several occasions about

Harrison's murder. The detectives in charge of the case appeared frustrated and under a lot of internal pressure at the lack of progress and suspects. It was reported that some class A drugs were found in Harrison's car, and there were also traces of PCP discovered in the boot.

Even though Frank's wife had been involved in a relationship with Harrison before her death, there wasn't any other evidence linking Frank to the murder—no mobile calls. Only the texts that Harrison had sent to Gill's mobile and the replies from Frank asking the identity of the person who had sent the text.

Also, it was considered highly unlikely that Frank would implicate himself by sending a letter to the victim's wife on the day of the murder, if he had in any way been involved. So, with the lack of suspects, the case was eventually left in police files as an unsolved drug-related murder by person or persons unknown.

Unfortunately, because of the investigation, Tom and Eli found out about their mum's affair—and found out in the worst way possible. This was the last thing Frank had wanted, and he was devastated when he recovered and found out about all the media coverage. It was bad enough that Tom and Eli found out about their mum's affair, but seeing it reported all over the newspapers for everyone to read about and pass comment on was shocking.

Both Tom and Eli had been interviewed by the police and questioned about where their dad was on the day he was attacked and what had he done. Did they know any reason why anybody would attack their dad? Also, had they known their mum was having an affair with Harrison? Had their father ever discussed the affair with either of them? The interviews had proved fruitless, as both of them had been completely and honestly in the dark about all the questions they were asked. They came over as honest decent young adults who were from a good middle-class family. Finally, the police were reluctantly satisfied with both interviews.

After the interviews at the police station, Eli and tom had gone for a drink. Eli hadn't wanted to go straight home. Tom thought it would be good for Eli to talk about her feelings after all that had happened. They discussed their mum and how they felt about what she had done. It was good for both of them. They could say things to each other that they felt they couldn't say to their dad. They discussed the attack on their dad. Tom didn't say anything about Max. He didn't want Eli to know about the poisoning. She would be too upset; she still missed her beloved dog.

What did concern Tom was a question that Eli asked him. It hit a nerve. She asked Tom if he thought their dad had anything to do with Harrison's murder. The question shocked him even though the same thought had crossed his mind too. But he had dismissed it, just as he dismissed Eli's question with fake shock and horror.

When Frank was strong enough, after he realised Harrison's murder and especially Harrison's affair with Gill, had been all over the newspapers, he spoke to Tom and Eli about everything.

He talked to them about the affair and how he had found out about it. He told them it that learning about it was one of the hardest things he had ever had to do, both mentally and, in his current weakened state, physically also. It was right up there with having to tell them about their mothers' death. He was still recovering in hospital. Dealing with all the revelations had sapped the strength from his body and soul. Frank told them their mother's relationship with Harrison was just a fling, and unfortunately that sort of thing happens in life. Maybe he shouldn't have been away from home so much on business. He wasn't sure that they believed him, and he hated them knowing. He didn't want them thinking badly of Gill despite what had happened. He answered all their questions honestly. Eli's were the most penetrating: Did Gill love Harrison? Didn't she love Frank anymore? Why would she have an affair when she had a loving family? Her questions were harder on him than his interview with the police, but he did his best to answer them all, some honestly, some not so much: No, her mum didn't love Harrison it; was just a fling. Yes, her mum did love her dad. "Your mum probably regretted having the affair," he told his daughter. "And she loved her family very much."

David and Sue were interviewed by the police about Frank's attack. They answered "honestly" that they didn't know of any problems that Frank had or who would attack him. Of course, they failed to mention that they were aware of Frank's run-ins with Harrison when they were questioned about the relationship between the men. They were shocked at Harrison's murder but couldn't bring themselves to believe for a minute that Frank was involved. They had visited Frank several times in hospital when he was conscious and was allowed visitors. It was difficult for them to speak to him, though, about anything because Tom and Eli were always there by the bedside. Sue had been wonderful as she always was in an emergency. She was at the house every day tidying, cooking, and looking after Eli. Poor Eli was devastated by everything that had happened and especially with all the press interest. One day when they were in the lounge talking, Eli came straight out and asked Sue if she had known about her mum's affair. Sue felt so guilty lying to her, but she denied any knowledge of what had gone on. She was worried how Eli would have reacted if she had admitted that she had known. Sue couldn't bear it if Eli had ending up blaming her for being involved in her mum's affair. Eli needed Sue to be there for her now. Sue told Frank that she had not let Eli know that she'd been aware of Gill's affair. Eli finding out that Sue had lied to her would have surely ended their close relationship.

Chapter 36

CONVALESCING

Frank sat in the lounge looking out across the road onto the Common. He was going over the events that had changed his life forever. He was recovering, albeit slowly, from the attack on the Common by that lunatic Harrison. Still weak, but now clear of infection, he had been discharged and allowed to go home.

Frank was still housebound and had been ordered to rest. A private nurse called every day to attend to his dressings. Eli was fussing over him even though she looked as if she was the one who needed looking after. She had lost a lot more weight, and her face looked gaunt. Frank was so worried about her. Tom had come home for the weekend, and they had all enjoyed a lovely dinner prepared by Eli. Later in the evening, talk turned to what they had all gone through recently. Eli said she was okay and didn't want to talk about. She just wanted to go to bed and get some rest.

Frank wasn't strong enough to walk Eli upstairs, but he told her that he was so sorry that she had to find out about her mum. He told her not to let it spoil all the lovely memories she had. He gave her a goodnight kiss and said it wouldn't be long before he was tucking her in like he did when she was a little girl. She smiled and told him it was good to have him home. Tom joined them in the lounge. Eli kissed him, said goodnight, and went upstairs to bed.

"How is Eli? Is she okay?" Tom asked his dad, who was sitting in his favourite chair.

"I don't know, Tom. After everything she's been through ... and then the affair obviously came as a big shock to her. Then there was the strain of having our family business splashed all over the newspapers. It's all taken its toll on her. Let's talk about you. You've been through it all too. How are you doing, son?" Frank wished he was allowed to have a drink of his favourite scotch.

"I don't really know how I feel, to be honest, dad. Shellshocked is probably the best way to describe how I feel after everything that's happened." Tom rubbed his chin and staring blankly at the wall above Frank's head. "What with you being attacked and then finding out about mum ... and you're right—all the media coverage was really shitty. Mum's affair certainly came as a massive shock, Dad. I suppose, as you said, these things happen, but it was still a shock. How did you find out?" Tom focused his attention back on his dad's face.

"He sent a text to your mum's phone after she died, and I saw it when I was in the process of charging the phone. I was planning to give it to Eli. Apparently, he had been away on holiday with his family and didn't know that your mum had died." Frank was surprised at how easy it was to truthfully discuss the matter with Tom.

"I've got a few things I would like to talk to you about,

Dad, if that's okay. But first there's something you should know." Tom put his glass down and leaned forward towards his dad. "Eli recognised Harrison from his pictures in the papers. She told me he came to the house one day to see you and that you seemed upset after he left. Did he threaten you, Dad? Also, did Harrison kill Max? it was him, wasn't it?" asked Tom, answering his own question before his dad could reply. Tom looked annoyed at the possibility of his dad being threatened in their home.

Frank looked enviously as Tom took another sip of his drink and thought to himself, *Shit! I could really do with a drink right now!* He let out a deep sign and replied, "No, he didn't threaten me when he called, Tom. It did upset me, though, that he had the nerve to come to our home. And to answer your question about Max, yes, he killed Max as a warning to me."

Tom was shocked at Frank's admission about Max's death even though he had worked it out himself. It was still a jolt to his senses to hear his dad confirm it. He was puzzled at his mum's choice of a lover and asked his dad, "How could Mum ever have had anything to do with a bastard like that, Dad? How? I can't get my head around that at all. After reading what a shit he was, I can't imagine what Mum could have seen in him!"

"I don't know, Tom. I really don't. I didn't have a lot of dealings with him, to be honest with you," lied Frank, quickly adding, "But to kill a dog ... you're absolutely right—you have to be a real evil bastard to do that to a poor, innocent animal."

Tom explained that he had taken a call from the vet when he had phoned for his dad with the news that Max had to be put down because he had been poisoned with PCP. Tom told his dad that he never mentioned it to the police at the hospital after his dad was stabbed, and not only because Eli was with him. He felt that, if he had told them, they would have jumped all over the fact that Max had been poisoned with PCP because traces of the same drug had been found in Harrison's car. Tom continued that the picture had become clearer with the news of Harrison's murder and the PCP.

Tom figured that Harrison had poisoned Max as a warning to his dad! Tom had been confident he had pieced it all together correctly, but there were two other points he wanted to know. "It wasn't a mugging on the Common that evening, was it? It was Harrison. Or he had arranged for someone else to stab you, possibly with intention of killing you. Isn't that right, Dad?"

Frank sat in silence listening to Tom's assumptions and questions about that evening's events. He looked at his son. He was worried where this conversation was leading now. He was aware that Tom was waiting for a reply. He cleared his throat and finally said, "Honest answer, Tom—I don't know. As I told the police, I didn't see who stabbed me. I suppose he was mad and evil enough to do it himself or to arrange for someone else to attack me. But what you suspect, son, isn't it all a bit Hollywood? I mean come on ... this is Wandsworth!"

Tom was shocked and angry at his dad's flippant reply. He shouted straight back at his dad, "Hollywood? My mum's lover comes to our house and threatens you, although you say he didn't. Then he kills our family pet shortly before you get stabbed in broad daylight! Later that evening, he gets shot through the head! And all you can say about it is, 'Come on … this is Wandsworth'? Well, it certainly sounds like fucking Hollywood to me, Dad."

"I just told you he didn't threaten me. Please, Tom, keep your voice down. Let's put all this nonsense behind us. We've all been through so much. I don't want to talk about it anymore. It's all over now," lied Frank as he slowly stood up to go to the toilet.

"One last question before I go to bed, Dad. I was in a bar in town after work when you were taken hospital after the attack. I ran into Mattie Patterson. He asked how you were. He said he liked you and told me you are a cool dad. Why would he say that, Dad?" asked Tom. He had stood up and was looking his dad straight in the eyes.

Frank just smiled and replied, "Maybe I handled myself well in our meeting, Tom. I told you not to worry. I told you I'm very good at negotiating in meetings, didn't I?"

Tom half smiled, half smirked and just shook his head. Turning to go out of the lounge, he said, "Goodnight, Dad. If you're going to continue to lie, there's no point talking, but I know what happened that night, despite what you say."

Tom lay in bed looking up at the ceiling. He was certain he had worked it all out. He just couldn't bring himself to believe the fact that his dad had initiated Harrison's murder! His dad didn't know the sorts of people who go around killing people. He was a company director for God's sake, not a gangster. The only person he had met who would be capable of doing something like that was Mattie Patterson. When he bumped into Mattie in the bar that evening, he seriously thought about asking him, but thought better of it. Asking something stupid like that could get a person killed!

Frank sat looking out over the common at nothing in particular. He was thinking about his conversation with Tom. His son was a clever young man, and he appeared to have worked out what had actually happened. Tom didn't know as much as David and Sue knew, but it looked as if he had arrived at the same assumption David had.

David and Sue had come around to have dinner with Frank and Eli. Frank was still weak, but he thought the company and cooking dinner would do Eli good. After they ate, Sue and Eli were tidying up in the kitchen. Frank and David moved into the lounge. It was the first time they had been alone. David was staring at Frank, which made Frank uncomfortable. Frank finally broke the silence by asking if David was okay. David got up, closed the lounge door, and came back to his seat. He came straight out with the question: "Frank, what the hell happened that evening? Did Harrison stab you on the Common because of the letter you sent to his wife?" Frank gave him the same stock answer that he had given Tom and the police.

David's next question did shock Frank: "Did you have anything to do with Harrison's murder?" Frank feigned horror at the question and said it was absurd that David could think he had anything to do with it. He added that he wasn't a member of the bloody Mafia, and that it was crazy that David would think something like that. The look on David's face told him he hadn't convinced him one iota. For all it was worth, he may just as well have said that he had had him killed.

Sue and Eli joined them in the lounge with mugs of

coffee. David was withdrawn and snapped at Sue when she asked him what was wrong. They said their goodbyes and left thirty minutes afterwards. It was obvious that David didn't believe that Frank was innocent in Harrison's death.

After that evening, Frank saw less and less of David and Sue. When Sue called to pick up Eli for their occasional shopping trips, the atmosphere was awkward and the conversation strained—so much so that even Eli asked her dad what was going on. She wondered if he'd had an argument with them.

Eli went back to Nottingham University to complete her final year after all she had been through in Wandsworth that summer. Frank just hoped she could get back into some kind of a happy, normal student life with her friends and hopefully one day put everything behind her. She didn't offer to stay at home and look after him when it was time to go back to uni while he was in recovery. It seemed to Frank that she couldn't wait to get away from Wandsworth and home, and who could blame her? It really broke Frank's heart thinking about all she had been through since that fateful day when he told her the news of her mum's' death. What he didn't realise was that his daughter's worse thoughts were not that her mum was unfaithful but that her dad was a murderer. Even if he hadn't shot her mum's lover himself, she believed he had somehow arranged for it happen.

Frank thought that, if any good came out of all that had happened on that fateful evening, it was the fact that, if Harrison really was Eli's dad, then the truth had died with him, and neither she nor anybody else would ever know. At least poor Eli was spared that heart-breaking news.

So, Frank sat there alone with his thoughts as he looked out the lounge window at the dog walkers, friends strolling along, families with their children playing in the sunshine on the Common, all as normal. The same question was going through his head over and over again!

Should he have let it go as David and Sue had told him to? If only he had, he could have prevented all the heartache Eli had been through in the past and now having to live with the hurt of finding out about her mum's affair.

Should he have let it go? If he had, Tom wouldn't have distanced himself from him. Tom was a clever young man and knew the truth about Max. And he knew that his dad had been involved in Harrison's murder, probably through Mattie Patterson. Frank knew that Tom had worked out what had happened. Frank believed that had changed their relationship forever. When Frank spoke to Tom on the phone, he knew their relationship just wasn't the same; there were awkward silences. There wasn't any warmth in Tom's voice, even when he asked about his dad's health. Frank felt his son couldn't wait to hang up.

Should he have let it go? David and Sue had both begged him to on many occasions, but he'd just ignored their advice. If he had listened to them, they wouldn't have all but deserted him. It was difficult. Frank had stopped phoning David because he stopped returning Frank's calls despite all the voice messages he left. Frank had never felt so alone. David and Sue had been good family friends for many years, and he missed them terribly.

Should he have let it go? Also, another innocent victim in all this mess was poor Max. If Frank had taken a different path, the dog would still be there; he wouldn't have deserted

Frank. Old faithful Max—all he ever wanted was nothing more than to be fed, walked, and patted. He was never happier than when he was falling asleep at Frank's feet. If only Frank had done things differently and not been conceited. If only he hadn't reacted to the indignation of finding out he had been cheated on by Gill and then wanting some kind of revenge. If only …

The situation and events had just snowballed out of control, especially after Max's death. By the time Frank's conscience finally kicked in again and he realised what he had arranged, it was too late. He was on his way across the Common to telephone Mattie Patterson to call off the deal he had made to have Harrison murdered. He had decided that a letter to Harrison's wife was revenge enough. He realised that hatred had turned him into a monster, and he couldn't live with himself for doing something like that. He still couldn't despite all that had happened.

If that stupid bastard Harrison hadn't got to him before he had made the phone call, the lunatic would still been alive today. Also, Frank would still have the principles that his mum and dad had instilled in him all those years ago, and more importantly he would still have his loving family and good friends around him as well as the will to go on living.

Printed in Great Britain
by Amazon